Faking Reality

AUG 2011

CH

Faking Reality

Zaria Garrison

www.urbanchristianonline.com

Urban Books, LLC
78 East Industry Court
Deer Park, NY 11729

Faking Reality Copyright © 2011 Zaria Garrison

ISBN 13: 978-1-60162-799-5
ISBN 10: 1-60162-799-8

First Printing September 2011
Printed in the United States of America

10 9 8 7 6 5 4 3 2 1

*This is a work of fiction. Any references or similarities
to actual events, real people, living, or dead, or to real
locales are intended to give the novel a sense of reality. Any similarity in other names, characters, places,
and incidents is entirely coincidental.*

Distributed by Kensington Corp.
Submit Wholesale Orders to:
Kensington Publishing Corp.
C/O Penguin Group (USA) Inc.
Attention: Order Processing
405 Murray Hill Parkway
East Rutherford, NJ 07073-2316
Phone: 1-800-526-0275
Fax: 1-800-227-9604

Faking Reality

Zaria Garrison

Dedication

This book is dedicated to the ministers,
evangelists, and preachers who've been a
part of my life and inspired this story.

Acknowledgments

As always, I must begin by thanking God who is the head of my life and the true author of all of my books. He is the reason I do what I do, and the reason I am who I am. I give Him all the glory and all of the praise.

Sandra K. Poole, my friend whom I refer to as "Miss Editor Lady" because she edits everything I write before the paid editors get a chance to see it. She even edits my e-mails. I love you, "Auntie," for all that you do for me and for the person that you are.

Sophia Garrison, Kanika Payne, and Sandra Cheek, who are my advance readers, thank you for giving me your thoughts and opinions that helped make this story the best it could be.

To Anthony Bunch, the love of my life, thank you for loving and encouraging me. To my son John, my family, and friends, who inspire and support me, I also thank you immensely.

To those people who read and enjoyed *Prodigal* and *Losing It*, thank you for reading my stories and continuing to support me as a writer. I strive to do my best for you.

Chapter One

Julian Washington, owner of the newly formed Washington Broadcast Network, walked briskly up the hallway to his new office. As each step echoed in the expansive hallway, he walked with excitement and pride. When he'd made the decision to get into television, Julian wanted to offer original programming primarily aimed at minority viewers. Currently, his network existed solely by rebroadcasting old sitcoms and syndicated programming. He was making an obscene amount of money and garnering lots of accolades and attention, but as a perfectionist, Julian wanted to make even more. Instead of being a successful small network, Julian wanted to have the most successful network in the country. It was never enough for him to be great; he had to be the absolute best. He was excited that he'd finally hired an executive producer who seemed to have just as much vision and ambition as he possessed.

Anderson Carter was a young, energetic producer looking to make his mark in television. He had attended Morehouse College with a major in marketing and a minor in broadcasting. He had very little experience, but he possessed a huge amount of talent, drive, and arrogance. At his interview, he'd convinced Julian that he had the answer that would catapult his new network to major success.

"Mr. Washington," Anderson had stated, "American viewers are excited about only one thing on television these days, and that's reality TV. If you want to become a powerhouse as a television network, you've got to add reality programming to your station."

Julian agreed with him in principle. Reality television was certainly sweeping the nation. He knew that almost every network carried at least one reality program. They were inexpensive to produce, and the viewers seemed to love them, no matter what the content. However, unlike Anderson, Julian had worked in television for many years. He began as an intern at the local television station in his hometown of Greenburg, S.C., and had been promoted to station manager within two years. By the time he had reached his thirtieth birthday, Julian had several dozen producer and executive producer credits on his résumé.

After he purchased the television station, his critics felt that a thirty-five-year-old man was too young to own and operate a network, but he had been determined to prove them wrong. He felt the only way to do that was to offer programming that no one else was offering. Jumping on the reality TV bandwagon did not fit into his plans of being original.

"I've come up with a reality concept and market that is virtually untapped," Anderson had said as he sat in Julian's office, trying to convince him he was the right man for the job.

"It's all been done before. There are reality shows for finding love, losing weight, dancing, having babies, getting married, being housewives. It's all been done before," Julian answered.

"My concept has never been done before. It's original, and I think it will be a huge hit."

Julian sighed and leaned back in his huge red leather chair. "Fine. What is your big idea, young man?" he asked.

"It's called *Revelations*. It will be a one-hour show that goes behind the scenes in the lives of local ministers. We are going to take them from their pulpits and follow them through their everyday lives."

As Anderson paused to gauge his reaction, Julian sat up in his chair and began to pay closer attention. "Go on," he urged.

"I want us to profile four well-known local pastors. The cameras will follow them as they interact with their families and go through their normal routines. I grew up in a religious family. We attended church every Sunday. You wouldn't believe the kind of scandalous things that some ministers do once they step out of their pulpit." Anderson grinned with excitement.

"While I agree with you that there are plenty of crooked preachers in the city of Atlanta, I'm not sure how you propose to get them to allow cameras to follow them around while they are doing their dirty work. We'd end up with a cleaned up version of their lives."

"With all due respect, Mr. Washington, do you realize that reality television is not real? It doesn't matter how much they try to clean up the dirt, our cameras will be there to uncover it. I've got a buddy from college whose editing skills are phenomenal. He can take any humdrum situation and create drama from it. Not only that, but I also believe that if we make the right choices, these ministers will create a wealth of drama of their own."

Julian was so pleased with the sales pitch that he'd hired Anderson Carter on the spot. Anderson's assistants then put notices on Craigslist and in all of the local newspapers. After interviewing hundreds of candidates, they'd finally narrowed the choices down to four. As he opened the door to his expansive office, Julian thought back on that fateful day and meeting.

Julian took off his suit jacket and hung it on the rack near the door before moving across the room to sit behind his desk. He felt more anxious than a five-year-old at Christmas as he waited for Anderson to arrive with the contracts.

On his way to the office, Julian had stopped by the barbershop to have his hair trimmed. The barber touched up the line on his fade and neatly trimmed his beard, while Julian watched a bootleg movie playing on the shop television. After he had left the barbershop, he stopped at the nail salon for a manicure and pedicure. Julian prided himself on being one of the most well-groomed black men in Atlanta. In his opinion, he had not been blessed with great looks. His skin was dark and blotchy in spots, his hair was nappy and unruly, and his nose was wide and flat. However, he'd learned early in life that with a proper haircut, his hair looked neat. Growing a full beard hid the uneven blotches on his skin and made his nose look smaller. He bought expensive body lotions to pamper his skin and stopped weekly for a mani-pedi. In addition, he had a gym built into a spare bedroom of his home where he spent at least one hour per day working out. His six feet four body was chiseled, sculpted, and firm. Several of his dates had remarked that a person could bounce a quarter off his abs. All of these rituals, combined with expensive clothing and shoes, made Julian feel as if he'd created the illusion of being an attractive man.

He licked his index finger and gently brushed down his arched eyebrows just as Anderson knocked on his door. "Come in," he called out.

Anderson Carter sauntered in and placed the proposed contracts of Reverend Brandon Kitts, Evangelist Danita Hyatt, Apostle Zack (Bo) Morton, and Bishop Jimmy Snow on the desk. "I've had our attorneys go over these with a fine-tooth comb. As soon as they are signed, we can begin shooting," he said.

"That's great," Julian replied excitedly. "Tell me about our candidates."

Carter outlined the background of each pastor as he presented their paperwork. "Reverend Kitts has a congregation of close to two thousand members. He's a former professional football player-turned-minister. He met his wife while he was still in the NFL. She was the wife of one of his teammates until their affair."

"Awesome, there is plenty of potential for drama there," Julian answered.

"Our one female pastor is Evangelist Hyatt. Her congregation is much smaller, with fewer than one thousand members. She lost almost half of her members last year, after the murder trial of her husband. However, she was acquitted on all charges and is dating again. She's tentatively agreed to allow us to follow her on every date."

"Let's hope she's easy," Julian said, and then laughed. He flipped through the paperwork. "What about the civil suit her late husband's family has filed against her for wrongful death?"

"Look on the last page. Once she signs, we'll have clearance for the cameras to follow her to court when it comes to trial."

Julian smiled broadly. "Tell me about Dr. Morton. His profile seems pretty typical."

"He's our token," Carter laughed. "Dr. Morton has sandy-blond hair and blue eyes, but he's full of soul. He has the charisma of T. D. Jakes, combined with the movie-star good looks of Matthew McConaughey. The ladies are going to love him."

"You are a genius, Anderson. This show is going to put us on the map," he said excitedly. "I can hardly wait to hear about the last pastor."

"Well, he's kind of a snooze. When his wife first approached me, I thought they'd be a good fit. She told me she's a former actress. Now I'm not so sure about them."

"What's the problem?" Julian wrinkled his brow in concern.

"I found out that she was only in one movie, and it was a really small part. I'm sure nobody has ever heard of her."

"What's his background?" Julian asked.

Anderson shrugged. "He's just the average Southern minister, as far as I can tell. I've only met him once."

Julian picked up the paperwork and read over Bishop Snow's profile. "This is interesting. They've been married ten years, but they have teenage children. What's the story on that?"

"His first wife died, and Mrs. Snow adopted the children after they were married."

"Every reality show has to have that one seemingly normal person. Let's move forward. If there's no drama going on with the bishop and his wife, we'll find a way to create it." He winked at Anderson.

"Great. I plan to get the signatures today, and we'll start filming tomorrow. I have camera crews ready for each of them. We'll film everything, and then be ready to air in about four months."

Julian rubbed his beard with his right hand. "No, I want this done totally different. If we want to be cutting edge, then we have to change up the game. I want the shows that are airing to be filmed no more than two weeks prior."

"Are you sure about that? We're going to have to do editing on a daily basis in order to accomplish that."

"I don't care. You said your buddy was an editing expert. Besides, I've found that all of these other reality shows have one flaw. The gossip blogs print what's going to happen before it's aired. I don't want that on this show. I want something fresh and new."

Anderson grinned. He was twenty-seven years old, but still wore braces like a preteen. "You got it boss." He reached over the desk and happily shook Julian's hand.

After Anderson left his office, Julian casually leaned back in his chair and thought about his life. In addition to the television station, Julian owned a ten-room mansion in one of Atlanta's most affluent neighborhoods. Each morning before heading in to his downtown corporate offices, he had the luxury of choosing how to arrive. On the days that he felt conservative and reserved, he drove to work in his slate-blue BMW sedan. If he was feeling adventurous, he'd speed out of his driveway behind the wheel of his candy-apple-red Porsche. Then there were days when he just felt lazy, and that's when he'd allow his chauffeur to drive him to work in his custom-designed limousine.

He traveled regularly to destinations throughout the United States, as well as took vacations in such exotic places as Paris, France, and Milan, Italy. To the naked eye, it appeared that Julian Washington had it all. Julian, however, did not share that opinion. From his perspective, his life was empty. He knew that he should be elated about his new show and the fact that he was steadily becoming one of Atlanta's most powerful moguls, but his success was bittersweet.

During his lifetime, Julian had dated many women, including several runway models, a soap-opera actress, and two Grammy Award–winning singers. He was considered by most people to be one of Atlanta's wealthiest and most eligible bachelors, but Julian didn't care about any of those things. Sitting alone in his office, Julian felt melancholy as he stared out of the window at the city below him. *Of all the things I own, I'd give it all back in a heartbeat if I could just have you back in my life,* he thought.

Chapter Two

Sitting in his office, Bishop Jimmy Snow slowly read over the contract in front of him. He looked up at his wife, Yolanda, as he came to a portion he did not completely understand. "I think we need to let a lawyer read this over before we decide," he said.

"What for, Jimmy? It's a standard contract," she answered.

Anderson Carter, the executive producer of the show, sat next to her, smiling broadly. "Go ahead and let your attorney look over it, Bishop. That's fine with me. Or if you have any questions, I'd be happy to answer them for you."

Bishop Snow pointed to a line in the contract. "It says here that you have final approval over what is shown on television. I think that I should have the final say."

"That simply means we'll do some editing before it's shown. We are going to have cameras running almost twenty-four hours per day. We have to edit it for content."

"Twenty-four hours a day?" Bishop Snow shook his head. "No, we wouldn't have any privacy at all."

Yolanda Snow looked back and forth between the two men, desperately trying to hide her deep desire to do the television show. "Jimmy, you promised me you'd consider this. I mean, I think it would be good for the church."

"Yolanda, do you *really* want a camera crew following us *everywhere* we go?" He turned to Anderson. "I think it would be better if the cameras just followed me at the church. That would be a lot less intrusive."

Anderson sat quietly for a few seconds before responding. "Well, that's not the show the network wants, but I guess I could talk to them about it."

Yolanda suddenly sat forward in her chair. "What about me? If the cameras only follow you at the church, I won't be on the show," she said anxiously.

Bishop Snow and Anderson looked at her surprised, as they both suddenly realized just how much she wanted to do the television show. Before their marriage ten years earlier, Yolanda Snow had aspirations of being a movie star. She had participated in theatre in high school and college. In her hometown of Greenburg, S.C., she had a key role in a local production of August Wilson's play *Fences*. Right after that, she had moved to Atlanta and immediately had been cast in a low-budget independent film. Yolanda's on-screen time was less than two minutes, yet she sincerely hoped it would lead to more roles and a successful acting career.

Instead, she had met and fallen deeply in love with the young, dynamic pastor, Jimmy Snow. At the time, he had been a widower with a five-year-old son and seven-year-old daughter. After only an eight-month courtship, they were married. Yolanda believed that the love she felt for him and his children far outweighed her acting aspirations. She was content to head the church drama department and occasionally act in a local theatre group.

However, when she'd seen the posting on Craigslist advertising a new reality show for ministers and their families, she felt chills of excitement coursing through her veins. To Yolanda, it represented the chance to fulfill her long-dormant dream of being on television, while at the same time, feeding her secret passion for reality TV shows. She'd contacted the show's producer and tentatively agreed to do the show without telling her husband. Now, all she had to do was convince Jimmy it was a good idea. She tried to be nonchalant and discreet, but as she sat in his office watching the chance slip through her fingers, she'd suddenly become frantic.

Seeing the look in her eyes, Bishop Snow tried to soothe her. "Yolanda, you will be a part of the show. As the first lady, the cameras would also have the opportunity to follow you as you work in ministry as well." He looked over at Anderson for help. "Isn't that correct?" he asked.

Anderson looked over at Yolanda, then back at Bishop Snow. He'd promised the network that this show would dig deeply into the personal lives of all of the ministers it featured. There was no way he was going to settle for a watered-down version, filmed only at the church. Mentally, he began going over the other names on his list, feeling the Snows were a waste of his time. "Listen, Bishop Snow, I have to agree with your wife. If we only film at the church, the show will be nothing more than your sermons and you sitting in the office."

"That should be enough," Bishop Snow answered.

"The viewing public wants to see more. They can walk into any church in America and hear a sermon or observe their pastor at his desk. We want to take them into your home and show them what goes on in your everyday life. This will be a groundbreaking television series."

"That's right, Jimmy. You've watched *Run's House* with me. He's a minister, and you enjoyed watching him interact with his wife and children," Yolanda said.

Bishop Snow sighed heavily. "That's different. Rev. Run was a celebrity before the reality TV show. You know I have no aspirations to be a celebrity pastor. I have nothing against anyone who does, but it simply isn't me." He picked up the contract and held it out toward Anderson. "I'm sorry, but my wife and I will not be able to do this."

Before Anderson could take the contract, Yolanda snatched it from her husband's hand. "Why, Jimmy? You are always talking about how you want to reach more people. Now that you have the opportunity to reach millions, you are saying no."

"I would love to bring millions to Christ. You know that, Yolanda. But I don't want millions of prying eyes coming into our home. I'm a simple, private person. Most of all, I'm a man of God. I will not allow TV cameras to come into our home and disrupt our lives."

"We don't want to disrupt your lives at all. Of course, having cameras around will be an adjustment, but I promise that we'll do our best not to be too intrusive," Anderson said.

Bishop Snow shook his head. "I'm sorry. I just don't see how that's possible."

"I'm sorry too, Bishop. I was really looking forward to you and Mrs. Snow being a part of this venture." Anderson stood up to leave, while holding his hand out for the contract that Yolanda was clutching tightly.

"Maybe you should leave us alone for a few moments. My husband and I need to discuss this in private," Yolanda suggested. She walked over to the office door and opened it. "Give me a few moments to talk him into it," she whispered to Anderson before closing the door.

"Yolanda, I know you love reality TV shows, but let's just stick to watching them, okay?"

Plopping down in a chair, Yolanda folded her arms across her breasts. "You're being unreasonable, Jimmy."

"I don't think I am. You watch those shows all the time. You know they are full of nothing but drama. Why in the world do you want to be a part of that?"

"You can't blame the show for the drama in people's lives. Besides, we don't have any of that going on in our house."

He gave her a side-eyed look. "We have two typical teenagers at home. I love them both, but they are not perfect kids. We don't have a perfect life."

"So what? We are a real family with real problems. That's what the show is going to be about. You know some people think ministers and their wives never go through anything. This is our opportunity to show that we are just like everybody else."

"I don't know about this. What will my parishioners think of me being involved in a reality television show?"

Yolanda stood up from the chair and walked over to her husband. She stood behind his chair and lovingly wrapped her arms around his neck. She whispered sweetly in his ear, "They will be proud of their pastor. Besides, just think of all the people who will never walk into this church that you can reach? Instead of them watching other reality shows full of drama and sin, they can watch us deal with our family in a godly manner."

"You do have a point. There needs to be another choice in programming."

"Exactly," she purred. "Our show will be something that people can watch with their family. And the money we'll be paid can be donated directly to the church."

"Am I ever going to win an argument in our marriage?" he jokingly asked.

She smiled as she slid the contract onto the desk in front of him. "Not this one."

Jimmy Snow awakened the next morning to the sound of his doorbell ringing over and over again. He leaned over and checked the clock. "It's six in the morning. Who in the world could that be?" he wondered aloud.

"It's the camera crew. You should be up and dressed by now," Yolanda answered.

Jimmy rolled over in bed and suddenly noticed that she was fully dressed with her hair and makeup done. "You look great, baby," he said.

"Thanks, sweetie, now get up and get dressed. I'm going to let them in so they can start setting things up." She rushed out of the bedroom, leaving him alone.

Jimmy slowly rolled out of bed and went to the bathroom to shower. As he stepped out of his master bathroom several moments later, wrapped in only a towel, he was startled to find a tall, lanky white man in the middle of his bedroom.

"What are you doing in here?" he demanded.

"I'm setting up. We won't be standing around in your bedroom. I'll just set the camera up, and we'll control it remotely."

"No, you are not putting a camera in my bedroom. Get out of here right now!" Jimmy pointed toward the door, but the young man ignored him. He continued setting up the camera equipment. "Did you hear what I just said?" Jimmy yelled.

Yolanda suddenly burst into the bedroom. "What's going on in here?" she asked.

"He doesn't want me to set up the camera," the young man replied. He rolled his eyes behind Jimmy's back.

"Honey, just leave this man alone and let him do his job," Yolanda said. "Come downstairs and eat your breakfast."

Jimmy looked down at himself and back at Yolanda several times. "I'm not dressed, and there's a camera in the middle of my bedroom. I knew this show was going to steal all of our privacy," he huffed.

Yolanda sighed; then she slowly walked to the other side of the bedroom. Quietly, she unfolded a room divider and set it up. "You can get dressed right here, Jimmy. I know it's a bit inconvenient, but there's no need to make such a big deal out of it."

Jimmy retrieved his clothes from the closet, then slowly walked behind the screen. As he dressed, he heard the cameraman quietly chuckling at him under his breath.

Chapter Three

"Summer, hurry up. You are going to be late," Danita Hyatt yelled. She stood at the base of the staircase waiting for her three daughters to come down. "Vivian, can you get the girls down here now!" she yelled to her nanny.

She stood impatiently tapping her feet until finally ten-year-old Summer, eight-year-old Autumn, and six-year-old Winter came bounding down the steps. "Good morning, Mommy," each of them said. Danita smiled in spite of her anger and bent down to gently hug each one.

"Vivian, what took you so long? The driver is waiting to take the girls to day camp."

"I'm sorry, Mrs. Hyatt. Winter wanted to wear her pink Chanel outfit this morning, and I had to search for it."

Danita look surprised. "What do you mean you had to look for it? All of her things should be in her closet. That's hardly an excuse."

Vivian glanced over at the cameraman standing about five feet from them. "Um, well, it was in the closet, but it was way in the back, and um . . ."

Danita noticed that Vivian's eyes were darting back and forth between her and the cameras. "Ignore them," she ordered. "I told you we are doing this show. If you are uncomfortable with that, then you need to find another job."

"No, ma'am. I'm sorry," Vivian answered.

"Forget about it. Get the girls to the car and have Philippe stop by McDonald's so they can eat breakfast."

"Yes, Mrs. Hyatt." Vivian grabbed the younger girls by the hand and motioned for Summer to follow behind them.

A red-haired cameraman put his camera down and began packing things into a black leather bag. "We're going to follow the girls to school, but Gerard and his crew will be waiting to follow you to the church. All of the other stationary cameras are positioned around the house," he said.

Danita smiled politely at him and nodded. "That's great. I'll be ready to go in just a few moments."

An hour later, Danita finally walked out of her front door and climbed into the waiting limousine. Her driver, Philippe, had returned from dropping off the girls and was patiently waiting for her. He stepped onto the driveway and opened her door, then stood politely by, waiting for her to get in.

Earlier that morning, the reality show camera crew had attached a camera to the dashboard of the limo. As Danita sat down, she scooted over to the mark they'd placed on the seat so she'd be sure to be in camera range. She smoothed out her clothes, fluffed her wig, and pressed her lips together to even her lipstick, and then settled back in her seat.

"Are we going directly to the church, Mrs. Hyatt, or do you have some other stops to make this morning?" Philippe asked.

Danita hesitated before answering. There was a camera pointed directly at her face and she took a moment to carefully choose her words. "Let's stop by Piedmont Hospital. I'd like to take a few moments to visit some of my sick parishioners and pray with them. After that, we'll go to the church."

Philippe gave her a strange look. He'd been her driver for several years, and they'd never stopped at any hospitals to visit any sick parishioners. When he'd asked the question, he expected her to suggest her usual route. They normally stopped by Starbucks coffee, Lenox Square Mall, and a myriad of specialty shops. Danita would spend hours shopping, eating, and socializing before finally arriving at the church around noon. He glanced over at the camera on the dash, thankful that he was out of its scope. "Yes, ma'am," he answered. He put the limousine into drive and slowly drove down the expansive driveway to the front gate.

As they rode through the hectic Atlanta traffic, Danita sat quietly in the backseat thinking. She was so excited that she'd been chosen to be a part of the new reality series, *Revelations*. The past year of her life had been tumultuous. The man who she'd believed was the love of her life had gone fishing early one Saturday morning and never came home. Two days later, his capsized boat had been found several miles down the shore. His body washed up onto the banks of Lake Lanier less than a week later. At first, it seemed to have been a tragic accident. However, autopsy reports showed there was no water in his lungs. This indicated that he'd been dead before his body went into the water. Two months later, Danita found herself on trial for his murder.

Danita had been livid that the police actually thought she had something to do with his death. Of course, she didn't have an alibi. She'd spent the day at home alone while the girls visited with their paternal grandparents. She readily admitted to the police that she and her husband were having problems, and that it was true that he'd asked her for a divorce a few weeks prior to his death. It was also true that she was in line to inherit several million dollars in insurance money due to his death. But she still felt that didn't add up to murder.

Following her arrest, her children were removed from her home, and after spending three days in foster care, they were finally picked up by Danita's sister. Danita endured an exhausting three-month trial that consisted mostly of circumstantial evidence before being acquitted on all charges. Thankful for her freedom, she had picked up her children, then gone home feeling grateful that the nightmare was finally behind her. That's until her late husband Ben's family decided to file a wrongful death lawsuit against her. Danita was crushed by their betrayal. Following his death, she believed she'd been very generous to his family. She'd given his parents $10,000, and they had the option to share it with his two brothers and three sisters. Instead, she felt they'd allowed a sleazy lawyer to talk them into suing her, based on what happened to O. J. Simpson following his acquittal on murder charges.

Over half of her parishioners had left the church, and Danita had begun to think that her life was headed in the same direction as O. J.'s. Then she received the call from Anderson asking her to be a part of his new reality show. He explained to her that this show would help bring positive publicity to her church, rather than the negative publicity she'd received for so many months. He promised to be respectful when filming her children and to treat her like a lady at all times. He also encouraged her to start dating again and allow the cameras to tag along. Lastly, he told her that he felt with cameras in the courtroom, she'd have a better chance of gaining sympathy during her wrongful death lawsuit.

It only took her one day of thinking before she happily agreed to an interview. When she received the call that she'd been chosen out of hundreds of candidates,

Danita jumped so high she almost popped right out of her brand-new Beverly Johnson lace front wig.

As her driver pulled off of the freeway onto the exit that led to the hospital, she smiled contentedly to herself. The cameras were rolling, and she intended to show the viewing public a whole new Evangelist Danita Hyatt. For over a year they'd seen a monster presented to them on the evening news. The woman whom the police had portrayed as a murderous gold digger was going to be erased from the community's memory. She planned to be a loving, caring, praying, praising, and sacrificing minister. The viewers would love her and how well she got along with her daughters. They would cheer for her as she went on dates with handsome, eligible men of God, and feel sympathy for her if the dates went wrong. Danita had it all planned out in her head and felt that being on *Revelations* was the best thing that could have happened to her.

Philippe pulled up to the front of the hospital and stopped the limousine. He hopped out and walked around to the side door and opened it for Danita. She stepped out, slowly placing her designer Louboutin boots gently onto the sidewalk. Opening her new black Louis Vuitton Sobe Clutch purse, she reached inside and pulled out the piece of paper her secretary had given her. It contained the name and room number of the parishioner she planned to visit. As she walked inside the hospital, she desperately tried to remember what the old woman looked like. *Let's hope she's in a private room*, she thought to herself as she and her camera crew boarded the elevator.

When she arrived at the room number that had been listed on her paper, Danita took a deep breath, then lightly tapped on the door. "Come in," she heard a woman's voice say.

Slowly, she pushed the door open. "Hello, Sister, how are you feeling?" she said cheerily.

Inside the room, Sister Maxine James sat up in her bed. "Evangelist Hyatt?" she asked with a surprised tilt in her voice and a look of shock on her face.

"Yes, it's me. I came by to visit and pray with you. I hope you don't mind, but I'm doing a new television show. Is it okay if I bring my camera crew in?"

Sister James suddenly noticed the camera crew that was standing behind Danita, who'd already begun to film her. "Well, um, I guess it's all right," she answered.

Danita walked over and gave the woman a big bear hug. Stunned by the sudden display of affection, Sister James stiffened up, then cautiously returned her embrace. "I really appreciate you stopping by to see me. I feel so honored," she said.

"You don't need to thank me. I'm just so glad to see you sitting up and doing so well." Danita sat by the bed and took Sister James's hands into hers. "I was really worried when I heard that you'd suffered a heart attack."

"Oh no, I didn't have a heart attack. I'm here to have my appendix taken out."

Danita glanced over at the cameras and quickly recovered from her mistake. "Yes, of course. I'm so sorry. I've visited so many people this week it's hard for me to keep them all straight. Please forgive me, Sister." She smiled sweetly.

Danita sat and talked with Sister James for several moments before bowing her head in an insincere prayer. As the cameras rolled, she asked God for healing power, grace, and mercy. When she was finally done, she hugged Sister James again before leaving the room.

On impulse, she decided to pop into a few other patients' rooms to visit and pray with them as well. It was easy enough to pacify them for a few moments, then repeat her prayer she reasoned. She leisurely strolled from room to room, visiting and praying.

Finally, before leaving the hospital, she asked a nurse if she could speak with the hospital administrator. A tall, thin, blond woman joined her in the patients lounge. "How may I help you?" she asked.

"I'd like to make a donation to this hospital," Danita announced.

The blonde looked at her strangely. "Um, sure, I'd be happy to give you an address where you can send donations."

"I don't think you understand. I'm Evangelist Danita Hyatt. I'd like to make a donation in memory of my late husband, Ben Hyatt."

The blonde's eyebrows suddenly shot up as she realized why Danita looked so familiar to her. She'd watched her on the news nightly throughout her murder trial. Like most of the residents of Atlanta, she believed that Danita was guilty and should have gone to jail for a very long time. "I see. Exactly how much of a donation are you interested in making?"

Danita reached inside her purse and pulled out a check written on her personal account. She held it up while the cameraman took a shot of it before handing it over to the administrator.

"You want to donate $25,000?" the administrator asked. Her voice was full of surprise.

"Yes, as I stated, in memory of my late husband. His full name was Benjamin Franklin Hyatt."

The hospital administrator softened her stare as her negative opinion of Danita Hyatt began to fade. *Perhaps she's not as big of a gold digger as we all thought*, she mused. "This is extremely generous, Mrs. Hyatt. Thank you so much."

"There's no need for thanks. I'm sure this would please Ben very much." Danita stood and shook the administrator's hand. Then she casually walked out of the hospital and got back inside her waiting limousine.

They arrived at Danita's church several moments later. Hyatt Evangelical Temple was housed inside an expansive building that she and her late husband had purchased for less than $2 million. Its sanctuary was large enough to accommodate four thousand people. Adjacent to the sanctuary, they'd built an educational wing that held thirty-seven classrooms, a dining hall, a library, a gymnasium with an indoor swimming pool, a computer lab, and several offices, including Danita's.

As usual, her driver stopped directly in front of the doorway that sat closest to her office door. She stepped out of the car just as the camera crew's SUV pulled up beside her.

"Is there a good place where we can park our van?" the leader of the crew asked.

"Um, yes, go ahead and drive around the side of the building. There is plenty of parking there. I'll have Philippe wait here for you, and then he'll show you where my office is," she answered.

The crew leader nodded at her then drove off in the direction she had indicated. As soon as he was out of sight, she dashed inside the church building and rushed down the hall to her office. Her secretary was sitting behind her desk typing a letter. "Karyn, are there any cameras set up in here yet?" she asked.

"No, not yet. I thought the camera crew was coming in with you."

"They are. I mean they did. They are parking their vehicle. I need you to take care of something quickly before they get in here."

"Sure, what it is?"

"Call my bank and cancel payment on a check. It's for $25,000, and it was written to Piedmont Hospital."

Without another word, Danita walked into her office to freshen her makeup before the camera crew arrived inside.

Chapter Four

Zack Morton trotted up his basement steps, walked into the kitchen, then turned and locked the basement door behind him. After pulling his key from the lock, he turned the tumblers on three deadbolts, ensuring they were also locked securely. Next, he pulled an iron bar into place and clicked a padlock onto it. When he was done, he turned to his wife and smiled. "Good morning."

His wife, Charlene, shook her head at him before placing a plate on the table. "Why do you go through all of that every morning? Nobody has any desire to go down there, least of all me."

He sniffed his egg white omelet, which was sitting on the plate, before answering her. "I've told you before, that equipment could be dangerous if one of the children were to play with it. I just prefer being safe, rather than sorry."

"One lock could keep them out. Besides, they are old enough to know better."

He sniffed his breakfast again. "This smells funny. The eggs must be bad. Throw it out and fix me another one."

Charlene took the plate away and tossed the contents down the garbage disposal, then dutifully went to the refrigerator to retrieve more eggs.

"Throw the whole carton away," Zack instructed. He picked up his newspaper to read while he waited.

Charlene tossed the carton into her tall, white kitchen trash bin; then she returned to the refrigerator and pulled out an unopened carton of eggs from the three remaining on the shelf. She made a mental note to purchase more. As she worked, she had to remind herself that she loved her husband dearly, but his eccentricities got on her last nerve. On their first date, they'd left two restaurants before settling on one that he felt was an acceptable place for them to eat. He'd told her that the first one smelled strange, although her nose didn't detect any scent. They'd been together for twelve years, and in that time, they'd walked out of restaurants, movies, plays, and even people's homes because Zack's nose didn't agree with the atmosphere. He seemed to be able to smell things that no one else could, and if it bothered him, they had to leave.

The second restaurant they walked out of that night had too many white chefs. "I'm no racist," he'd said. "I am white, for goodness' sake, but black people are just better cooks. I haven't eaten a meal cooked by a white person in years, and I don't plan to." She'd often wondered if he had issues with his own skin. He'd never dated a white woman, and 90 percent of his congregation was black. When she questioned him, he stated that he just wasn't attracted to white women. It wasn't a bigoted thing; he just loved the beauty of darker hued skin tones, rounder hips, buxom breasts, full lips, and thick hair. Charlene fit his type perfectly.

His quirkiness didn't end with smells and people. He never wore the same pair of underwear or socks more than once. He'd told her that those items could never be properly cleaned; therefore, he insisted that they be disposed of after use.

Every morning, he spent two hours in his private gym working out, and no one, not even Charlene, was allowed to interrupt him. Afterward, he showered in his private basement bathroom and changed into a white wife beater T-shirt and white cotton underwear that Charlene referred to as tighty whiteys. His daily attire consisted of a white button-down dress shirt, black slacks, black socks, and black shoes. On Sundays, he added a black tie and suit jacket.

After he was done each morning in the basement, he'd enter the kitchen, lock the door, and wait for Charlene to serve his breakfast. They had a housekeeper and a nanny, but he refused to allow either of them to cook his meals. That was his wife's duty, he'd told her.

Charlene set a new egg white omelet on the table and waited for Zack's approval just as their front doorbell rang. "That must be the camera crew," she said.

Their housekeeper escorted the crew into the kitchen before returning to her duties. "Good morning, Reverend Morton, I'm CiCi." The crew leader smiled and stuck out his hand to greet him. He was a tall, stocky, African American man with a bald head. Charlene watched her husband's nose wrinkle up.

"What's that cologne you are wearing?" Zack asked.

"Uhm, Lagerfeld. It's my favorite," he answered.

"Don't wear it again in my house. It's offensive. As a matter of fact, don't wear it in my presence ever again."

CiCi gave him an odd look before pulling his hand away. "Um, yeah . . . So can we get a tour of the house so we can get these cameras set up?"

Zack continued eating his breakfast. "Have a seat. I'd like to talk and set down some ground rules."

CiCi pulled out a chair at the table and sat down while the rest of his crew stood looking around awkwardly. Charlene offered him a cup of coffee, which he declined. He sat patiently, waiting for Zack to speak.

"I'm really excited about this new show," Zack said. "My wife and I have talked with our children, and they are excited about it as well. But, of course, there have to be some boundaries so that things run smoothly."

"Of course." CiCi nodded his head in agreement.

"First of all, there will be no cameras following my sons to school. Twin boys don't do anything but go to class. I will, however, allow the cameras at their sporting events. They both are on the school soccer team. Luther is on the peewee football team, and Martin is studying karate. Those activities should be interesting to your viewers." Zack paused and took the last bite of his omelet. He drained his glass of orange juice before turning and pointing at his wife. "As you can see, she is pregnant with our third child. There will be no cameras at the hospital before, during, or after her delivery."

"But Reverend Morton—" CiCi began to protest, only to be stopped as Zack stood up from the table.

"That's not negotiable. My wife is the first lady of my church. Remember that she is first in my life, and she is always to be regarded as a lady."

Charlene smiled as he gave her a quick peck on the cheek and motioned for the crew to follow him as he showed them the rest of the house. Zack Morton was eccentric, sometimes he was demanding, and Charlene's family still had not gotten over the fact that she married a white man, but none of that mattered to Charlene. He was also kind, generous, and compassionate. With sandy-blond hair, piercing blue eyes, and skin that glowed almost golden when he tanned, he was drop-dead gorgeous. He was a wonderful father to their sons, the best lover she'd ever had, and most important of all, a man of God. Her love for him was deep. She believed that was all that truly mattered.

Charlene felt her baby kick, and her stomach growled, begging for sustenance. Quietly she sat down at the table and ate her breakfast alone, as she did most mornings.

She'd just finished eating and was rising from the table when she heard a tapping at her back door. Cautiously, she walked over and peered out the window of the door.

"What are you doing here? How did you get past Marty, the guard at the gate?" she asked through the glass.

"Marty loves me. Open up, Charlene," her cousin, Vanessa, answered.

"Zack is upstairs, and the camera crew for the new show is here. What do you want?" Charlene looked nervously over her shoulder, praying that Zack would not walk in.

"What's he still doing here? I didn't see the Jaguar in the driveway."

"I just told you, the camera crew for the new show is here, and Zack is giving them a tour of the house. He sold the Jaguar last week."

"I don't care if he's here. Let me in. This morning air is chilly," Vanessa whined.

Charlene glanced over her shoulder once again before finally unlocking the door and letting her cousin enter. Zack wasn't very close to his own family, and he was not a fan of Charlene's family either. She knew he would not be pleased to see her cousin standing in the middle of his kitchen.

"Look at you, cow. You are about to pop." Vanessa rubbed Charlene's protruding belly and laughed.

"Be quiet. You know Zack can hear a rat pee on cotton a block away."

Vanessa covered her mouth to stifle another laugh. "I bet he can smell it too," she said sarcastically.

Charlene laughed out loud, then quickly covered her mouth, but it was too late. Zack was on his way down the stairs, and within a few seconds, he was staring at the two of them in the kitchen. "Did I miss the joke?" he asked.

"Hey, Zack, what's going on?" Vanessa asked innocently.

"Hello, Vanessa. What are you doing here?" he asked.

Vanessa looked cautiously over at Charlene before answering. "I just came by to visit with my cuz."

Zack gave her a disapproving look before turning to Charlene. "What are your plans for today?"

"I have a doctor's appointment at ten; then I have a meeting with Luther and Martin's teacher at eleven. After lunch, I was planning to go to the mall and look at baby furniture for a while, then back here before the boys return from school."

Vanessa rolled her eyes and sucked her teeth as she listened. It irritated her that whenever she came to visit, she always heard a similar conversation. Zack needed to know where Charlene was every hour of the day.

"Okay, fine. I'll tell the camera crew leader to meet you back here around noon. They can follow you this afternoon." He leaned in and kissed her gently on the lips before turning to leave the kitchen.

"Zack," Charlene called after him, "I need the credit card."

"I thought you were just looking at furniture today. When you are ready to buy, I'll go along with you."

"My car is low on gas . . . and um . . . I wanted to buy a card for the twins' teacher. It's her birthday next week, and I thought I'd take it with me today."

Zack reached into his back pocket and pulled out his wallet. He bypassed the credit cards and pulled out a twenty-dollar bill. He handed it to Charlene. "This should cover the card and a small gift. You can drive my car today; it's full. I'll take yours and make sure it's full when I return." After kissing her once more he walked out of the kitchen.

"Why do you let him—" Vanessa screeched before Charlene interrupted her with a look that said, "Shut it up right now."

"You are divorced, and you don't understand. Zack is my husband, and he is the head of our house. I have no problem with that, so why do you?"

"Let him be the head of the house, but that's *your* money he's controlling. You married a poor country boy from Asheboro, North Carolina."

"It's Asheville," Charlene corrected her, before taking a seat at the table.

"Whatever. He was still broke." Vanessa sat down and helped herself to a glass of orange juice. "He had nothing, and you had plenty. That's what I'm saying. Now *you* have to ask *him* for every dime you spend. It's not right."

Although she hated to admit it, her cousin had a point. Charlene was the daughter of one of Atlanta's most prominent physicians. Their family was considered to be among Atlanta's African American aristocracy. Following in her dad's footsteps, she'd graduated from John Hopkins School of Medicine. She had just completed her residency and was enjoying her first month on the job as a physician in her father's clinic when Zack entered her life and changed everything.

Zack Morton came in carrying a four-year-old black girl who'd twisted her ankle on the steps of his church. As the pastor, he felt responsible for her accident and accompanied her parents to the doctor and offered to pay for everything. The problem was, Zack couldn't afford to pay for a Band-Aid. He took one look at the bill and begged Charlene to put him on a payment plan so that the child's parents would not know.

Since then, he'd taken a small run-down church in the ghetto with fewer than twenty-five members and built his congregation into a supermegachurch with more than ten thousand members. Following their marriage, Charlene gave up her medical practice and became a full-time wife, first lady, and mother. She loved Zack, and she loved their life. Without hesitation, she let Vanessa know that. "He's not broke now. Zack's church brings in close to $1 million in revenue each Sunday. So what we have now is ours. He's never refused me anything that I needed. Mind your business, okay?" She gave her cousin a sly smile.

Vanessa smiled back, and the tension floated from the room. "Fine. Get that housekeeper down here to fix me some breakfast. I'm starved."

Chapter Five

"This waiting is driving me crazy. Has it been fifteen minutes yet?" Brandon Kitts paced back and forth in his bedroom while glancing at his watch. His wife, Tia, had just taken a pregnancy test, and he was anxious for the results.

"No, it's only been about ten minutes," Tia said.

"The camera crew from the new show is due here any second. Why didn't you buy the test that only takes a few minutes?"

"This one is new and supposed to be more accurate. Just relax and wait."

Brandon glanced out of the bedroom window and let his eyes scan the length of their driveway. "Oh great," he said sarcastically. "I see a van pulling up. It must be them."

Tia pressed the intercom button on the wall near their bedroom door. She waited until her housekeeper, Sophia, answered. "Sophia, I think the camera crew is here. My husband and I will be down in a few moments. Please let them in and have them take a seat in the great room." Tia released the intercom button and went into her expansive bedroom to retrieve the pregnancy test she'd left sitting on the counter. She closed the door behind her, leaving Brandon waiting in their bedroom. Without looking at the test, she tossed it into the trash. There was no need to check it; Tia was positive that she wasn't pregnant. Sitting down at her vanity table, she lay her head in her hands as she waited.

Tia had known since the day she'd married Brandon five years earlier that more than anything else in the world, he wanted to be a father. His mother had given birth to three girls and four boys, with Brandon being the youngest. All of his siblings had followed his parents' lead and also had large families, with each of them having four or more children. Brandon doted on his nieces and nephews and dreamed of the day when he'd have children of his own to spoil. He'd shared his dreams with Tia on the night he proposed. The two of them had just shared a moonlit picnic on the beach in Hilton Head, S.C. Tia was enjoying the warm night air while sipping on a glass of red wine. Brandon knelt in front of her and took her hand into his. "I love you, and I want to share the rest of my life with you. I want to make babies with you and just spend the remainder of my life making you and our children happy," he said.

Tia was stunned. Their relationship had begun as a casual fling, and she honestly was not in love with him. It wasn't his fault. Brandon was very handsome with shoulder-length locks and cocoa-brown skin. As a member of the NFL, he worked out religiously, and his body was toned to perfection. He was also sweet, charming, and a great catch. Tia simply wasn't interested in being caught.

Brandon wasn't the only one of her former husband's teammates she'd had flings with. Brandon just happened to be the one her husband caught in bed with her. When he asked for a divorce, she moved in with Brandon because she didn't have anywhere else to go. Tia felt she wasn't the kind of woman who could commit to one man. She enjoyed variety, and she loved sex. As soon as her divorce was final and she received her settlement, she had intended to live it up and enjoy herself. Marrying another football player and having his babies did not fit into that plan. Rather than break Brandon's heart, she told him that she needed time to think about it.

Four days later, after returning to Atlanta, Tia called Brandon and accepted his proposal. That was after she'd received a call from her attorney letting her know that she would not receive anything in her divorce settlement. Her prenuptial agreement had a clause in it that stated she would get nothing if she was caught cheating. Her attorney suggested that they fight it out in court, but Tia declined.

Two weeks after her divorce was final, she became Mrs. Brandon Kitts. Although she didn't have love, Tia was content to know that she had security. Brandon was wealthier than her first husband, and he loved her. For a few months, Tia was almost happy. Until the night that Brandon told her he was leaving the NFL. He'd found God and felt the call into ministry. Before she knew it, Tia found herself standing beside him as he purchased his first church.

Tia struggled with going from being the perfect NFL trophy wife to being the first lady of a church. Being a trophy wife came easy to Tia. She was five feet four, with peanut-buttery skin and chestnut eyes. Her hair was a perfectly coifed black weave that hung midway down her back. *Voluptuous* was the word most used to describe her body that was toned and curved in all of the right places. Most men considered her to be exceptionally beautiful.

Tia believed that she'd been born to be someone's perfect black Barbie doll trophy wife. But she knew nothing about being a first lady. Until she married Brandon, Tia had never even been inside a church. It took some time, but eventually she learned to fake her relationship with God and the church. She watched television and mimicked the way other first ladies and women in the church acted. Tia was able to copy their every move and action successfully, except for getting pregnant. They never used protection, and Brandon often remarked that he could not understand why God had not blessed them with a baby.

"Tia, I need to go speak with the camera crew. What does the test say?" Brandon impatiently knocked loudly on the bathroom door.

Taking a deep breath, Tia stood up and went to the door. She took another deep breath before finally opening it. She greeted her husband with a huge smile. "It's positive. I'm pregnant," she said.

Brandon picked her up and spun her around as he grinned excitedly. "Hallelujah!" he yelled. Then he suddenly put her down. "Oh, I'm sorry. Did I hurt you?" he said, gently touching her stomach.

"No, I'm fine," Tia said laughing. She had never seen him so excited.

"It's a boy. I can feel it. You are carrying Brandon Kitts Jr. in there. Let's go downstairs. I want to share this news with the camera crew. It will be a great start for our first show."

"Honey, wait. I don't want to tell everyone just yet."

Brandon looked at her strangely. "Why not? This is incredible news."

"It's too soon. What if . . . well, what if I miscarry again? Let's at least wait until my second trimester before we spread the news."

Brandon smiled; then he reached out and pulled her into a hug. "You're right. Forgive me. I was so excited I forgot about what happened last time." He released her from the hug and gently kissed her on the lips.

As they left their bedroom and walked downstairs to greet the camera crew Tia's mind was spinning like an expensive clock. Her thoughts went back to her first marriage. *She had awakened one morning feeling nauseous. After checking her calendar, she realized that her period was late. She immediately rushed to the drugstore and bought a pregnancy test. The time period that she waited for the results seemed like sheer agony to her until, with relief, she read the negative results.*

Tia had decided as a teenager that she did not want children. In her opinion, they were loud, messy, and expensive. For that reason, she began taking birth control pills at seventeen, and they were a constant part of her diet, except for the rare occasions that she forgot. Her brief pregnancy scare convinced her that she needed to make sure that she never conceived a child with anyone.

Tia was home alone as her husband was away at spring training camp for his football team. Before he returned, Tia had her tubes tied. She did not regret her decision, as being a mother was not something that she ever dreamed of. Even though Brandon constantly talked about being a father, Tia knew it would never happen.

She'd faked a pregnancy during their second year of marriage, and she eventually had to fake a miscarriage. It was her hope that this would pacify Brandon for a while, but its effect was only temporary. Tia grew weary of the lies and pretending to be a great first lady and decided that divorcing Brandon would be her best option. Although she'd signed a prenuptial agreement, there was no evidence of infidelity and she felt there was a good chance that she'd receive a nice settlement. Her lawyer saw things differently. At that time, they'd only been married a few years and her lawyer felt her settlement would be minimal. He advised her that the

most effective way for her to walk away from the mar-
riage with a substantial settlement was to give Bran-
don at least one child, maybe two.

Tia was furious as she left his office. Not only did
she not want any children, there was no way that she
could give birth even if she wanted to. Instead of go-
ing home, she'd stopped at a local interior design stu-
dio, The Periwinkle Palace. The owner, Quincy, was
flamboyant, loud, bossy, and gay. He was also Tia's
best friend in the whole world. She sat in his private
office and begged him to give her answers to all her
problems.

Quincy's plan was so over-the-top that it had taken
Tia over a year to put all the pieces into place, but she
was sure she'd found a foolproof way to not only fake
her pregnancy, but to also give Brandon the child he'd
always wanted.

They reached the bottom of the stairs where the
camera crew was waiting for them in the front entryway. Brandon reached out to shake each person's hand
before turning to Tia. He politely introduced them.

Lights, camera, action, Tia thought, as she began to
"act" like the perfect first lady.

Chapter Six

The lights dimmed, and Julian settled back comfortably in his chair. It wasn't the usual screening procedure, but he had become excited about his new reality series. For that reason, he'd decided to go over the footage personally in his home theatre with just him and Anderson in attendance. Anderson arrived right on time with the reels tucked safely under his arms. After setting up the video to play on Julian's fifty-inch screen, the two of them waited patiently to see the raw footage before it went to their editors.

They shared a bowl of popcorn while they watched the tapes. Julian felt disappointed. All of the footage he'd watched so far had been bland and boring in his opinion. "What is this? I thought we agreed that we didn't want a sanitized version of their lives. Where's the dirt?" he demanded.

"This is just the first day of shooting, Julian. The camera crews were settling in and getting to know the ministers and their families. Trust me."

Julian turned his attention back to the screen, still feeling severely disappointed. He watched for several more moments; then he abruptly grabbed the remote control and turned the television off. "Get out. Get out now!" he suddenly screamed.

Anderson jumped from his seat. He was so startled that he turned over the popcorn bowl and scattered popcorn all over the floor. "I'm sorry, Julian. It *will* get better, I promise. Just let me clean up this mess and then we—"

Julian interrupted him. "I said get out! I don't want to watch anymore." He pointed toward the door.

Slowly Anderson walked to the door feeling defeated. "Does this mean we are not moving forward with the show?" he asked quietly.

"Leave me alone. I need time to think."

"Okay, man, that's good. Just think about things, and I'll call you tomorrow. Is that okay?" He stared at Julian waiting for an answer, but none came. Julian stood stoically staring at the blank screen.

He was still standing staring at the screen long after Anderson had left the room. As hard as he tried, he couldn't get his feet to move. Inside his head he heard voices from his past, and his heart began beating rapidly. His pulse quickened, and he felt as if he might faint. Finally, he returned to his seat and picked up the remote control. The tape started again—and he saw her face.

He knew she had moved to Atlanta, but in all of the years that he'd been there, he couldn't find her. He checked phone records and bought public records accounts online. He had poured over the information, but there was nothing there. It was as if she'd disappeared off the face of the earth. He had given up hope that he'd ever find her again when he received a letter from a high school friend. In the letter, the friend told him that his beloved Ophelia Guzman had left Atlanta and died in a car accident while traveling from South Carolina to her new home in Florida. The friend had even sent along a newspaper clipping verifying the story.

That weekend, Julian flew to Florida and placed flowers on her grave. He sat in the cemetery and wept for hours before finally going home. Although he'd dated many women in his lifetime, Julian made a vow that he would never marry. The one true love of his life was gone, and no one could replace her.

Is it really her? Is she alive? he wondered. *Maybe it's just someone who resembles her. I'm tripping. She's dead. Ophelia is dead.* He settled into his seat and re-started the tape. She was descending the staircase on her way to the kitchen. The woman on the tape had long, dark brown hair that wasn't a weave. He could tell by the way her hair bounced as she walked down the steps. Her luxurious hair was one of the things he had adored most about Ophelia. Julian fell asleep at night with his hands wrapped in it and woke each morning still entwined.

As he watched her, he recognized the familiar sway of her hips. This woman's hips were a bit wider than his Ophelia, but she wasn't fat. He believed it was just possible that she'd filled out in all the right places. Although she was in her late thirties, the woman on the screen still looked youthful and vibrant. She looked the way Julian imagined Ophelia would look, if she had lived.

For the next two hours, Julian watched the tapes and studied the woman. *My mind is playing tricks on me. She looks like Ophelia, she sounds like Ophelia, she smiles like Ophelia, but there's no way she could be Ophelia.*

Exasperated, he left the theater room and went into his home office. Julian sat down behind the huge mahogany desk and pulled out the contracts Anderson had given him for all of the show's participants. Tossing papers aside without noticing they were scattering all over the floor, he searched until he found her profile. Slowly he read it.

Yolanda Smalls Snow had met and married Bishop Jimmy Snow ten years earlier. She was a stay-at-home mom to his teenage children. She was active in church activities and was head of the dramatic arts ministry of her congregation. After reading this, Julian thought back to the first time he'd seen Ophelia on stage. Their small hometown was predominantly white so whenever there was a high school play, it was inevitable that the black actors would be cast in very small roles. That didn't matter to Julian. He felt his beloved Ophelia stole the show, even if she didn't have many lines. Her mere presence was breathtaking.

Years later, he was excited when he learned she'd gotten a principal role in a play. He read an article in the newspaper that said she would be playing Rose Maxon in August Wilson's play *Fences* at the local community theater. Julian sent roses to her dressing room and showed up every night with another armful of roses to present to her. But that had been so many years before. One day, Ophelia had walked out of his life and never returned. There had been no explanation and no long good-byes. She just disappeared from his life, leaving Julian devastated.

His heart desperately wanted to believe that he'd found her again, but his mind would not stop asking questions. *Who is Yolanda Smalls, and if she's really Ophelia, why is she using that name?* Julian dug deeper into his desk until he found the newspaper clipping announcing her death. Although he had it memorized, he read it again.

A one-car accident claimed the life of a local woman. The driver of the car, and victim, has been identified as twenty-four-year-old Ophelia Guzman, of Tallahassee, Fla. Ms. Guzman was heading north on Hwy I-85 in South Carolina when it is believed she fell asleep at the wheel. Her car veered off the road and crashed into a tree. Guzman was pronounced dead at the scene. Investigators state that there were no other occupants in the car, and no other vehicles involved in the accident.

It is believed that Ms. Guzman had no living family. A memorial service will be held for her at Mt. Temple Mortuary, and her remains interred at Forestdale Cemetery. If you wish to make donations to cover funeral costs, please contact the mortuary.

Julian received the letter and clipping two weeks after Ophelia's burial. It was too late for him to say good-bye. Ophelia's parents had died when she was a small child, and her grandmother, who raised her, had passed away while she was in college. Julian felt horrible that she had died alone and sincerely wished he had been there for her.

After placing the newspaper back inside his desk, Julian picked up his phone and dialed Anderson's number. "Hey, it's me," he said solemnly. Julian felt drained, as if he'd relived Ophelia walking out of his life and her death all over again.

"Hey, man, I'm so glad you called. Listen, I talked with my editing guy, and we can fix this. We can punch it up and find some drama. Even if we have to twist their words, there is nothing in the contracts that can stop us. Just don't give up on it yet."

"I'm not giving up. That's why I called. I overreacted, and I'm sorry."

Anderson was too wrapped up in his own thoughts to notice the sadness in Julian's tone. He began rattling off details of the next few days' shooting schedules. He continued on for several moments before he realized Julian was not answering. "Are you there?"

"Yes, I'm here. Listen, what do you know about Bishop Snow's wife, Yolanda?"

"Nothing really. She's a former actress that nobody's ever heard of. I know they are boring, but we can't kick them off just yet. Give me some time to work on them. I can get some investigators digging. Maybe there's some dirt in their background that we don't know about yet."

Julian pondered what Anderson was saying for a moment and realized that he could help him. An investigator could dig up all the information he'd need on Yolanda Smalls Snow. Deep inside, he believed that she was Ophelia, but there were too many holes and unanswered questions. He knew he had to play his cards just right if he was going to get the truth.

"That's a great idea. Dig up anything and everything that you can find on her. I mean on them."

"I'll get right on it," Anderson answered excitedly.

Julian hung up the phone and went upstairs to his bedroom. His mind was still reeling, and his heart ached. He'd grieved for Ophelia every day since he learned she died. Reaching into his nightstand, he pulled out the last photograph he had of them together. They were happy and smiling at a church picnic. He remembered that she'd brought the potato salad that he loved so much. It was her grandmother's special recipe that contained mayonnaise, mustard, and a secret ingredient she refused to tell. Several of the members requested it for church functions. It was the best he'd ever tasted.

Finally, he returned the picture to its drawer and prepared for bed. As he showered, he found himself reminiscing about their first kiss. It wasn't in the shower, it was in the rain. But whenever he felt water pelting his head, he remembered her lips and her kiss. After changing into his pajamas, he climbed into bed and stared up into his skylight. *Have I really found you again, Ophelia?*

Julian wasn't sure, but he made another vow to himself that if Yolanda Snow was indeed his beloved Ophelia returned to him, he would never ever let her go again.

Chapter Seven

As she stood in her kitchen preparing dinner, Yolanda tried to contain her excitement. It had been over a month since the camera crews began filming them for *Revelations,* and after dinner, she and her husband would join the rest of the cast for the premiere party and screening at the W Hotel in Buckhead. Earlier in the day she'd laid out the new dress she purchased just for the party. She'd chosen a white one-shoulder chiffon gown with flattering ruching and iridescent beads at the empire waist. Yolanda felt it was reminiscent of Michelle Obama's inaugural gown. Although she wasn't the first lady of the United States, she wanted to look just as beautiful as she represented her church as their first lady. It had taken some time, but she'd finally convinced Jimmy to rent a tuxedo for the occasion.

"Momlanda, my dress doesn't fit," her stepdaughter Priscilla said. She walked into the kitchen carrying the blue A-line empire dress she'd worn to her junior prom just a few weeks prior.

When Yolanda met and married their father, Priscilla was seven years old, and her younger brother Jimmy Jr., or JJ as he was called, was five. Neither of them had many memories of their natural mother, but both she and Jimmy felt it was important that they not erase her from their hearts. She wasn't comfortable being called Mom or Mommy, but she also felt it would be disrespectful of them to call her by her name.

So they'd come up with a compromise, and she'd been Momlanda since that day.

"It fit when you wore it to the prom, and you haven't gained any weight. What's the problem?" Yolanda asked. She turned the gas down on the chicken she was cooking so that it would not burn while she spoke with Priscilla.

"I don't know. It just won't fit. If I left now, I could get a new one and be back before it's time to leave for the party."

"What about dinner? They are only serving drinks at the party."

"I'll grab something at the mall. Please?" she begged.

Yolanda knew that the dress probably fit fine. Priscilla just wanted a chance to see her friends at the mall and get a new dress for the party. She hesitated for a moment, but then realized it was a special occasion for them all.

"The car keys and the Visa debit card are in my purse. Do not spend more than $200," she said.

Priscilla hugged her and gave her a kiss on the cheek. "Thanks so much." She rushed out the back door to the garage.

"Hurry, we don't want to be late tonight," Yolanda yelled after her.

A few hours later, just as the family was completing dinner, Priscilla excitedly burst through the back door. "I found the perfect dress. I can't wait for everyone to see me in it."

"You'll still look like a pencil with a black eraser," JJ said. He began laughing loudly.

"You're just jealous because I'm not fat like your girl-friend," Priscilla shot back.

"Teresa is not fat. She has a gland problem," JJ snapped. He turned to his father for help. "Dad, make her stop saying that." JJ folded his arms across his chest in anger.

"JJ, stop teasing your sister, and Priscilla, you know better than to call Teresa fat. I need to hear apologies from both of you," Jimmy replied.

"Sorry," they both mumbled.

Priscilla grabbed a chicken drumstick from the serving platter and sat down at the table. "I can hardly wait until the show premieres. That's all people were talking about at the mall. There were publicity posters all over the place."

"Oh yeah, and I heard there might be some celebrities at the party tonight," JJ added.

"Really? Like who?" Yolanda asked eagerly.

"Sharmaine Cleveland is a definite because she's a member of our church. I also heard that we might see BeBe and CeCe Winans, Jill Scott, and maybe even Tyler Perry."

Yolanda's eyes grew wider with excitement. "Oh my goodness, I would love to meet Tyler Perry and be in one of his movies."

"Dad, aren't you excited too?" Priscilla asked.

"Sure, honey," Jimmy answered halfheartedly.

"I'm gonna finish this chicken in my room. I need to get dressed," Priscilla said as she stood up from the table.

"Wait, I need you to retwist my locks. I want to look good tonight," JJ said.

"Why do you always wait until the last minute? Come on," she answered.

Jimmy sat quietly at the table while the children rushed out; then he began helping Yolanda clear the dishes.

"Honey, you don't have to do that. I laid your tuxedo out on the bed. Go ahead and start getting dressed. I'll be up in a minute."

Jimmy left the dishes on the counter, but instead of going upstairs, he sat down at the table again. "Yolanda, I have a bad feeling about this. Something in my spirit is telling me that we should not go to this premiere tonight."

Yolanda spun around and stared at him. "Are you *serious?*"

He slowly nodded his head. "God has been nudging me ever since we signed those contracts. I don't quite know what it is, but I just can't shake this feeling."

Yolanda walked over to the table and sat down with him. She sighed loudly. "Jimmy, I know being on TV is not important to you, but please don't spoil this night for me. I've been looking forward to it for too long."

"I'm not trying to spoil it. Besides, it's only been a month of filming. You haven't been looking forward to it for that long."

"I've dreamed of being on television or in movies since I was five years old. Tonight, we are going to walk the red carpet and rub elbows with Atlanta's elite. There will be photographers and reporters all vying for a chance to see us. This could be my big break."

"Your big break? I thought you gave up on being a movie star years ago. I thought you were happy being a wife and mother."

"I am happy. You know that I love you and the children. This is different."

Jimmy leaned back in his chair. "How is it different? For ten years you've led me to believe that those were just childhood fantasies. Now I find out that all along you've been waiting for your 'big break.'"

Yolanda stood up and began pacing around the kitchen. "I gave it all up. I stopped going to auditions and looking for parts in movies. I gave it all up the day I became your wife and mother to your children."

"*My* children?" Jimmy pointed at himself. "I thought they were *our* children?"

"They are. You know I love them both as if I'd carried them myself. I didn't mean it like that. All I'm saying is that when I fell in love with you I gave up that dream. Now, God has given me a second chance. I now have the unique opportunity to be both. I never thought that I could."

Jimmy stood up and walked over to her. He stepped in her path to stop her frantic pacing. "Listen to me. I'm not trying to crush your dreams. I'm just concerned for our family."

"Our family will always be my first priority. You should know that."

He nodded his head. "You're right. Tell you what, I'll finish up in here, and you start getting dressed. You know it takes you women longer to dress than us men," he teased.

Yolanda stood on her tiptoes and gave him a kiss. "Thank you for understanding."

He smiled when she said it, but Jimmy truly did not understand. He had dreams once too. While he attended college he'd played All-Conference Baseball and dreamed of one day pitching for the Atlanta Braves. When he'd received the call into ministry he fought it. All he wanted to do was play baseball, not preach God's Word.

Then one morning as he was taking his usual morning jog around campus, he noticed a stray dog running in his direction. He tried to swerve to avoid it, but instead, he tripped over the dog and landed on the ground, injuring his pitching arm.

He lay in his hospital bed that night and said an anguish-filled prayer, "Okay, God, you have my attention. You wanted me to preach, so you fixed it so that I can never play baseball again. Fine. I get it. I'll preach if that's what you want me to do."

Over the next several months as he recuperated he began to listen to God's call and study the Word. Jimmy enrolled in seminary classes and resigned himself to live the life that God had chosen for him. The following spring, he went in for a follow-up visit with his doctor.

"Your arm looks great," the doctor had said.

"Yeah, it feels a lot better too. I don't wake up at night with that throbbing sensation anymore."

"That's because the muscle tissue has completely healed. It may take awhile, but with some physical therapy and hard work, you should be pitching again in no time."

Jimmy stared at the doctor. "Are you kidding me? I gave up baseball completely. I'm studying to be a minister now."

"Really? I had no idea. Well, your arm is fine. Maybe you can preach sermons from the mound like Jesus did on the mount." The doctor laughed lightly at his own bad joke, but Jimmy did not join in.

That night in his dorm room, Jimmy had a peculiar dream. All through the night he prayed and wrestled with God. Surprisingly, he awoke the next morning feeling fresh and renewed. Then finally he made his decision. Being a minister was his calling, and he no longer cared about being a baseball star. His relationship with God was all that mattered. Jimmy knew then that God had given him a choice so that he could serve Him fully, and not because his other choices were taken away.

When he'd married Yolanda, he believed she'd made the same choice. He believed that she had married him because she loved him and knew that being his wife was the right choice. Now he wondered if she chose him only because she felt her movie career was impossible. The same as he'd originally chosen God only because he thought being a baseball star wasn't possible.

Jimmy placed the last dish in the dishwasher and started the machine. As he climbed the stairs, a feeling of foreboding filled his entire spirit. Stopping on the stairs, he prayed. "Lord what are you trying to tell me?" He paused and waited. "Father, is my wife unhappy with our marriage?" Again he paused and waited.

Yolanda stepped out of their bedroom and yelled to him as he stood lost in prayer on the stairway. "Jimmy, hurry up. I'm almost dressed."

Jimmy suddenly looked up at her. "I'm coming."

Later that evening, they stood arm in arm with their children on either side of them as the paparazzi's flashbulbs went off. Then the four of them walked the red carpet and entered the hotel. Jimmy only wanted to find their seats and wait for the screening to begin, but Yolanda insisted on mingling in the crowd and searching for celebrities. Priscilla thought she spotted Spike Lee on the other side of the room, and she, JJ, and Yolanda rushed over to investigate, leaving Jimmy all alone. This was the part Jimmy hated the most, but Yolanda reveled in the attention.

"Bishop Snow?"

Jimmy turned around as he heard his name. "Um, hello," he said. Jimmy took the woman's outstretched hand into his. He stared at her with a perplexed look on his face.

"I'm Charlene Morton. We met at the photographer's studio last week when Zack was there doing his publicity photos."

Jimmy smiled broadly, "Oh, yes, I remember. Where is your husband? He isn't going to miss the premiere, is he?"

"No. He left something in the car, so he went back for it. How have you been?"

"Fine, just fine."

Charlene looked him up and down. "No offense, Bishop, but you don't look fine. Frankly you look a little uptight and out of place. Is everything all right?"

"I'm just not real comfortable in this type of crowd." He laughed nervously.

"I'm not either. Being on television was Zack's idea. I'm just glad that the wives only get a few minutes of screen time. I'd hate it if the focus was on me." Charlene closed her eyes and suddenly winced with pain.

"Are you all right?"

"Yes, I'm fine. I've been having false labor pains all day."

Jimmy took her lightly by the arm and steered her toward a chair. He lowered her into the seat, then sat down beside her. "Are you sure they are false? When are you due?"

Before she could answer, Zack suddenly appeared standing over them. "Charlene, what's going on?" he asked.

"Nothing. I just had another pain, and Bishop Snow helped me sit down."

Standing up, Jimmy extended his hand to Zack Morton, but he did not take it. "I was just asking your wife about her due date. Maybe these are not false contractions."

Zack sneered up his nose as Jimmy's cologne found its way into his nostrils. "I'm sorry, I thought your doctorate was in religion, not medicine," he answered.

"It is, but I have two children and I just thought—"

"So do I, Bishop. My wife and I have this under control, thanks so much for your concern." Zack turned to his wife. "Let's go find our seats. The viewing will be starting soon."

Charlene smiled and politely said good-bye to Jimmy, then followed her husband to their seats. "What was that all about? You were rude to him," she said.

Zack stretched his long legs trying to get comfortable in his seat. "That was nothing, Charlene. The producers asked that I create a little tension between cast mates. It makes for good ratings. I'll call him tomorrow and explain. It's not personal, just business."

After his encounter with the Mortons, Jimmy decided it was time to find Yolanda and the kids and go to their seats. The room was huge and people were everywhere, but finally he located them. They were chatting with a young up-and-coming actor that they'd seen featured in a movie the previous year. JJ was excited that the actor, James J. Johnson, also shared his nickname. Jimmy waited patiently while he signed autographs and posed for photos with them before walking over and extending his hand to James. "I'm Bishop Jimmy Snow. It's a pleasure to meet you, Mr. Johnson. My entire family enjoyed *Too Saved*."

"Thank you. I really appreciate that. I'm a preacher's kid, so I'm looking forward to the show."

Jimmy flashed his big smile. "So are we. That's why I came to get my family so that we could find our seats."

"It was a pleasure meeting all of you," James answered as he waved good-bye.

The viewing lasted only an hour, as the premiere was for only the first episode. The crowd cheered, laughed, applauded, and everyone seemed to be having a wonderful time. For the first time since he'd agreed to do the show, Jimmy felt a sense of pride in what he'd done. His scenes involved him visiting one of his parishioners in jail. It was very dramatic as the cameras followed him through check-in, and the microphones amplified the sounds of the gates locking behind him.

Jimmy felt it showcased the prison ministry he felt so steadfast about. When it was over, the entire room stood and gave the show a standing ovation.

When they returned home, Priscilla and JJ rushed to their rooms, anxious to post the photographs they had taken on to Facebook. Jimmy made sure the house was locked and secure before joining Yolanda in their bedroom. Surprised, he found her angrily snatching her earrings and necklace off and throwing them on the dresser.

"Honey, what's wrong?"

Without answering, she walked into their bathroom and slammed the door. Several moments later she emerged, wearing her slip with her dress balled up in her hands. She tossed it on the floor and sat down at her vanity to remove her makeup. He watched her roughly applying cold cream to her face. Jimmy walked over and placed his hand on her shoulders. Gently he began to massage them. "Talk to me, Yolanda. What's going on?"

Angrily, she spun her vanity chair around and looked at him. "Forty-five seconds, *that's* what's wrong. I was on screen for no more than forty-five seconds. All those hours of camera time and that's all I got."

Jimmy suddenly realized that she was correct. The cameras went back and forth between the four ministers' lives, and his segment was primarily spent at the prison. Yolanda and the children had only been featured very briefly. Silently, he struggled for the right words to say to comfort her. "Honey, it was just the first show. Mrs. Morton and Mrs. Kitts were only shown briefly as well."

"I don't care about them. You didn't even want to do the show. *I* did, and *you're* the one who's becoming a star. Didn't you hear the crowd applauding?

They loved you, Jimmy. They barely even noticed me."
Yolanda turned her back to him as tears began to rush
down her cheeks.

The feeling of foreboding returned to Jimmy's spirit,
and he wondered if being a star was more important to
Yolanda than he was. Throughout their marriage there
had never been any form of competition. He preached
the Word, and she worked diligently in her ministries.
They each had separate roles. Now suddenly, she was
upset that he was garnering more attention. Quietly,
he sat down on the bed. "Yolanda, come sit with me."
When she didn't move he asked her again. "Please, just
come here."

Finally she got up and walked over to where he sat.
Still crying, she lay her tearstained face on his shoulder. He was torn apart watching her pain. "Listen, I'll
talk to the producer tomorrow and see if I can do something about this."

Suddenly she perked up. "What do you mean?"

"I'll call Anderson. No. I'll call his boss, the guy who
owns the network. I don't remember his name, but I
have his business card. I'll call him tomorrow and tell
him that either you are featured more prominently or
we won't do the show."

"Jimmy, do you mean it?" she said, suddenly looking
at him and smiling.

"Of course I mean it. I don't care about this show, but
it's important to you, and I want you to be happy. I'll
give him a call in the morning."

As promised, as soon as he entered his church office
the next morning, Jimmy dug in his desk for Julian's
business card, then dialed the number. Patiently he
waited until Julian's secretary connected him.

"Mr. Washington, this is Bishop Jimmy Snow. I need
to talk with you about last night's show premiere."

"I thought that it was a fabulous party. Is there a problem?" Julian asked.

"No. Not really. Well, it's my wife."

Julian's ears perked up. "What about her?"

"I'd rather not go into over the phone. Can you meet me at my office for lunch at the church later this week?

"I'd be glad to," Julian answered. There was nothing he wanted to do more than to meet with Bishop Snow and discuss his wife.

Jimmy smiled broadly. "Great, I'll have my secretary call you back in a few days to confirm."

Chapter Eight

Danita sat in her living room lounging on the sofa and sipping on a diet soda. Leisurely she picked up the *Atlanta Journal Constitution* and perused the pages. Her phone had been ringing almost nonstop since the premiere event the night before, so she was certain there would be good reviews in the paper. Gleefully, she read the glowing reports. When she was done with the paper she opened her laptop to check the online blogs. One columnist called her gorgeous and captivating. Another spoke of her sincerity and obvious humility. There was only one who dared mention her having been on trial for murder, but they did so only to state that they now believed Danita was innocent.

Fantasia's "Even Angels" began to play as Danita's ringtone. Closing her laptop, she picked up her pink BlackBerry phone. "Hello."

"Hi, Danita, this is Tia Kitts. How are you?"

"Um . . . fine," Danita said. She tried her best not to sound surprised.

"That's great. Listen, I was wondering if you'd like to have lunch with me and a friend today."

Danita was flabbergasted by the invitation. She knew that Tia was the wife of Brandon Kitts, as they'd met at the premiere. But they had barely said five words to each another, and she wondered what was behind the sudden lunch invitation. "Wow. I have to admit I'm surprised that you would invite me to lunch."

"Yes, I know, but Anderson feels that there needs to be some interaction between the cast of the show. So we both felt it would be great if you and I had lunch together. The cameras will catch all of it. What do you think?"

"Sure. Where would you like to meet?" Danita was willing to do anything that would garner her more camera time.

"How about Vonnie's Soul Food. I'm in the mood for some ribs and mac and cheese. Is one o'clock good for you?"

"Great." Danita hung up the phone and hurried upstairs to get dressed.

When she arrived at the restaurant Tia was nowhere in sight. Danita asked the waitress to seat her in an area where they were sure to be seen by most of the restaurant's other patrons. The waitress took her drink order and had just returned with it when Tia and Quincy finally entered the restaurant.

"Quincy, it's been ages," Danita said, as she stood up to greet him.

Quincy had redecorated Danita's home right after her murder trial. It was his idea to put purple drapes with pink and white accents in her living room. He'd also boldly suggested that she put a chandelier in her master bathroom, as well as designing the mural on her daughter's bedroom walls. Danita thought it all looked fabulous.

"When Tia told me she was having lunch with one of the ministers from her show, I had no idea it was you. You look fierce," he said.

"Thank you, Quincy. You are looking fine as ever. I love the new hair color," she said, commenting on Quincy's short Afro which had been dyed a very loud shade of burgundy.

"You know how I do," he grinned before taking a seat.

Tia joined them at the table, and before saying hello to Danita, she summoned the waitress. "I'll have a glass of white wine." She turned to Quincy. "What are you having?" she asked.

"I don't think you should be drinking wine in your condition," Quincy answered, then turned to the waitress. "Bring us two of Vonnie's famous peach lemon teas.

Tia rolled her eyes at him, then nodded at the waitress that she agreed. "Sorry, I forgot."

"What condition? Are you pregnant?" Danita asked.

"Yes, I am, but I'm only a few weeks along. It's still new to me."

"She's almost three months. I'm surprised that she isn't showing by now," Quincy gave Tia a wink, then picked up his menu.

The leader of the camera crew came over and approached the trio, just as their meal was being served. "This small talk is cute, but Anderson wants you to talk about the premier party last night, and dish some dirt on your cast mates."

"I don't really know them," Danita answered.

"It doesn't matter. Just talk about your first impressions of them. Our editors will take care of the rest." He walked away, leaving them to their meals.

"It's not my show, but I just want to say that Apostle Zack Morton is probably the finest white man walking around in Atlanta. That man gave me the vapors," Quincy said, fanning himself.

Tia and Danita both laughed loudly. "He is fine," Danita agreed. "His wife is gorgeous also, but she seemed a little . . ." she hesitated.

"Dish the dirt," Quincy encouraged her.

"Well . . . weak. She seemed very weak. As if she never makes a move without his permission. It was "Yes, Zack . . . No, Zack . . . Of course, Zack." Danita paused to take a bite of her chicken fried steak.

"He gave me the creeps," Tia said.

"Why?" Quincy and Danita asked in unison.

"He wouldn't shake anyone's hand, and he kept sneering up his nose as if he smelled something bad. Then when they did his segment, I saw all the locks on his basement door. I bet he's hiding bodies down there." Quincy and Danita laughed loudly. "I'm serious," Tia continued. "I mean, who really needs to lock up their gym like *that?*"

They dissed Zack Morton and his wife before the subject turned to Jimmy and Yolanda Snow. Danita's ears perked up at the mention of one his parishioners, Sharmaine Cleveland. "She attends his church?" she asked.

"Yes, she does. From what I've heard, he was one of the few who stuck by her when her publicist framed her for attempted murder," Quincy answered.

"At least she never had to actually go to trial, like *I* did," Danita replied. "But we do have the same attorney. Victor is one of the best in the business."

Just then, a tall, thin, dark-skinned woman approached their table. "Mrs. Hyatt, I'm Sandy Thorne. You may have read my blog, Sandy Thorne.com. It's an online gossip blog. I was at the premiere of your show last evening, and I'd like to ask you a few questions, if you don't mind."

Danita looked up at the woman with her pad and pen waiting to take notes. She felt flattered. "Of course, ask me anything."

"Although the show has not yet aired, there is already quite a bit of buzz about it following last night's party and premiere. I especially enjoyed the segment of the show that showed you making a donation to Piedmont Hospital in your late husband's memory."

"Thank you. Ben meant the world to me. I just wanted to do something to show the world how much I still love and miss him."

"If that's true, Mrs. Hyatt, why did you cancel payment on the check?"

"Oh, snap!" Quincy yelled. He and Tia began laughing hysterically, while Danita tried desperately to regain her composure and think of a plausible answer.

"I . . . I don't know what you're talking about," she stammered. Out of the corner of her eye she noticed that the camera crew had moved in closer.

"This morning I called the hospital to find out exactly what they intended to do with your donation, and a hospital spokesperson informed me that payment was cancelled on the check the same day it was written."

Danita stood up from the table. "Turn the cameras off. Don't film this," she ordered.

Respecting her wishes, her cameraman turned off his camera. Tia turned to look at the leader of the crew who'd come along with her. "Don't you *dare* stop filming this," she ordered.

Danita grabbed her purse and covered her face with it as she rushed out of the restaurant. Tia and Quincy doubled over in laughter as they watched her running frantically to her limousine.

Once safely inside, Danita ordered Philippe to take her straight home. It had never occurred to her that reporters would call the hospital to verify the check. She felt like a complete fool. As soon as the limousine pulled up to her home, she hopped out and rushed to the door. A large manila envelope taped to the front stopped her in her tracks.

"Now what?" Danita snatched it off the door and hurried inside. Immediately she went into her downstairs parlor. It was the one room where she knew no cameras would be filming her every move. Quietly she lay back on her chaise lounge and fought back tears. Then she suddenly remembered the envelope. Sitting up, she opened it and read the contents.

The envelope contained a summons, advising her that she was due in court on the twelfth of the month to face her late husband's family and their wrongful death lawsuit. When she signed on to do the show, Danita had agreed to allow the cameras in the courtroom along with her. But as she read over the summons, she began to wonder if that had been a huge mistake. Ben's family was adamant about proving her guilty, even if a jury had not. Danita believed it had very little to do with Ben's death. They just wanted the money he'd left her.

Reaching into her purse, Danita retrieved her phone and dialed her attorney's number.

"Hello, Danita, I assume you received the summons today," he said.

"Yes, and I've made a decision. I don't want to fight it out in court. I want to settle. Find out how much money Ben's family is asking for."

"I don't think that's a good idea."

"You don't understand. I just had one of the most embarrassing moments of my life this afternoon, and it was all caught on camera. I thought doing this show would be a good thing for me, but the media checks up on everything. I don't want to go through the embarrassment of another trial." Danita took a deep breath. "Let's just give them what they want."

"Danita, they don't want your money. Didn't you read the entire summons?"

Picking it up off the floor, Danita glanced over it. "Not really, I just know the date I'm supposed to face those bullies in court."

Victor hesitated before answering. "They want full custody of the girls. If you are found liable for wrongful death, they have waived all rights to the money. They want the judge to revoke your parental rights so that they can raise the girls."

"They can't do that, can they? I mean, they can sue me for money, but not for my kids," Danita shrieked.

"It's unprecedented, but it's possible. If the judge rules that you are liable for Ben's death, then they have good cause to request custody."

Danita Hyatt didn't care about many things or many people, but her three daughters meant everything to her. Since Ben's death, she'd allowed her husband's family to continue to be a large part of their lives. The girls had done sleepovers at his parents' house, attended the birthday parties of their cousins on Ben's side, and gone sailing with them on July 4th. Her former in-laws had wanted the girls for the entire summer, and Danita had consented to allow them two full weeks. She was livid that with all of that they *still* wanted to take her children away from her.

"There is no way I'm giving up my daughters. Is there any way I can stop the cameras from being in the courtroom? I know I agreed to it, but now I've changed my mind."

Victor thought for a moment. "If the judge bans all cameras, that will certainly include reality TV show cameras as well. I'll start working on a motion to make sure that happens. I don't know what happened earlier to embarrass you, but I suggest you find a way to fix whatever it was. You need to look your best when you go into court."

Danita thought back to the bogus check she'd written to the hospital and the embarrassment of the blogger finding out. "Okay, I'll find a way to fix it."

"Good, I'll be in touch," Victor said before hanging up.

Danita put her head in her hands and tried to think up a plan. In her mind she replayed the entire day's events, searching for a way to fix things. For a brief moment she considered praying, but quickly dismissed the idea. Danita had stopped speaking to God the day her husband died. Before he left for his fishing trip, she'd prayed that he have a safe trip and that when he returned they could fix the problems in their marriage. The reason she was home alone was because she was fasting and praying for her marriage. They'd been having issues, but she desperately wanted for things to work out. She begged God for help in saving her marriage. When she received the call that he was dead, she was furious that God did not answer that prayer. Later, when she was arrested for his murder, Danita's anger at God intensified. She couldn't fathom how a merciful God would not only take her husband, but also allow her to be charged with his murder. Danita began to believe that God wasn't helping her, so she had to find a way to help herself. A sudden knock at the parlor door interrupted her thoughts.

"Come in," Danita called out.

"Mrs. Hyatt, I was just about to pick the girls up from day camp. Do you want me to stop and get dinner for them?"

"No, Vivian, I want the family to eat together tonight. Please ask the cook to prepare the girls' favorite dishes."

Vivian smiled. She'd begun to worry about how often the girls were eating fast food, and was glad that

Danita seemed to be coming out of her grief cloud and spending more time with them. Seeing an opening, she decided to make a suggestion. "Mrs. Hyatt, earlier this week Summer asked if they could have a barbecue out by the pool. It's a beautiful day out."

Danita looked at her as if she'd just given her the cure for cancer. "That's a wonderful idea, Vivian. But let's not do it today. Let's plan it for next Friday. And on second thought, go ahead and feed the girls. I need to make plans." She dismissed Vivian with a wave of her hand and grabbed her cell phone to call Anderson. "Hey, it's Danita Hyatt. I've got a great idea," she said.

After telling him her plan, she hung up the phone and grinned with delight. Anderson had agreed to set up a cast party at her home the following Friday. Danita reasoned that would ensure her lots of air time as she prepared and played hostess to everyone and their families. She'd also requested that he invite the hospital administrator to attend. Danita planned to present her with a new check at the barbecue while claiming it was a clerical error that cancelled the first one.

Danita pressed her intercom and summoned Philippe. He was just leaving with Vivian to pick up the girls. "Tell Vivian to take her own car. I need you to take me shopping for my barbecue next weekend."

Grabbing her purse, she rushed outside to meet him.

Chapter Nine

At the restaurant, Quincy nibbled on a sparerib while Tia picked at her salad. "You have to eat more," he said.

After Danita's sudden exit, Tia had instructed her camera crew to leave and they were now able to speak freely. "I'm not a big eater," she answered.

"All pregnant women are big eaters. Do I have to tell you *everything?*"

Tia pushed her plate away and sighed. "I'm not hungry right now. I'll pretend to eat more when I'm around Brandon. Is everything going okay with the surrogate?"

Quincy put down his rib and wiped the barbecue sauce from his fingers on a napkin. "Yes, I went with her to the doctor yesterday." Quincy paused. "Can I ask you something?"

"Sure, go ahead," Tia said nonchalantly.

"Why don't you just tell Brandon the truth? I mean, tell him that you can't have kids and the two of you could do this surrogate thing together. You know he'd be willing. I just don't understand why you keep lying to him."

Tia rolled her eyes. "I don't want Brandon having any doctors poking around on me asking fertility questions. I know why I can't get pregnant. If he knew my tubes were tied since before we met, then he might divorce me for lying to him. I can't risk that. Now tell me what's going on with the surrogate."

Shaking his head at her, Quincy continued. "The surrogate is almost three months along and starting to show. So we need to pick up some padding for you today. Have you figured out how you are going to hide your body from Brandon for the next six months?"

"Yes, about four months ago I started insisting that we only have sex in complete darkness, and I always change clothes in my private bathroom. Brandon hasn't seen my body in a long time. He thinks I've become a modest Christian woman." Tia laughed at the thought.

"Speaking of sex, you know you can't do that after you start wearing the padding."

"Don't you mean I can't have sex with *Brandon?*" Tia laughed again. "I've already started refusing him, by telling him it's pregnancy hormones. Don't worry. I got this."

"Tia, I know you need to get your swerve on from time to time, but if you expect this plan to work, you have to be careful. Taking your padding off to fall into bed with some random dude is *not* a good idea."

"Quincy, you are like a mother hen. You worry too much." Tia raised her hand and summoned the waitress to retrieve their check. After placing her credit card in the black folder, she pulled out her compact and checked her makeup in the mirror.

"You can call me what you like, but I'm knee-deep in this with you. If Nicky finds out what I'm up to, he'll leave me."

Putting her compact down, Tia looked over at him and noticed the look of concern in his eyes. "I promise you, I will be careful. Besides, our plan is foolproof. The surrogate was impregnated with Brandon's sperm, so if he requests a DNA test, we're covered. I'm glad he bought my story about needing to freeze our eggs and sperm, in case we have fertility issues later on. Now, I just wish there was some way that we could make sure it's a boy. That's all he talks about."

"He'll get over it. My dad wanted a son too, but he got me." Quincy gestured as if to fling pretend hair over his shoulder, and then dramatically put on his pink-and-rhinestone-encrusted sunglasses, causing Tia to burst out with laughter.

The two of them left the restaurant and got into the front seat of Quincy's Lexus convertible. "I have a friend who works in movies, and he's going to give us the padding we'll need to make you look pregnant over the next few months. Do you have a place to hide it? If not, I'll keep the bigger ones and you can just take home the one you'll be wearing."

"With the cameras in the house, I think it's best if you hide everything. Brandon signed a release that says if it's caught on camera they have a right to show it."

"Why in the world did you agree to do this show? I mean, it's hard enough pulling this off without having cameras watching your every move."

Tia leaned back in the plush leather seats and laughed. "You know why. It's for the money. Besides, the show is about the ministers. The wives are just window dressing."

After meeting with Quincy's friend and receiving the padding, the two of them drove back to his design firm so that Tia could try it all on.

"I hate this thing. It's too bulky," she whined.

Quincy adjusted the straps on her back. "Tia, this is only the padding to make you look about three months pregnant. It will get heavier as your pregnancy progresses. Stop complaining already."

Waddling as if she were nine months pregnant, Tia found her way to a chair. "Maybe this wasn't such a good idea after all. Why don't I just divorce Brandon and take whatever small settlement he gives me?"

"Are you *kidding* me?" Quincy asked, with his hand over his chest faking a heart attack like Fred Sanford.

Tia leaned back in the chair and began examining her fingernails. "What's the big deal? If we stop now, Nicky will never find out, and you're in the clear."

"What about the surrogate? There is a woman out there carrying your husband's baby. If we quit now, she might get *your* settlement."

"What do you mean?" Tia suddenly sat up and stared at Quincy. "Does she know about our plan?"

Quincy was afraid to answer. He'd tried his best to find an anonymous surrogate, but Tia was putting entirely too much pressure on him. Many of his friends had used surrogates to become parents, but none of those women were willing to help him. And although they were surrogates, they also insisted on being involved in the lives of the children they carried. There was no way that could happen in this case. Just when he'd decided to give up and tell Tia that her plan could not be done, the perfect person showed up on his doorstep.

Myrna was a former girlfriend of his from high school. At the time, Quincy was still struggling with his sexuality and dating both men and women. After the breakup, they'd remained good friends. Originally, Quincy didn't plan on asking her to become involved, he just needed a shoulder to cry on. After he told her the entire story, he was shocked when she volunteered to carry the baby. She told him she was between jobs and really needed the money.

Quincy knew that he could trust Myrna explicitly, but he also knew better than to tell Tia the truth. If she found out that the surrogate knew all of the intimate details of the plan, she would freak out.

Taking a deep breath, Quincy quickly made up a lie. "Of course she doesn't know about our plan. But if you abandon things now, she'll be angry that she wasn't paid."

"So we'll go ahead and pay her. I have full access to all of Brandon's money. She can put the baby up for adoption, and I can move on with my life. Now help me get this stupid pad off," Tia said as she stood up and began struggling with her protruding belly.

"That's fine with me." Quincy reached for the straps of the padding. "I was just wondering where you planned to get that kind of money. I mean, after you divorce Brandon, how can you pay a surrogate ten grand?"

Free from the padding, Tia took a deep breath. "Whew, I don't know how women deal with stretching their bodies out of shape like that." She sat panting like a St. Bernard for several minutes. "Quincy, I appreciate you helping me, but I just realized that this isn't going to work. I wasn't meant to be pregnant, pretend or otherwise. I will pay the surrogate before the divorce is final." Without another word, she gathered her purse and left the studio.

As she parked in her garage, she noticed that Brandon's car was there. *That's odd. I wonder why he's not at the church*, she thought as she walked into her home.

As soon as she entered, she remembered the cameras and quickly went into "perfect wife" mode. "Hi, honey," Tia said to Brandon.

Sitting on the sofa in the great room, he didn't look up. Tia stood for a moment before she realized he was praying. Impatiently, she waited until he noticed she was in the room.

"Tia, honey, I'm sorry. It's been a difficult day," he said as he finally looked up.

She walked over to him and sat down, then put her arms around him. "What's wrong, sweetie?"

"One of my parishioners passed away this morning." Brandon brushed away a tear.

As a minister, Brandon lost parishioners to death several times per year. Each time he grieved, Tia wondered how he was able to become so consumed in their lives. He claimed they were his family, but there was no way she could fathom having that many family members.

Faking concern, she rubbed her hand up and down his back. "Oh, sweetie, I'm so sorry. Who was it?"

"I don't think you ever met him. He'd only been a member a few months."

Hearing this made his sadness and grief even more puzzling to Tia. If the man was a new member of only a few months, it made no sense that he would be so upset.

As if reading her mind, Brandon began to explain. "He was the same age as me, Tia. Actually, he was a few months younger. He left a wife and son behind. They wanted more children, but he had prostate cancer."

"Sometimes people die young. That's no reason for you to worry. You eat right, and you work out daily. I'm sorry he died, but, honey, it wasn't you."

Brandon pulled her closer to him. "I know, honey, it just made me think. I realized how blessed I am to have you and a new baby on the way." He reached out and began to rub her empty belly. "You and this child mean everything to me, Tia. I was just sitting here praying and thanking God for our blessings."

Although her acting skills worked for her in other situations, Tia always found herself tensing up whenever

Brandon touched her stomach. It wasn't rational, but she worried that he somehow could tell there was nothing inside. Pushing her belly out as far as she could, her mind briefly wandered to the padding she'd left lying on Quincy's studio floor.

Brandon suddenly released her and grabbed a stack of papers that was lying on the coffee table. "I want you to see this," he handed the papers to her.

"What is it?"

"I had my attorney draw this up. It's a trust fund account for the baby. In case . . . Well, in case anything ever happened to me, I want to be sure he's taken care of."

Tia read over the paperwork, but she was still confused. "Is this your will?"

"No, sweetie, basically, it says that a third of everything I have belongs to our son." Brandon laughed. "Or daughter, but you know I'm hoping for a boy. Anyway, the moment the baby is born, this money belongs to the child. It transfers from me."

"What would an infant need with all that money?" She looked at him strangely.

Brandon shrugged his shoulders. "I don't know. I don't even care. Tia, I realize this may be our last and only chance to be parents. I want to be a good father, but if for some reason I can't, this will ensure that he or she never wants for anything."

"What about me?" she asked.

Brandon pulled her back into his arms. "You would get everything else, sweetie. Besides, if it belongs to a minor child, it's essentially yours." He kissed her gently on the forehead.

The next morning, Tia took the paperwork and made a visit to her attorney's office. Although Brandon had tried his best to explain, she wasn't satisfied. Instead, she wanted answers from someone she trusted.

After reading the paperwork over, her attorney's face spread into a wide grin. "This is exactly what I was talking about, Tia. This is why I knew it would be in your best interest to get pregnant."

"How can this be good for me? Brandon is giving our baby a third of everything. That's more than I could ever get in a divorce settlement."

"Tia, this says that the moment your child is born, an account is established in his or her name, and one-third of everything Brandon owns automatically transfers to that account. You don't need to get the money in the divorce; your child will have it."

Tia rolled her eyes. "So what? Brandon has to die for me to get to it?"

Her attorney shook his head. "No, he doesn't. If you divorce him, you will get your settlement as outlined in the prenup. If you get sole custody, you also get any and all assets that belong to your minor child."

Snatching the paper from his hands, Tia stared at it. "That can't be true."

"Do you remember all of the so-called fathers who showed up after Anna Nicole Smith's death? It was because they all wanted control of the assets her minor child was due to inherit."

"I understand that, but like I said, Brandon has to die for me to get it."

"Your husband didn't stipulate that your child gets the money upon his death. Your child gets the money the moment it's *born*. Whoever is legal guardian of the child gets control of that money."

Tia left her attorney's office and made a beeline for Quincy's studio. Speeding through Atlanta traffic, she ran a red light and almost sideswiped three cars. Finally she arrived and rushed inside. Quincy was with a client, but she rudely interrupted them and pulled him into his private office. "Please tell me you didn't throw away my padding?" she asked breathlessly.

Chapter Ten

Zack gently kissed his newborn daughter on the forehead before placing her into Charlene's waiting arms. Sitting in a white wicker rocking chair in their newly decorated nursery, Charlene began to gently rock her back and forth.

"She's beautiful, Mommy," her son Luther said.

"No, she's not. Babies are smelly," his twin Martin interjected. "But I love her anyway," he said with a shy smile.

Charlene and Zack both laughed. Zack had just brought Charlene home from the hospital with their newest family addition. Zack did not want the boys to visit the hospital because he felt it was no place for children, so this was their first introduction to their little sister. They were delighted that both boys seemed very excited to meet her.

Although Zack tried to brush him off, Bishop Snow had been right when he questioned whether Charlene's labor pains were false the night of the premiere. While the audience cheered and enjoyed the show, Charlene sat wincing with pain and praying that the evening would end as soon as possible. After the show, Zack posed for several cast photos while she sat down on a plush sofa and tried to remember the breathing exercises she'd learned in birthing class. When that didn't work, she tried walking around since she'd once been told that false contractions could be subsided that way.

It didn't help at all and actually seemed to increase her discomfort. Just when she felt she couldn't take anymore and was on her way to drag Zack out of the room, he told her he was ready to go. Once inside their car, she finally began to relax.

Zack was ecstatic about the premiere and the audience's reaction to the show. In his excitement he chattered on in the car about how many influential contacts he'd made and how many new parishioners he was expecting as a result. While he talked Charlene smiled and nodded and thanked God that the pains had finally subsided.

Just as they entered their house, Charlene felt a gush of wetness down her legs as her water broke. "Oh my God!" she screamed.

Zack turned around and looked at the water trickling through the entryway. "Don't panic, honey. I'll grab your bag, and we can call the doctor in the car on the way to the hospital."

While holding her belly, she waddled toward the stairs and began to protest. "No, I need to change clothes first. I can't walk into the maternity ward in a ball gown. A completely *ruined* ball gown!" she shrieked.

"There's a pair of leggings and a T-shirt in your bag. Change in the bathroom down here, and I'll let the nanny know what's going on." He dug inside the bag and pulled out the clothing, then handed it to her before trotting swiftly up the stairs.

Charlene barely had time to remove her gown and pantyhose before Zack was standing in the bathroom ready to help her. "The boys are asleep. I told Sierra we'd call her as soon as possible."

He took the T-shirt from her and began to dress her the way one would dress a child. Carefully, he put the shirt over her head, then straightened the hem around her stomach. Next, he sat her on the commode while he placed her legs inside the leggings, and then stood her up and helped her pull them up over her hips. Last, he placed socks and sneakers on her feet and tied the shoestrings.

"Thank you, sweetheart," Charlene said. Smiling, she relished in his pampering.

Less than three hours after they arrived at the hospital, little Coretta Morton came screeching into the world with a head full of jet-black hair, pudgy round cheeks, her father's wide nose, and Charlene's brown eyes. It had been a fairly easy delivery, and Charlene fully expected to be discharged the next day. But Coretta began to run a low-grade fever and the pediatrician recommended that they remain another day.

Staring into her daughter's precious face, Charlene felt grateful to finally be home.

"Can I hold her, Mommy?" Martin asked.

"We have to wait until she's a little older," Charlene answered. "But I want both of you to learn how to help take care of your sister."

Luther's eyebrows went up. "We won't have to change any poopy diapers, will we?"

"You might. As a matter of fact, you can help me with that right now if you want," Charlene teased.

Martin grabbed his brother by the arm. "Let's go, man. I don't want to hang around for that."

Charlene and Zack laughed at them again as the two of them left the room.

Since the boys were gone, Charlene decided it would be the perfect opportunity to breast-feed Coretta. Zack sat in a nearby chair and just stared at the two of them.

"Stop looking at me like that," Charlene said.

"Like what?" he asked. He tilted his head and smiled at her.

Charlene blushed and giggled. "Like you have stars in your eyes or something."

Zack grinned. "I can't help it. I love you both so much."

Charlene blushed again and giggled even more.

When Coretta was done nursing, Charlene continued rocking her until she noticed that she'd fallen asleep in her arms.

"Do you want me to put her in the crib?" Zack offered.

"I'll do it. You've been with us all day. Shouldn't you be at the church?" Slowly, Charlene stood up and walked over to Coretta's crib that was decorated in bedding with Disney's the Princess and the Frog imprinted all over it.

"I want to be here with you and the baby. Church business can wait."

Although she loved it when her husband was attentive, Charlene felt that he was wasting his time watching the two of them. "She's asleep, and to be honest, I'd like to take a nap also. It's okay if you leave for a few hours."

Zack wrapped his arms around her from behind and stared lovingly into the crib. "Are you sure? I won't leave if you need me."

"I'm sure."

Instead of leaving immediately, Zack walked with Charlene to their bedroom. He fluffed the pillows on their king-sized bed and helped her put on her favorite pajamas. After she was comfortable on the bed, he covered her with a lightweight blanket. "Do you need anything while I'm out?" he asked.

"No, I'm fine." She leaned forward to kiss him. When their lips parted she lay back on the bed.

Curled up in a ball with her head resting on the pillows, Charlene thought that sleep would come quickly. It had been impossible to get a good night's sleep at the hospital. Even with the baby in the nursery, the nurses seemed to wait until the moment she dozed off to rush in and check her blood pressure, temperature, or just to ask if she was okay. All she thought about was finally returning home to her own comfortable bed.

Now that she was in it, she tossed and turned, unable to stop her mind from wandering. Maybe it was nothing, like Zack said, but the exchange she'd witnessed at the hospital was still bothering her.

The morning after Coretta was born, Zack had returned home to do his two-hour workout and to check on things at the house. Charlene wasn't surprised by this as he'd done the same thing when the twins were born. Zack never missed his workout. Even when they were on vacation, he'd make sure that wherever they were staying had a full gym, and that he could have it closed while he had his private workout time.

While he was away, a hospital employee brought Charlene her breakfast. The middle-aged black woman peeped into the bassinette and complimented Charlene on her new baby. Then she spent another ten minutes telling Charlene about her son and grandchildren.

They were still chatting when Zack returned. His nose immediately sneered up as he smelled the hospital breakfast sitting on the tray. "Ugh. I brought you some grits and eggs from that restaurant you like so much," he said.

Barely noticing the woman, he removed the hospital breakfast tray and set it on the other side of the room. *Then he put the take-out plate on the serving table, and opened it for Charlene.*

"Zack Morton, as I live and breathe," the woman said unexpectedly.

The look on his face as he turned and studied the woman worried Charlene. She was sure he recognized her, but his face was contorted as he stared at her. The only time she could remember her husband's face turning that shade of red and twisting in such a manner was when he'd been constipated.

"Do I know you?" he asked.

"It's me, Mabel Joe Stevens. I used to live right next door to you and your grandmother."

Zack gave her a strained smile. "Um . . . how are you?"

"I'm just fine. I've been seeing you on TV and stuff preaching at that big megachurch. Your granny would be so proud. I always told her that you was gonna do big things for the Lord one day." She pointed at Charlene. "Is this lady one of your church members?"

Charlene stared at him waiting for him to introduce her, but he seemed to be suspended in another dimension, unable to move or speak. "I'm his wife," she answered for him.

Mabel Joe grinned. "I always knew you'd marry a sista. She's beautiful, and so is your new baby."

"Um, thank you," Zack said. He was still staring at the woman as if he'd just seen a ghost.

"Aren't you on that new TV show, Revelations?"

Zack nodded. "Yes . . . but we didn't want them filming the baby's birth."

"I'm glad you didn't bring the cameras into the hospital. A family moment like this should be private. Well, I better go. I have a lot more folks on this floor to

feed." Mabel Joe grabbed the discarded food tray and headed toward the door. "By the way, I love the new look. It's different, but I like it."

After she left, Zack suddenly snapped out of his trance and began arranging Charlene's food as if nothing had happened.

"What was that?" Charlene asked.

Feigning innocence, he tore the wrapper off of her fork and began stirring salt into her grits. "What was what?"

"That woman said she lived next door to your grandmother. You told me your grandparents died before you were born."

"So she must be mistaken." He held a forkful of grits up. "Here, taste this. I may have put too much salt in it."

Charlene opened her mouth and took in the food. "It's fine." She took the fork from him and ate her breakfast while he picked up Coretta and held her.

As she ate, the woman, the look on his face, and the conversation kept playing over and over again in her mind. "What did she mean by she likes 'the new look'?"

"Huh?" he asked. He looked up from cooing at Coretta.

"That woman said she liked your new look. What did she mean by that?"

Zack sighed. "How am I supposed to know? You've known me for twelve years. Has my look changed?"

"Well, no, but the whole exchange was really weird."

"Honey, people see me preaching on TV, and in their minds, they know me. That's going to happen a lot more now that we're doing the new show. But I don't want it to upset you. Trust me, it was nothing."

Lying in her bed, Charlene knew that it most certainly was something. She just didn't know what.

***

At the church Zack paced back and forth in his office. He'd told the camera crew that he was just going to write a sermon so there was no reason for them to turn the cameras on. That was his plan, but there was no way he could accomplish it. Instead, he paced back and forth and to and fro and round and around his office until he was exhausted. Inside his head, he heard his late grandmother's voice. *You are who you are, Zack Morton. That's who you were when you were born, and that's who you gone be until the day you die. God help you if you try to be someone else."*

Zack suddenly wished he'd understood her words back then. Now it was too late. He sincerely wished he could turn back the clock, but he knew that he couldn't. Feeling defeated, Zack lay his head on his desk and prayed.

"Father, I thank you for my wife and my new daughter. Thank you for my strong and beautiful sons. You have blessed me so much that I have no right to ask for more. My love for Charlene is surpassed only by my love for you. If I lost her, I would lose myself. I know I don't deserve her, but she loves me, Father. Things are closing in on me, and I don't know what to do. Dear God, I beg of you, help me . . . please help me."

When he was done praying, Zack picked up the phone book and searched through the pages. He stopped when he located the phone number for the hospital where his daughter had been born. "I'm trying to get in touch with one of your employees," he said to the operator. "Her name is Mabel Joe Stevens . . . Yes, I'll hold." Impatiently, his fingernails tapped against the desk as he waited. After almost five minutes on hold, she finally picked up the line.

"This is Mabel Joe. Make it quick, I'm on the clock."

"Hello, Mrs. Stevens, this is Zack Morton."

"Well, well. I haven't seen or heard from you in years, and now I get the pleasure twice in one week. What can I do for ya, Zack?"

He hesitated before speaking. "It was such a surprise seeing you. I was hoping we could get together and talk about old times."

"Ain't that a blip? I'd like that, but I won't have a day off until next week. How about I come to the church? I've been dying to see that new building you put up. I heard it's spectacular."

"It is, and I'd love for you to see it someday, but it's not a good meeting place. There's so much going on, there would be constant interruptions. I have a better idea. Let's meet for lunch somewhere downtown. It would be my treat."

Mabel Joe smiled broadly. "That would be really nice. Thank you so much for inviting me."

After choosing a restaurant and a time, Zack hung up the phone and continued his pacing. Over and over he repeated in his head as he paced, *It's the best thing for my family. It's the best thing for my family.*

Soon, Zack realized that he wasn't going to get anything done, so he decided to leave his office and return home. He was just getting into his car when his phone rang. "Hello," he answered.

"Good afternoon, Apostle Morton. This is Jacob Robins. I called to let you know that your necklace is ready. You can pick it up this afternoon if you'd like."

Seeing Mabel Joe again had rattled Zack so deeply that he'd completely forgotten about his wife's gift. While he was away from the hospital the morning following Coretta's birth, he'd stopped by the jeweler's and ordered Charlene a platinum baby's foot pendant hanging from a platinum chain. It also had a flawless emerald stone, which was Coretta's birthstone, encrusted in the big toe.

"Thank you, Jacob. Can you have it gift wrapped for me. I will be stopping by within the hour."

"Certainly, it will be ready when you arrive."

Filled with excitement, Zack yelled out Charlene's name as soon as he entered the house and bounded up the stairs. He ran so fast the cameraman had trouble keeping up with him. First he went into their bedroom, and when she wasn't there, he rushed to the nursery, still yelling loudly. Charlene was leaning over the crib, as she laid Coretta down.

"Charlene, I have a surprise for you," he said. His voice boomed with enthusiasm.

"Shhh," she put her index finger up to her lips. "She just dozed off."

"I'm sorry," Zack whispered. "Come here. I have something for you."

Grinning, Charlene rushed over to where he stood. "What is it?" she asked excitedly. Charlene had begun to think that she wasn't going to receive anything. Seven years earlier, after she had given birth to the twins, Zack had surprised her at the hospital with a charm bracelet. The bracelet contained two charms in the shape of little boys with Martin and Luther's birthstone on their chests. The stones were cheap glass, the gold was plated, and it looked as if he'd purchased it at Kmart, but she loved it just the same. Now that their financial outlook was better, Charlene had expected a gift to celebrate Coretta's birth, but Zack returned to the hospital that morning with only grits and eggs. Until he showed up with the gift she had not realized how disappointed that had made her.

"Close your eyes," he said.

"No, just give it to me," she squealed.

Zack reached into his jacket pocket and pulled out the package. Charlene snatched it from his hands and started ripping the ribbons and wrapping. Finally, she reached the center and pulled out the velvet jewelry box. She looked at him and grinned before opening it. "Oh, Zack, it's beautiful," she exclaimed.

"Do you really like it?" he asked.

"I love it," she gushed. "Put it on for me."

Turning around, Charlene held on to her ponytail while Zack placed the pendant around her neck. Lovingly, he kissed the nape of her neck when he was done.

Spinning around to face him, she wrapped her arms around him and kissed his lips. "Thank you, sweetie."

Zack held her tightly in his arms. He realized he wasn't the easiest man to live with considering his oddities and idiosyncrasies. But Charlene did it with a smile on her face. She'd given up a lucrative medical practice and a spacious condo to move into his tiny two-bedroom apartment after their marriage. Family was very important to Charlene, yet she didn't listen to her family or friends when they warned her not to marry a white man. "I fell in love with a man, not a color," she'd told them. Nothing they said affected her feelings about Zack. Without a shadow of a doubt, he knew that she loved him completely and unconditionally. There was nothing that he wouldn't do for her. *It's the best thing for our family.*

Chapter Eleven

Hello, Mr. Washington, thanks so much for meeting me." Jimmy Snow stood up and extended his hand.

"Thank you for the invitation. I know most station owners don't get directly involved with their cast, but I set out to do something totally different with *Revelations*. By the way, I gave your camera crew the afternoon off. This meeting doesn't need to be filmed."

"That's fine with me. Frankly, the cameras make me nervous. Please have a seat," Jimmy offered, then sat down also. As he did, he noticed Julian looking around the room. "I hope you don't mind meeting here at The Spiritual Blessings Café. Since it's a part of the church, I have lunch here often."

"No, I don't mind at all. I was just admiring the atmosphere."

The Spiritual Blessings Café was one of the ideas that Jimmy Snow was adamant about being a part of his church's recent expansion. It was reminiscent of a college coffee house with bistro-style tables and chairs. The ambiance and décor were warm and inviting. Gospel artists such as Yolanda Adams, Byron Cage, and Kirk Franklin were gently piped through the speakers, offering subtle background music. Near the back of the café was a computer lab that also featured free Wi-Fi service. The café served specialty coffees and teas, as well as an assortment of soft drinks and juices. During the morning hours, they offered a continental breakfast of homemade muffins, pastries, rolls, and bagels which were baked and donated by church members. The lunch menu consisted of an assortment of cold sandwiches and salads.

"This is one of my favorite spots at the church. All of the food is prepared by church members, and it's extremely delicious," Jimmy said.

A lanky teenager with long micro braids approached their table and handed them two menus. "Are you having the usual, Bishop?" she asked.

"Yes, thank you, Lena." He turned to Julian "What would you like, Mr. Washington?"

Julian looked up from his menu. "Please call me, Julian. Um . . . What's the usual?"

"I usually have a Rueben sandwich with potato salad," Jimmy answered.

"Sounds good to me." Julian closed his menu and handed it back to Lena. When she was gone, he turned to Jimmy. "Why are there no prices on the menu?"

"That's my favorite part about this place. It's operated totally on donations from the members. There are no set prices. If you can afford to pay something, we have an offering box. If you can't, then you've just received a blessing."

Julian raised one eyebrow. "You mean to tell me that any bum off the street can come in here and eat for free? I'm surprised the place isn't overrun with deadbeats and homeless people."

"You know, that opinion isn't rare. Some of my own members shared the same sentiment when I first suggested this place. We have some homeless people who are regulars, but this isn't a soup kitchen." Discreetly, Jimmy pointed to a young lady sitting nearby with her laptop computer. "It's for the college student on a budget." He turned slightly in his seat and motioned toward the computer lab. "It's for the single, unemployed mothers with kids to feed. She's using the computers to search for a job, and her kids will have something nutritious to eat."

Unimpressed, Julian continued. "I'm sorry if I sounded harsh. My point is how can you afford to keep this place running? I know the food is donated, but you have overhead. I mean, this place is nice, really nice. The money has to come from something besides donations."

Jimmy nodded his head. "I understand your point. But there's something I've learned over the years. It doesn't take money to have ministry. If you concentrate on ministry, the money will come. God will provide it. If you chase the money, your ministries will suffer."

Lena returned with their lunch just as Julian was about to protest further. He held his tongue as she laid the plates on the table and returned to the kitchen. "That sounds good, Bishop, it really does. But it's not realistic."

Jimmy turned around in his chair and pointed toward the front door. On the wall directly above the entrance Julian saw a beautifully etched verse of scripture. "But seek ye first the kingdom of God, and his righteousness; and all these things shall be added unto you" (Matthew 6:33).

Unable to argue with scripture, Julian decided that further protest was futile. Instead of speaking, he picked up his sandwich and took a bite. The corned beef inside was tender and juicy. Grabbing a napkin, he caught the juice before it began to dribble down his chin. "This is delicious," he commented.

"My wife makes them. They are my favorite."

The mention of Bishop Snow's wife brought Julian's thoughts back to the real reason he'd agreed to the meeting. "Oh, yes, your wife. Isn't she the reason you wanted to speak with me?"

Jimmy put down his sandwich, then chewed and swallowed the bite he'd just taken. "My wife, Yolanda, was very disappointed after the premiere last week. It's gotten even worse since the first episode aired to the public last night."

"I don't understand. Your segment was one of the most popular."

"You may not know this, but I never wanted to do this TV show. It was all my wife's idea, and you know how wives can be when they really want something."

Julian shook his head. "No, I don't. I've never been married." *I was saving myself for my beloved Ophelia,* he thought.

"Oh, well, anyway, Yolanda was insistent that we do the show, and I only agreed to it in order to please her."

Julian nodded his head, encouraging him to continue.

"You see, my wife has always wanted to be an actress. At one time that was all she dreamed of. So this show is really important to her, and she was really disappointed that she had such little camera time."

Julian was taken aback. The reason she wasn't featured more prominently was because all of her footage was sitting in his theatre room and the editors did not have an opportunity to work it into the show. Realizing he couldn't explain that to Jimmy, he faked concern. "Really? Are you sure it wasn't more?"

"I'm sure. My wife has been screaming, ranting, and mumbling 'forty-five seconds' over and over again since the premiere."

"Well, I understand her concern. Although it's primarily a show about the ministers, we want to include the families and wives as much as possible. I'll speak with the producer to see if we can add in a little more of her footage."

"Thank you. I understand that the show is primarily about the ministers, but a large part of my ministry is keeping my wife happy," Jimmy laughed.

Chuckling politely, Julian reached for his potato salad cup, then took a bite. As soon as it hit his palate, his taste buds grabbed him and dragged him backward in time.

"Ophelia, you make the best potato salad in South Carolina." He grinned at her and took another bite.

"I bet you say that to all the girls. It's my granny's recipe. I just threw it together. Besides, you said you loved my chicken supreme and my lemon pound cake. You love everything I cook."

"I know I shower you with compliments, but this is different. When we get married, I want you to serve me potato salad for dinner every night."

Ophelia's eyes grew wide, and she stared at him. "Married? But we've only been dating a few weeks."

He took her hand into his. "I know, but this is right. I can feel it. There is no other woman for me on this earth. You are everything and the only thing that I want. Marry me, Ophelia. Be my wife." That was the first time he proposed, but it wouldn't be the last.

Jimmy Snow's hand waving in front of his face brought him back to the café.

"Are you okay? You spaced out for a minute."

Julian struggled to regain his composure. He pointed at his plate. "This potato salad is wonderful. Which one of your members donated this?"

Jimmy beamed with pride. "My wife made this also. She's a wonderful cook, don't you think?"

The potato salad sealed everything for Julian. Anderson had done as Julian asked and gathered as much background information on Yolanda Snow as he could. Julian had learned that she had the same birth date as Ophelia. Just like Julian and Ophelia, Yolanda was a native of Greenburg, S.C. Ophelia moved to Atlanta after college, the same as Yolanda Snow.

While looking over the information, Julian tried to convince himself that it was all just a bizarre coincidence. Ophelia was dead; he had visited her gravesite many times. He'd also considered the possibility of identity theft. It wasn't unheard of for someone to forage through the obituaries and assume another person's life story. That theory sank when he realized there was no reason for Yolanda to assume Ophelia's life, unless she also took her name.

So he'd agreed to meet with Jimmy Snow in the hopes that he could fill in the holes in the story and somehow get confirmation or denial that Yolanda was or was not his beloved Ophelia. He'd only caught a glimpse of her during the premiere party, and he was reluctant to approach her unless he was positive of her identity. During lunch, he'd planned to coyly ask questions about her without letting on his true intentions. Gobbling down another bite of potato salad and savoring the flavor, he realized there was no doubt. Yolanda and Ophelia had to be the same person.

Leaning forward, he began his rehearsed line of questioning. "Yes, your wife is an amazing cook. Tell me, Bishop, how did you two meet?"

"We were introduced by a mutual friend. After my first wife passed away, I spent my time concentrating on raising my kids and didn't get out much. So my friend invited me to a cookout, Yolanda was there, and the rest, as they say, is history."

Although he was telling the story of meeting his wife, Julian noticed that a sad look washed over Jimmy's face. "Is everything all right, Bishop?"

"Yes, I just get a little sad when I think of it. I mean, meeting Yolanda was the best thing that could've happened to me. It just saddens me that our friend who introduced us never got to see how great it turned out." Jimmy took a slow sip of his tea and sighed. "I still can't believe that a guy can walk into a TV news station and open fire on innocent people like that. Greg never even saw it coming."

"Greg Foster? Are you telling me Greg Foster introduced you to your wife?" Julian's mouth was gaping open.

"Yes. Did you know him?"

"Um . . . no . . . but I used to watch him on the news. Everyone in Atlanta remembers the night that gunman shot him on live television."

Jimmy nodded. "Yolanda went to high school with Greg, and he was one of my members right here at the church. I still miss him."

Julian had also attended high school with Greg Foster. They'd kept in touch over the years, and it was Greg who had sent him the letter telling him that Ophelia was dead. *It was a conspiracy. He introduced Ophelia to this guy, while telling me she was dead.* Seething with anger, Julian took another bite of potato salad and reveled in its calming effects. "Well, he must have thought that you two were perfect for each other."

Jimmy laughed. "Yes, he did, but I wasn't so sure at first. I thought she was just another flaky wannabe actress. Atlanta is full of those types of women, and I didn't think it would be good for me or my children. I mean, Yolanda even changed her name to try to get more acting roles."

Tea spewed all over the table as Julian abruptly and violently spit it out. *I was right. She changed her name.* Feeling embarrassed, he grabbed napkins and began cleaning it up. "I'm so sorry. I thought I tasted a bug, but I guess it was just a piece of ice."

Lena rushed over with a dish towel and helped the two men clean up the spill. Noticing that they were done eating, she offered to remove their plates.

"Yes . . . thank you," Julian stammered. "Um, do you do takeout? I'd love a cup of that potato salad."

"Well, no sir, I'm sorry, but we don't," Lena answered.

"It's fine, Lena. Mr. Washington is my personal guest today. Please go ahead and give him the potato salad. He loves it," Jimmy said.

After Lena left the table, Julian felt that he finally had enough courage to ask the question that was burning his heart, tongue, and soul. He swallowed hard and took a deep breath. "What was your wife's name before she changed it?" he asked.

"Oh, I don't think I should tell you that. Yolanda was so embarrassed by it that she hates it when she runs into old friends and they refer to her by that name."

Just then Lena returned to the table with the takeout cup full of potato salad. "This is the last of it. Bishop Snow, can you tell Ms. Yolanda we need more?"

"I certainly will. Thank you, Lena."

Julian carefully took the cup and held it lovingly in his hand as if it were a very fragile and priceless piece of crystal. After staring at it for several minutes, he suddenly looked up as he felt eyes on him. Jimmy and Lena were staring as he tenderly caressed the side of the cup. Quickly he set it down on the table. "Um . . . yes, thank you."

Lena gave him another side-eyed look, then walked away giggling.

"Are you okay, Julian? I don't mean to pry, but you've seemed sort of out of it this afternoon," Jimmy said. "Is there something you need to talk about?"

Laughing nervously, Julian shook his head. "No, it's nothing. I'm a bachelor, so it's not often that I get good home-cooked food. Now, you were about to tell me your wife's real name."

"Oh no, I wasn't." Jimmy shook his head emphatically.

"You know, Bishop, this is typical. You called me here to ask me to feature your wife on the show, and I have graciously agreed to that. But you are not willing to cooperate. I really don't see how I can feature her, unless I know everything." Julian was growing tired of beating around the bush with Jimmy. Inside, he was a bundle of emotions.

"I don't understand. What difference does it make to you what her real name is?"

Julian reached into his pocket and pulled out his wallet. He threw a twenty-dollar bill on the table as a tip. "Before we began shooting this show, I had my producer run background checks on all of the participants. The reason we do that is to make sure that there are no surprises. We ran a check on Yolanda Snow, and now I find out that's not even her real name." He stood up from the table. "It's in our best interest that we keep her low profile. The last thing I need is for some overzealous reporter to find out her real name and then tell us she robbed three liquor stores back in 1999." He grabbed the cup of potato salad and turned in the direction of the door.

"Wait, don't leave. I didn't even think of that. You're right. Of course I'll tell you her real name."

An evil grin spread across Julian's face. Quickly erasing it, he tried his best to look disinterested; then he turned around and took his seat. "I'm an understanding man. We'll do our background check, but otherwise, I promise it will be just between the two of us."

Looking around, Jimmy made sure that none of the
other patrons in the café were eavesdropping on his
conversation. Then he leaned in close and motioned
for Julian to lean in as well so that he could share his
wife's secret. "It was Ophelia Guzman."

Underneath the table, Julian's legs quivered and
buckled. His eyes closed, and he slowly slipped out of
the chair and wilted onto the tile floor, passed out cold.

Chapter Twelve

"Momlanda, I'm home," Priscilla yelled.

Yolanda was surprised to hear voices in the house so early. She looked at the clock on the wall over her desk. It read 3:30 P.M. "I'm in the study," she yelled back.

"Hey, what are you doing in here, and where's the camera crew?" Priscilla asked as she bounced into the room wearing her red and black cheerleader's outfit. Pushing some papers aside, she sat down on the edge of the desk and let her long legs dangle off.

"Your dad reminded me that it's time to begin working on Harvest Sunday. It's hard to believe that it's November already. I've been so preoccupied lately that I completely forgot. This is boring stuff, so the crew is out in the truck, probably napping. What are you doing home so early?" Yolanda continued typing on her laptop.

"I got a ride home. Oh yeah, JJ said to tell you that he's going over to Teresa's after football practice, but he'll be home before dinner."

Still preoccupied Yolanda barely looked up. "That's fine. Who did you ride home with?"

Excited, Priscilla began speaking rapidly. "Julian Washington, you know, the guy that owns the TV station. When I got out of school he was sitting out front in a limo, and he asked me if I wanted a ride home. That limousine is crazy. You could have a party in there; it's so big, and he's got it stocked with sodas and snacks. Well, of course, liquor too, but I knew better than to drink any of that."

Yolanda suddenly slammed her laptop shut. "You rode home with Julian Washington? You know better than to accept rides from strangers."

"He's not a stranger, Momlanda. I met him at the cast pool party at Evangelist Hyatt's house. Besides, he's technically you and Daddy's boss, as long as you are doing the TV show. He even said to tell you hi."

"I don't care about that. He's a grown man, and you barely know him. Don't you ever get into a car with him again!" she screamed. "Do you hear me? Stay away from Julian Washington!"

"Why are you freaking out? It was cold, and I didn't want to wait for the bus." Priscilla stared at Yolanda as her face turned several different colors.

"Don't argue with me. Just promise me you'll never ever go near that man again. Promise me!" she shrieked.

Priscilla hopped off the desk and shook her head. "Whatever, Momlanda, I'm going upstairs."

As soon as Priscilla was gone, Yolanda lay her head on top of her laptop and began crying. She realized that she'd let things go too far.

It had been almost three months since she'd discovered that Julian Washington had found her again. The entire cast and crew of *Revelations* had been invited to the home of Evangelist Danita Hyatt for a pool party. Yolanda was aware that Jimmy had met with the owner of the television station, but until that afternoon at the pool party, she had no idea that it was her former fiancé.

Julian innocently sauntered up to her as she stood alone near the food table. Both of her kids were splashing around in the pool, and Jimmy was caught up in a discussion with Brandon Kitts about theology and football. "Hello, Ophelia," Julian had said.

The sound of his voice made the baby-fine hair on her arms stand on end. Her first instinct was to run away from him as fast as she could, but she realized it would make her look like a fool. Instead, she stood there holding her breath.

"It's been a long time. I never thought I'd see you again," he said.

She stared at him but still did not speak. Her voice was not gone; she just had no idea what to say to this man.

"You look wonderful." He smiled. "I mean, sometimes I run into our old classmates and it looks as if they had a wrestling match with Father Time, and lost." He smiled again and stepped closer. Instinctively, Yolanda backed away from him. "Ophelia, surely you are not afraid of me?"

"That's . . . that's not my name," she finally muttered.

"Oh, I'm sorry. You like to be called Yolanda now. Well, Yolanda, it's been a pleasure seeing you again." He smiled once more, and then he walked away.

A few days later, Yolanda opened her front door to a delivery man carrying two dozen red roses encased in a crystal vase. "Delivery for Yolanda Snow," he'd said.

Excitedly, she directed him to place the bouquet on her dining-room table. After tipping the delivery man and escorting him out, she returned to the flowers and dug in for the card.

I remembered how much you love red roses, Julian

Yolanda immediately grabbed the vase from the table and took it out her back door. Then she threw the entire thing into the trash can and slammed the lid shut. The same delivery man returned every day for the next week. Each time, Yolanda took the flowers, ripped up the card, and threw it all in the trash.

When *Revelations* aired that Friday night, Yolanda was surprised to see that the show had a new opening sequence. While all of the other ministers were featured in the opening without their spouses, Jimmy's had been changed to include Yolanda. She was also shocked to see her name alongside his in the opening credits. Feeling elated, she watched the episode and marveled as she received more screen time than any of the other wives. After it was over, she sat on the sofa with a goofy, proud grin on her face.

"Momlanda, you were great!" Priscilla shrieked. "My phone has not stopped buzzing with text messages. Everyone loves you!"

"That's right," JJ agreed. "My friends think you are hot!"

Jimmy reached over and hugged her. "Julian really came through for you, honey, just like he promised."

The smile suddenly fell from her face as she realized that Julian was responsible. "Um . . . you should call and thank him," she replied.

"I could, but I think it would sound better coming from you."

It took her several days, but finally Yolanda picked up the phone and called Julian. As soon as he answered, she got right to the point. "I just wanted to thank you for my extra role in the show. I appreciate it."

"You don't have to thank me, Ophelia. You know I'd do anything for you."

The thought of it made her cringe. "I told you before, that's not my name. It's Yolanda. Yolanda Snow," she said while putting extra emphasis on Snow.

"You don't have to remind me that you are married. I haven't forgotten, but we both know that you were supposed to marry me."

"That was a long time ago, Julian. I don't ever want to go back there. I only called about the show."

Yolanda heard Julian sigh loudly. "There's no way that country preacher can give you all the things that I can. I want to shower you with diamonds and furs and take you on exotic vacations. As my wife, you'd never want for anything. The world would be yours."

"I don't care about those things. I love my husband and our family."

Suddenly Julian began laughing hysterically. Yolanda felt humiliated and was about to hang up the phone when he finally stopped. "I know what you care about. Can that country preacher make you a star?" Just like Satan, he'd found her weakness and zeroed in on it.

"Um . . . well, no . . . but . . ."

"I own a television station. I have the power to give you your own show. I can put your name up in lights, Ophelia . . . I mean Yolanda. We both know Bishop Jimmy Snow can't do that."

Yolanda bit her lip to stifle a moan of temptation from seeping out. She wanted all of those things, just not from Julian. "But he's my husband," she protested weakly.

"Not for long," Julian answered. Then he hung up the phone.

For the next several weeks Julian set out to win her back. The daily flowers continued, but she stopped throwing them away. Instead she simply hid the cards from her husband, rationalizing that what he didn't know couldn't hurt him. Since she'd accepted his flowers, Julian stepped up his game and asked Yolanda out on a date. She immediately turned him down, but he refused to give up. He cajoled, begged, and pleaded for just a few moments of her precious time. Finally, against her better judgment, she agreed to have lunch with him. Every fiber of her being told her that she was wrong, but she wouldn't listen. For the next several weeks, her part on the show grew larger, and her lunch dates with Julian became more frequent. They laughed together, and she flirted, but still she continued lying to herself by saying it was all perfectly innocent.

Then one afternoon, Julian brought her crashing back to reality. They were sitting in his limousine outside her home after another lunch date together. Julian had impressed her by stating he had plans for her to star in a new movie. He'd even promised to get Morris Chestnut to be her costar. Yolanda stared into his eyes, falling in love with the idea while Julian mistakenly believed she was falling in love with him. Unable to contain his desire any longer, Julian leaned over and kissed her deeply on the lips.

She quickly pushed him away. "What are you doing? I'm a married woman."

"I'm tired of the games, Ophelia. You are mine. You have always been mine, and you will always be mine." Julian roughly grabbed her arm and tried to pull her closer to him.

Yolanda snatched her arm away and reached for the car door. Julian grabbed her arm again and dug his nails into her flesh. She looked at him and saw fire blazing in his eyes. That look should not have surprised her, as she'd seen it many times before during their previous relationship. After she'd left him long ago, she vowed that she never wanted to see that look again. "Let me go. You're hurting me," she whimpered.

"*I'm* the one in pain, Ophelia. It tears me apart every time I see you with him." He tightened his grip on her arm, twisting her flesh like a vise.

Panicking, she screamed out in pain, and within seconds, the glass separating them from the driver began to slide down.

"Is everything all right?" the driver asked.

Julian quickly released his grip on Yolanda's arm. "It's fine. Mrs. Snow just stubbed her toe on something."

While he was speaking with the driver, Yolanda pulled on the door handle and discovered that it was locked. She turned to the driver. "I think I'm locked in. Can you open my door, please?" she asked sweetly.

"Certainly, ma'am," he said. He rolled up the window and got out. As soon as he opened her door a few seconds later, Yolanda rushed out of the car and inside the safety of her home. When Julian called the next day, she told him that she didn't want to see him again and to stop calling her.

Over the next few weeks, Julian became progressively persistent and aggressive. He called and texted her over and over, but she refused to speak with him. One Sunday, Yolanda looked out over the congregation from the choir stand and noticed Julian had walked into the church. He took a seat in a front pew and spent the entire service just staring at her. She'd faked a stomachache and left service early.

One afternoon, later that same week, she was at the grocery store, and suddenly, she noticed he was behind her in line. "Ophelia, you can run, but you cannot hide," he growled in a low voice. Yolanda abandoned her groceries and rushed out of the store.

Repeatedly during the months of September and October as she drove around Atlanta running errands or doing church business, she'd glance into her rearview mirror and notice Julian's car following her. Once he'd let his car roll into her bumper while sitting at a red light, tapping her lightly. He backed up a few feet then drove forward, intending to hit her harder just as the light changed and she drove away. On another occasion, he sped up his car and drove into the lane beside her. Yelling out of his car window, he screamed her name over and over again until he'd caused her to run off the road and knock down three of her neighbor's mailboxes while he sped off up the street. Secretly, she'd paid the neighbors for the damage and prayed that Jimmy did not see the scratches on the car before she could get it repaired. Yolanda felt there was no way she could admit to him how the accident happened.

Her phone rang one morning at three A.M. Still half-asleep, she reached over her husband and answered. Then she dropped the phone after Julian screamed vile obscenities at her. Yolanda couldn't fathom what was going on inside his mind. One moment he was professing his undying love for her, and the next minute he was spewing venom like a rattlesnake.

As her head lay on her laptop crying, Yolanda could not believe that Julian was now trying to get to her through her own daughter. *What am I going to do? Dear God, what am I going to do?* she prayed. For two months Julian had made her life a living, breathing nightmare. She heard the front door close and suddenly realized that she had no choice. It was time to tell Jimmy the truth.

Jimmy walked into the study and immediately noticed that she'd been crying. "Yolanda, what's wrong?"

"I'm so sorry, Jimmy. I messed up. I messed up really bad," she cried.

He walked over and pulled out a chair to sit beside her. "It can't be that bad. Just tell me what's going on."

Yolanda took in several gulps of air; then she began speaking. "I know I should have told you this a long time ago, and I'm sorry that I didn't." She paused to wipe her face, but the tears continued to fall.

"Told me what?" he asked.

"I promised myself that I'd never talk about it, not with anyone."

Jimmy stared at her. "You're scaring me. Just tell me what it is."

"Before I met you . . . I was engaged to marry Julian Washington."

He didn't speak. Jimmy just stared at her. His eyes grew wide with surprise. "It was a long time ago, Jimmy. It seems like it was another lifetime."

"You were engaged to marry another man, and you never told me?" He stared at her in disbelief.

"I just wanted to forget. I wanted to move on and forget."

Jimmy shook his head. "How could you keep something like this from me? All of these months that we've been doing this show, and you never once thought it was important to mention that you almost married this man?" Jimmy stood up from his chair and walked to the other side of the room.

Yolanda could see the hurt and disappointment in his face. She dropped her head in shame. "There's more."

He turned to look at her, and Yolanda spilled out the story as fast as could. She began by telling him about seeing Julian at the pool party, and ended with the kiss in the limousine.

"You kissed him?" he demanded.

"No, no, he kissed me, and I pushed him away. I never meant for things to go that far. Honestly, I didn't."

Jimmy turned his back to her again. This time, Yolanda recognized his rage as he struggled to contain it. "I don't know who I'm angrier with right now, you or him. What made him think that he could manhandle my wife?"

"Because it wasn't the first time," Yolanda said softly.

"What did you say?"

Yolanda felt more tears streaming down her face. "That's why I left him. I couldn't take it anymore." She sniffed loudly and continued. "It started early in our relationship, and gradually it got worse. He never hit or punched me, but he would grab me roughly or shove me across the room. Sometimes it would be a hand pressed hard in my face, or his elbow in my side if I wasn't doing what he wanted, or acting the way he thought I should. I don't know why, but I told myself that if he didn't punch or slap me, it wasn't really abuse." She looked up as she realized that Jimmy was no longer facing the wall; he was staring at her as she spoke. "When he proposed, it didn't feel right. I knew I didn't love him, but he said he loved me, and he was all I had. My grandmother had recently died, and there was no one else I could count on. So I accepted his proposal and moved in with him."

Yolanda paused again. The memory she wanted to share with Jimmy was buried in a place she planned never to visit again. But she dug down into the caverns of her spirit and dredged it up. "One night he came home late, and I was already in bed asleep. He shook me really hard to wake me up. It was so hard I thought I heard my eyeballs rattling around in my head. Julian was feeling frisky and wanted me to give him some "good loving," as he liked to call it. Then he kissed me hard and rough. I told him no, because it was late and I was tired. "No" has always been a word he hated to hear. Hearing me say it just made him more forceful. I rolled over and turned my back to him so I could go back to sleep, but he grabbed my shoulder and jerked me down onto my back. I tried to squirm away from him, but he was too strong."

"Yolanda, stop." Jimmy held his hand up. "I don't think I want to hear anymore."

Ignoring him, she kept talking. Her words came out strained and choppy as she talked and cried. "He climbed on top of me and tried to kiss me again, but I turned my face away. Then he . . . he took his forearm and he placed it on my neck covering my throat. I squirmed until I realized that every time I moved he pressed his arm deeper into my throat to hold me down. I tried to scream, but his arm was choking me. No matter how I protested, he just pressed his arm harder into my throat and continued having his way with me. I guess I must have passed out because the next thing I remember was waking up with him lying next to me, snoring. I tried to get up, but his hand was entwined around my hair so tightly that I couldn't move."

Yolanda sniffed and wiped tears and snot from her nose. "So I lay there, and I prayed. I made a promise to God that if He helped me escape, I'd never go back. The next morning while Julian was gone to work, I packed all my things and left.

"At first I thought that he didn't care. I was gone for over a week, and I heard nothing from him. But one day as I was leaving work, I saw his car parked out front. Instead of going out that way, I left through a back entrance. The next day he was back with his car parked across the street. He sat there and stared at the building for hours. He was there every single day for about two weeks until he got a coworker to tell him where I lived. I tried to talk to him and tell him that it was over, but he wouldn't listen. Instead, he would come to my apartment and knock on my door over and over, begging me to let him in. I called the police, but all they did was ask him to leave. He would go away, but he always came back. It got so crazy that I moved, but he found me again. Wherever I went, I was looking over my shoulder. Even when I didn't see him, somehow I knew he was there."

Jimmy turned his back again and stared at the wall, fighting back tears. A part of him wanted to comfort Yolanda as she continued crying, but his disappointment and anger stopped him.

Yolanda continued to talk. Now that she'd exhumed the memory, she had to get it all out. "The final straw happened when I had a role in community theatre. Julian was there every night with roses. Then he told the director that he was my fiancé, and they gave him a backstage pass. I was so flustered I could barely go onstage. I decided that if I was ever going to be free of him, I had to leave Greenburg. So I moved to Atlanta, but he followed me here too."

"How long have you been talking with him? Has this been going on our entire marriage?" Jimmy asked, still staring at the wall.

"No, I never saw him or talked to him. About a month after I moved here, Greg told me that Julian called him and asked if he would help him get in touch with me. So I told Greg everything and begged him not to tell Julian where to find me. A few weeks later Greg showed me a newspaper clipping about a woman with my same name who'd been killed in a car accident. Our backgrounds were so similar that if I had not known better, I would have thought that woman was me. So Greg sent the clipping to Julian and told him that I'd died. It was the only way we could think of to get him to stop looking for me."

Jimmy spun around and glared at her. "None of this makes any sense. If you went through all the trouble of convincing this man you were dead, then why in the world would you want to go on national television. Even if he didn't own the station, didn't you think that he might watch the show?"

"Yolanda Snow is on *Revelations*. As far as I am concerned, Ophelia Guzman is dead. It never occurred to me that he'd connect the dots, or if he did, that he'd even care. That was so many years ago."

"That's it, Yolanda. We are off the show. Any relationship you may have had with Julian Washington is finished. It's over!" he screamed.

The only time Jimmy Snow ever raised his voice was to emphasize a point in his sermon or when he was really excited. In ten years of marriage, Yolanda had never heard him raise his voice in anger, and it frightened her. So much so that she was almost afraid to continue speaking, but she knew that she had to tell him everything. "It's not over. He's stalking me again. He's been calling and following me around for the past two months. And today, he was sitting outside the school, and he brought Priscilla home."

Jimmy suddenly bolted to the front door. He ran outside to the van where the leader of the crew was sitting inside enjoying a sandwich. "Get all your equipment out of my house right now!" he screamed.

Startled, the crew leader stared at him. "Bishop Snow, is everything all right?"

Jimmy snatched open the van door and pulled the crew leader out. "I said, get all of this stuff out of my house, and get it out right now!"

Yolanda stood at the front door screaming his name as he jumped into his car and drove away. "Jimmy! Jimmy!"

Jimmy sped through the streets of Atlanta until he arrived at the corporate office of The Washington Broadcast Network. Julian was on his way out of the front door. Jimmy left his car running with the door standing open and ran up to him. He stood so close that Julian could smell his tonsils. "My wife and I are through with your show. Tear up our contracts," he said through gritted teeth.

"Bishop Snow, what's wrong? Let's go inside my office and talk."

"I have nothing to say to you except stay away from my wife and away from my family. Stop the phone calls. Stop following them. Just stay away! Do you understand me? Stay away from them!" he bellowed. Then he turned and walked back toward his car.

"Hey, Bishop, I have just one question." Jimmy turned and looked at him. "Does she still scream so loud in bed that the neighbors complain?" Julian smirked.

Like a bull seeing red, Jimmy charged toward him, but he suddenly stopped when he thought he felt a hand on his shoulder holding him back.

"Be ye angry, and sin not; let not the sun go down upon your wrath," he heard a voice say.

"You are so not worth it!" he screamed at Julian before getting back into his car and driving away.

Chapter Thirteen

Danita hung up her phone and smiled. All of the details were coming together nicely. She'd just finished speaking with the caterer, and her next order of business was to confirm the decorations. After the success of her cast pool party in August, Danita was ecstatic that Anderson had asked her to host the season ending cast party as well. It would be held the last week of November in the grand ballroom of her estate.

The phone rang again, and Danita checked the caller ID before answering. "Hi, Anderson, how are you?"

"I'm great, Danita. I just called because there's been a change in plans for the finale party."

"What kind of change? I just got off the phone with the caterers, and everything is running smoothly."

Anderson sighed. "Julian has decided to move the party up a week. Instead of hosting after the show wraps, he wants the entire cast together to watch the final show the same night it airs to the public."

Danita smiled. "That's a fabulous idea. I'm sure the caterer will not have a problem with changing the date."

"Awesome! Julian has taken the liberty of ordering a huge projection TV. It should be delivered to your home in a few days."

After speaking with Anderson, Danita went back to planning the party. *This is going to be great.* Danita was hoping it went as well as the pool party. At that time, to ensure that things went well, Danita not only invited the hospital administrator, but also the blogger who'd approached her in the restaurant. With the cameras rolling, she presented the administrator with a new check and gave the blogger an exclusive interview. Her plan worked, and public opinion of Evangelist Danita Hyatt shot up 100 percent. The best part was that she didn't have to donate the money. Anderson found a loophole that allowed her to count it as a show expense.

Two weeks after the party was over she reported to court to face her former husband's family and the wrongful death allegations. Thankfully, the judge had banned all cameras, including the crew of *Revelations*. The trial dragged on for almost two months. Danita found it heart wrenching having to relive every moment of her husband's death in court yet again. Her attorney tried his best to fight it, but the judge allowed photos of his bloated dead body to be shown. Danita turned her head and cried as it flashed on the courtroom screen.

After the shock factor, his family went about the business of tearing down Danita's character. They called her a gold digger and pointed out the fact that she was working as a waitress prior to her marriage. Her attorney countered with the fact that she worked nights in the restaurant and spent her days in seminary, earning her ministerial degree. With that degree, she had assisted her late husband in building a large and well respected ministry.

Next, his family's lawyers called in witnesses to testify that Danita and Ben's marriage was on the rocks at the time of his death. Danita felt this was ridiculous as she'd never denied that they had problems. It was difficult leading a ministry together without some issues and tribulations creeping in.

Ben Hyatt had been the definition of tall, dark, and handsome. Those traits alone made him a magnet to most of the women that he met, including Danita. Add in personality, a good heart, and a multimillion-dollar ministry and Ben seemed to be walking chocolate Häagen-Dazs to most women. Many were drawn to his power and charisma, while others simply became caught up in the almost angelic aura that surrounded him. The fact that he was a married minister of the gospel didn't matter to the boldest of the women. Their pursuit of him was relentless and unwavering.

Danita never suspected her husband of infidelity, but she was well aware that an assortment of women would do virtually anything to take her place. Their tricks included dressing sexy for church services and programs, sending him gifts, and even stopping by his office or their home uninvited and unannounced.

During the trial, Danita was devastated when one of those women took the stand on Ben's family's behalf. After being sworn in, she proceeded to tell the court about her relationship with Ben.

"We were madly in love. Ben and I knew that God wanted us to be together, but Danita refused to let him go. It wasn't because she loved him. All she cared about was shopping and planning parties. Her focus was spending his money."

Unable to contain herself, Danita jumped up and burst out, "You are lying. Ben would never cheat on me!"

Her attorney pulled her down into her seat. "Calm down or the judge will throw you out," he whispered.

"But she's lying. I can't allow her to sully his memory like that."

"We'll get our chance to speak," he assured her.

On cross-examination, Victor questioned the alleged mistress. "In your testimony, you stated that you and Reverend Hyatt were in love, is that correct?"

"Yes."

"Are you also admitting that you and he were involved in an affair?"

The mistress hesitated and looked around before answering. Danita could have sworn she was looking at Ben's sister for direction. After prodding from the judge, she finally answered. "Our love was pure and chaste. Ben never violated his marriage vows."

"How long was your relationship?" Victor asked.

"We were together for six months. The week before he died, he asked Danita for a divorce. If she had not killed him, we would be together right now."

Victor remained calm while the rest of the courtroom began to swell into a frenzy of whispers. "Your Honor, I request that the witness's last statement be stricken from the record. My client was found not guilty in a court of law."

During his closing statements, Victor pointed out that during this case, Ben's family had not presented any evidence that connected Danita to his death. Instead, what they'd proved is that while Danita was busy trying to save their marriage, he was involved in an affair. He also stated that while they had attempted to prove that Danita did not love Ben, all they'd really done was cast doubt as to whether he loved her.

The entire process had drained Danita, but she felt confident that she would come out of court victorious. The case was due to close the following day, so Danita happily continued her party planning.

She arrived at court early the next morning feeling refreshed and ready to be vindicated by the verdict. Instead, she was stunned by what transpired. Danita sat lost in a daze of unbelief as Ben's family cheered the judge's ruling in their favor.

"How could this happen, Victor? I'm innocent. I did not kill Ben," she cried.

Victor tried his best to soothe her. "It's okay. This isn't a criminal trial. This only means that they feel that your actions may have contributed to his death."

Danita was about to say more when the judge banged his gavel and demanded that the court come to order. Ben's family looked over at her smugly, then quieted down their celebration.

"I've just been informed that this case has an unprecedented twist. Normally at this time, I would be called upon to make a determination regarding monetary damages. However, in this case, the plaintiffs have waived all financial claims. Instead, they are requesting a review of custody of the minor surviving children of Ben Hyatt. Those children are Summer Raine Hyatt, Autumn Brease Hyatt, and Winter Storme Hyatt."

Danita shook her head and began crying. "No, you can't take my babies. You just can't," she blurted out. Victor quickly shushed her.

"As I stated, because there is no precedence in this case, I will not make a decision at this time. Instead, this matter will be turned over to family court. It will be up to them to make a final ruling on custody in this matter. Court adjourned."

Victor rose to show respect for the departing judge and urged Danita to be quiet until he was completely out of the room.

"What does this mean? Are they going to get my children?" she asked as soon as the judge was gone.

Victor shrugged. "I can't answer that right now. I wish I could, but I can't."

Danita was beside herself with anguish. "What do you mean you can't answer that? I pay you to know the answers."

Victor noticed that several members of Ben's family were still in the courtroom. He pulled Danita closer to him and lowered his voice. "Normally, if you are found liable in a wrongful death suit, you are obligated to pay whatever monetary damages the court awards. In this case, the judge will simply advise family court of his verdict. It's up to a family court judge to decide." Victor paused and looked around again. "Let's get out of here and discuss this in the privacy of my office."

Danita looked over at her late husband's family as they filed out of the courtroom, smiling and jovial. "Mother Hyatt, Pop Hyatt," she called out, but Ben's parents ignored her and kept walking. "Joy, wait, please," she called out to Ben's sister. Victor tugged on Danita's arm to stop her, but she pulled away from him. "Joy, you and I used to be so close. Can't we come to some sort of settlement?" she pleaded.

"We don't want your money. It's meaningless to us," Joy answered.

"That's not what I mean. I've never kept the girls away from you, and I never will. Can't we work out a visitation schedule between us without involving the court?"

Joy looked her up and down, and then turned her nose up. "We don't want anything to do with you, and I will not sit idly by and let my nieces be brought up by a murderer." Without another word, she turned her back to Danita and left the courtroom.

Half an hour later as they sat inside his office, Victor tried his best to console Danita, without giving her false hope. "In order for grandparents or other relatives to get custody, they have to prove that you are unfit or unstable. Prior to today, you would not have been considered either one of those things. But the judgment in this case changes things."

"I did not kill, Ben. I was found not guilty. Doesn't that count for *anything?*"

"Of course it does, but today's verdict may hold equal weight. Listen, let's not panic. Right now, all we really have is a petition for custody based on today's verdict. That does not mean that you will lose your kids. Most judges still tend to favor the mother in these types of cases."

His words did little to ease Danita's worries. Instead of going home after she left her attorney's office, she went to the mall. Ordinarily, shopping would cheer her up, but she wandered from store to store without making any purchases. Finally, she returned to her limousine and asked Philippe to take her home. As soon as she entered the limousine she demanded that he turn off the radio.

"What's wrong?" he asked. Philippe was listening to T. D. Jakes choir singing, "This Test Is Your Storm."

Danita slumped back in her seat. "That music is working my last nerve."

Confused, he turned the radio off. For the past several months, Danita had insisted that the car stereo always be tuned to a gospel radio station or that he play only gospel CDs. Glancing back at her, Philippe reasoned that she was probably through pretending. Anderson had advised them that he had enough footage to complete the last two shows of the season and all of the cameras had been removed the day before. "Do you want me to play something else? I've got Beyonce's latest CD up here."

"No, I just want silence, please." She pulled her sunglasses down over her eyes and leaned her head back against the leather seat. The last few words she'd heard of the song continued to play inside her head.

this test is your storm, but it won't be long, go through, hold on.

Over and over it echoed like a commercial jingle that just wouldn't go away. *Whatever, God, I'm tired of your test*, she thought. By the time they reached her home, the song inside Danita's head had begun to annoy and anger her. Without waiting for Philippe to open her door, she jumped out of the limousine and rushed inside her house, slamming the front door behind her. Then she swiftly ran upstairs and into the master bedroom. The song continued playing over and over in her head as if her brain was a DJ stuck on repeat.

Danita grabbed a pillow from her bed. She hurled it across the room in frustration. "I'm sick of your test, God," she yelled. "This is not fair. First, you took Ben; then you let me stand trial for his murder. Now you want my children too?" Danita threw another pillow and watched it crash into her closet door. "Okay, I've made some mistakes, and I haven't done what I should all the time, but now you are just being cruel. What more do you want? I can't please you. I don't know how to please you." Grabbing the remaining eight decorative pillows from her bed, she fired each one off in succession across the room. They landed on her dresser, vanity, and floor. With nothing left to throw, Danita stared upward and began sobbing. "I can't take anymore. I can't. My God, why have thou forsaken me?" she cried as she crumbled onto the floor in a pool of her own tears.

Danita's bedroom door slowly creaked open, and Summer walked in. "Mommy, are you okay?"

Quickly wiping her tears, Danita tried to regain her composure. "Yes, sweetie, I'm fine. I didn't know you were home. Where are your sisters?"

"They're downstairs in the playroom with Ms. Vivian."

Danita stood up and straightened out her clothes. "Why aren't you playing with them too?"

"I came up here to ask for your help . . . with my lesson."

"Sure, baby, come sit with me." Danita wiped away the last remnants of her tantrum and sat down on the bed and waited for Summer to join her. "What do you need help with, math or science?"

Summer sat on the bed next to Danita and opened her book. "Neither, it's my Sunday School lesson. We're studying Joseph and the coat of many colors."

"Yes, that's a wonderful story. What do you need help with?"

"The teacher wants us to cut up strips of paper in different colors and make a coat with all the colors in it from the story. Can you help me?" Reaching into her pocket, Summer pulled out several colorful strips of paper and laid them on the bed. Then she pulled out a piece of paper that had a small man with a blank white coat drawn on it. She pointed at the man. "That's Joseph. When I find the colors in the story I'm supposed to tape them on his coat."

"Okay, sweetie, go ahead and read the story."

Summer picked up her workbook and began to read. "There once was a man named Jacob, and he had twelve sons. Of all his sons, Joseph was his favorite. Jacob gave Joseph a beautiful coat. Whenever he wore it, his brothers were green with envy." Summer stopped reading and put the green strip of paper on Joseph's coat, then went back to the story. "One day his brothers got so jealous that they took his coat and threw him down a well. All Joseph could see was black all around." Again, Summer stopped, and this time she added the black strip to the paper.

"Just keep reading, I'll add the colors," Danita suggested.

"Joseph's brothers took him from the well and sold him to a group of men from Egypt to be their slave. Then they killed a goat and splashed red blood all over Joseph's coat. They took it to their father and told them that Joseph had been killed. Joseph's father was blue because he thought his son was gone forever."

Danita added the red and blue strips of paper to the coat. Since there were no more strips to add she believed that she was done, but Summer continued reading. "But that isn't the end of this story. God was with Joseph and kept him safe. God had a plan for his life. God was watching over Joseph. Joseph wasn't the perfect child. He was probably spoiled and thought too much of himself. He was also a tattle-tale. His brothers were jealous and did a very bad thing. But we will learn next week how God took a very bad situation and made something good out of it. We will see how God can make bad things good again.

"Sometimes you have bad things happen in your life that you think just aren't fair. Maybe you have people that pick on you or call you names. Or maybe someone is sick in your family or doesn't have a job. God wants you to know that He is always with you no matter what happens. He is watching over you and your family. He is with you wherever you go and no matter what you do. He can take something bad and turn it into something good. So, when you have a problem or bad things are happening, just remember that God is with you. When you pray to Him, God is there to listen to your troubles. Next week we will learn how God helped Joseph and his family with their problems and made a bad thing good."

Danita began to cry again, unable to stop the tears. As the leader of a huge congregation, she'd preached sermons to thousands of people, yet it never occurred to her that her ten-year-old daughter would be the one preaching to her. She pulled Summer into a hug and held her tightly.

"Now we have to say the prayer together, Mommy," Summer said.

Wiping her tears, Danita looked over Summer's shoulder at the book, and they prayed together. It was the first sincere prayer Danita had uttered in over a year.

Dear God,
Thank you that you are with me
no matter what happens.
Thank you that you can take something bad,
and turn it into something good.
In Jesus' name,
amen.

Danita hugged her daughter tightly once again. "Hey, how would you and your sisters like to go out to dinner tonight?"

A big grin spread across Summer's face. "Can we pick the restaurant?" she asked.

"Of course, we'll go wherever you want. Now run downstairs and tell Vivian, so that you girls can get ready." Danita gave her daughter another hug and a kiss before sending her out. Once Summer was gone, Danita looked up. "Okay, God, I'm through fighting with you. I surrender to your will. Please help me. Please don't let them take my girls away."

Chapter Fourteen

As he did every morning, Zack Morton trotted up his basement stairs and locked the door behind him. He turned to greet his wife and noticed that there was a guest with her in the kitchen. "Vanessa, I'm surprised to see you here," Zack said as he sat down at the kitchen table.

"You always are," she said sarcastically. "Since they are through filming your TV show, I thought it was about time I met my new little cousin, Coretta." Vanessa bounced the baby on her lap and grinned at her.

"Your breakfast is ready, sweetheart," Charlene said. She placed a plate in front of Zack with scrambled eggs, country ham, and buttered toast.

"Thank you, sweetheart." Zack took a bite of his ham, then looked over at Vanessa. "Have you been watching the show? It's a ratings and viewer success."

"I detest reality TV," Vanessa answered.

Zack put his coffee cup down and leaned back in his chair. "Really? Why is that?"

"Not that it would matter to you, but most of the reality shows that are on television are degrading to African Americans. They are stereotypical and exploitive."

Zack nodded his head. "I actually agree with you on that, but our show is different. If it wasn't, then I would not be a part of it, and I certainly would not let my family be involved."

Vanessa laughed. "Do you really believe that? You are blond and blue eyed, so you bring in the right demographic. Then you have a beautiful sista as your wife, to add the controversy and drama."

Zack pushed his plate away and suddenly stood up from the table. "I'd better get going. I have an early meeting today." Taking his daughter from Vanessa's lap, he gave her a kiss on the cheek, and then handed her to Charlene. "I think she needs changing," he said. Then he kissed Charlene good-bye and walked out the back door.

Charlene glared at her cousin. "Why do you always have to start with him?"

"I didn't do anything but speak my mind. He should know better than to ask questions if he isn't prepared for the answers."

Charlene pulled out a chair and sat down while balancing Coretta on her hip. "You were just being difficult. You know you haven't missed an episode of our show. You told me that you really like it, and you thought that it was unusual."

"Well, you're family. Of course I'm watching your show, but I didn't have to tell *him* that. Hey, did you hear about the verdict in your cast mate's wrongful death trial?"

Charlene nodded her head and stood up with the baby. "Yes, I heard. Come upstairs with me. Zack was right. Coretta does need to be changed."

Vanessa followed Charlene up the stairs and into the nursery. "Wow, this looks so nice. I told you decorating with Princess Tiana would be a great idea."

"You only say that because people say you look like Anika Noni Rose, and you have the nerve to believe it," Charlene laughed.

Vanessa laughed too. "Don't hate," she said and winked at Charlene. "So, what do you think about Evangelist Hyatt's verdict?"

"I think it's sad. That poor woman has been through so much already." Charlene laid Coretta on the changing table and unsnapped her onesie.

"You're kidding, right?" Vanessa took a seat in the rocking chair and slowly began to rock back and forth.

"No, I'm not. Since we've been on the show together, I've had a chance to be around her quite a bit. I don't believe she killed her husband, and she adores her girls. You can just feel it when you are around her."

"I think she got away with murder, but I guess being around her, you have become friends or something. Does that mean you like all of your cast mates?"

"Um . . . I get along with most of them." Charlene finished changing Coretta's diaper and picked her up. Vanessa held out her arms for the baby, and she handed her over. Sitting down beside Vanessa in the matching rocking chair, Charlene pulled a basket of clothes closer and began folding tiny pink T-shirts and shorts.

"So, tell me . . . who don't you like?" Vanessa asked.

"Bishop Jimmy Snow and his wife are really nice. They have two great kids. Priscilla babysat the twins last week when the nanny was sick. JJ is a real jokester. Martin and Luther follow him around like he's the Pied Piper. We've all grown really close."

"So you like the Snows and Evangelist Hyatt. That must mean that you don't like Brandon Kitts and his wife. Maybe he should have stuck to playing football," Vanessa chuckled.

"Oh, no. Brandon is an anointed man of God. His ministry is powerful. Leaving the NFL was the best decision he could have made in his life." Charlene hesitated. Although she trusted Vanessa, she hated to gossip. "I just think his wife is . . . Well, she's kind of standoffish. I'm sure she's a lovely woman, but she just doesn't allow anyone to get close enough to her to find that out."

Vanessa looked down and noticed that she'd rocked Coretta to sleep. Quietly, she stood up and walked over to her crib and gently laid her down. Leaning into the crib, she kissed her forehead. Then she sat down and began helping Charlene fold the remaining clothes. "Listen, cuz, it's just you and me in here. Come on, you can be truthful. Girlfriend is a witch, ain't she?"

"No, I don't think so. She's expecting, so I thought since I have a new baby the two of us could bond. It's her first child; you'd think she'd want to hear from someone who's been through it."

"Yeah, so, did she want any advice from you?"

"Nope. As a matter of fact, she doesn't seem to want to discuss her pregnancy at all. And I respect a person's right to their personal space, but she went ballistic last week when Julian tried to touch her belly."

Vanessa nodded her head. "That's not so strange. I hated having my belly rubbed when I was pregnant. It's annoying."

"I guess so, but there just seems to be more to it." Charlene folded the last baby T-shirt from the basket. She walked over to the dresser and put all of the clothes away. Looking into the crib she saw that Coretta was sleeping soundly. "Come on. Let's go to the family room. I don't want to disturb her with our conversation."

When they arrived downstairs, Vanessa sprawled onto the sofa and grabbed the TV remote. "I want to watch the news and see if there's an update on Mabel Joe Stevens's disappearance."

"Who's that?" Charlene asked, as she sat beside her.

"Do you even listen when I talk? She's the woman from the hospital who's been missing for almost three months now."

Charlene felt nauseated as she suddenly remembered. "You mean, they haven't found her yet?"

Vanessa shook her head as she flipped channels. "It's almost like she's disappeared off the face of the earth."

Two months earlier, Vanessa had called Charlene to tell her about the latest hospital gossip. As the fourth-floor head nurse, Vanessa was familiar with almost everyone there. Although Charlene stopped working at the hospital after her marriage, there were still employees, doctors, and nurses that she was familiar with and they often chatted about them. When Vanessa first mentioned the name Mabel Joe Stevens, it did not ring a bell. It wasn't until Vanessa described her that it became clear to Charlene who the woman was.

Mabel Joe was a short, middle-aged woman with caramel-colored skin and a short Afro that had just a patch of grey up front. According to Vanessa, Mabel Joe left work one day, and when her two days off were over, she did not return. Her supervisor called her home over and over and got no answer, so she went to her house. It was empty, and Mabel Joe was nowhere to be found. The supervisor felt that something was wrong so she called the police. After a thorough search of the house, the police found no evidence of forced entry or theft. It just seemed as if Mabel Joe just disappeared. Some of her clothes were missing, and the police suggested that she probably went on vacation.

A month later, the supervisor called the police again. She stated that it was unlike Mabel Joe to just leave without telling anyone where she was going. In ten years, she'd rarely missed a day of work. The supervisor was convinced that foul play was involved and insisted that the police file a missing person's report. With the help of Mabel Joe's coworkers and neighbors, the supervisor taped flyers up all over Atlanta with Mabel Joe's picture on it. They'd had very few leads, and so far, nothing had panned out.

"What about her family? Have they heard from her?" Charlene asked.

Vanessa sighed. "I know Mabel Joe likes to talk about him in the present tense, as if he's still alive, but she doesn't have any family. Her son was killed in Iraq two years ago, and his children are with their mother in Hawaii."

Still feeling sick, Charlene decided to confide in her cousin. Taking a deep breath, she told her about the morning after Coretta's birth and Zack's reaction to Mabel Joe.

"That is so weird. Did you ask him about it later?"

Charlene shook her head. "It bothered me, but I decided it wasn't worth pursuing. Zack gets approached by strangers all the time. It's a part of being a well-known pastor."

"Then why are you so concerned? Don't try to deny it. I can see it in your face. What else is going on?"

Charlene left the family room and went upstairs to her bedroom to retrieve her purse. She returned several minutes later just as the news was ending. "Did they have any updates on her?"

"Nope, they didn't mention her at all. I think the police have probably given up hope of ever finding her alive."

"Don't say that. She's fine. She just has to be." Charlene plopped down on the sofa and tried to steady her trembling hands. She reached inside her purse and pulled out an old picture. Without a word, she handed it to Vanessa.

"Where did you get this?" Vanessa demanded.

Charlene looked down at her feet, then whispered, "Zack's car."

Vanessa stared at the picture of a much-younger Mabel Joe Stevens. She was standing in front of a wrought-iron fence wearing a blue and yellow dress with a big yellow hat. Standing on either side of her were two little boys who appeared to be around nine or ten years old. They were both wearing new Sunday suits, with ties and shiny black patent leather shoes. One of the boys was dark skinned with his hair cut into a fade. The other little boy was very light skinned with dark brown curly hair.

Turning the picture over Vanessa read the words aloud. "Easter Sunday, 1987." She slowly shook her head. "How long have you had this?"

"I found it a couple of months ago. Zack let me use his car to take Coretta to her first doctor's appointment. This was in the glove compartment."

"We have to call the police right now."

"What for? It's just a picture."

Vanessa's brow wrinkled up, and her eyes were open as wide as they could go. "It's a picture of the woman who's been missing for almost three months. This could be a clue."

"There's nothing in that picture that would tell the police where she is. It's an old picture."

Vanessa decided to try a different approach. "Charlene, this picture proves that Zack lied to you at the hospital about knowing Mabel Joe. Now she's missing, and he has a picture of her in his car. Don't you at least want to know what he's doing with it?"

Charlene slowly nodded her head. "Yes, but he never said he didn't know her. He just said that she was mistaken about living next door to his grandmother. There could be a perfectly logical explanation for that picture. I don't want to involve the police until after I talk to Zack."

"I hate to say this because you are family and I love you. But that man has your nose so wide open that you can't see the forest for the trees, girl. Mabel Joe could be locked in your basement right now, and you want to give him a chance to lie to you, again?"

Charlene snatched the picture away from Vanessa and put it back inside her purse. "I'm sorry that I told you. You've never liked Zack. I don't know why I thought you'd at least have an open mind about this."

"Your mind is the one that's closed. Zack could tell you the sky is falling and just like Chicken Little, you'd be running away scared."

"That's enough. I've put up with the snide comments about my husband for my entire marriage, and frankly, I'm sick of it. You and the rest of my family have given me no credit since the day you met him. I know that Zack is not perfect, but I love him, and I want our marriage to work. So instead of nagging him, I pray for him and with him. I'm not stupid, like most of you think. I just know how to choose my battles. In return, God has blessed me with a loving husband, three beautiful children, this exquisite home, and just about any material thing I could want. I'm happy, and I have learned to accept the fact that my family won't be happy for me. But I'm not about to sit here and let you disrespect me in my own home."

"Charlene, I'm sorry. That picture just has me freaked out. I've been concerned about Mabel Joe, and when you showed me that, it was just scary. I'm sorry. I didn't mean to hurt your feelings."

Charlene sighed loudly. "It's okay. I'm just not ready to accuse Zack of anything. All we really know is that he knew Mabel Joe. So did you and a lot of people."

"I've got an idea. Just promise you'll hear me out before you say no."

Charlene eyed her suspiciously. "What is it?"

"Let's just take a look in the basement. I've got a friend who's a locksmith, and I could have him over here in less than an hour."

"No way. That's an invasion of his privacy, and I won't do it." Charlene suddenly heard Coretta crying. She left the family room and rushed up the stairs to tend to her with Vanessa following closely behind her. Picking her up, Charlene bounced her and rubbed her back to soothe her. "Mommy's here, sweetie. What's the matter? Are you hungry?" She turned to Vanessa. "Will you get me a bottle from the minifridge please?"

"Sure, do I need to go downstairs and warm it up?"

"No, just take it to the bathroom and run it under the warm water for a few seconds."

Charlene was sitting in the rocking chair still trying to soothe Coretta when Vanessa returned a few moments later with the bottle. Vanessa handed it to her, then sat in the chair beside her. Silently, she watched her cousin lovingly feeding her baby while trying to think of a way to convince her to search the basement.

As much as she hated to admit it, Vanessa really did not dislike Zack. She was well aware that he was a good provider and a loving husband and father. She'd visited his church on numerous occasions and truly believed that he was a man of God who preached the Word. Those were not the things about him that bothered her.

She couldn't pinpoint it or give it a name, but something about him just didn't sit well with her. There was something about him that was bubbling just under the surface of his character that made her wonder who he really was. It had taken awhile, but she'd gotten used to the fact that he wouldn't shake hands with most people, and his nose worked like a bloodhound.

She believed his overprotectiveness of Charlene was his way of showing love, and she knew lots of men who had private home gyms. Individually, none of it was worthy of concern, but collectively, it made her skin crawl like hearing fingernails scratch across a chalkboard.

Because Charlene loved him, Vanessa had ignored her gut feeling for years, but she wasn't willing to do that anymore. Something in her spirit told her that Zack was connected to Mabel Joe's disappearance, and she just had to convince Charlene to go into that basement.

Charlene placed Coretta on her shoulder and gently patted her back until she let out a loud burp. Then she smiled and cradled her in her lap before looking over at Vanessa. "I see that look in your eye, but I've already given you my answer."

"You promised to hear me out before saying no, remember?"

"I heard you. You want to break into Zack's basement gym."

"But you didn't let me tell you why. Okay, I know I made that crack about Mabel Joe being down there. I was out of line. But in all these years, you mean to tell me you've *never* wondered what he's hiding down there?"

"He's not *hiding* anything. There is a gym and a full bathroom with a shower down there. He locks it to keep the boys out. For Pete's sake, I have the keys." Charlene walked over to the crib and laid Coretta down while Vanessa stared at her with her mouth gaping wide open.

"*You* have the keys? He won't be home for hours; we can go down there, look around, and be back upstairs in no time. If he has nothing to hide, what's the harm in looking?"

"I trust my husband. He's always trusted me with the keys, so I know that he isn't trying to keep me out. I've just never had a reason to go down there."

"Honey, you said yourself that he acted as if he didn't know Mabel Joe, but you found that picture." She walked over to the crib and looked Charlene directly in the eyes. "I'm not trying to destroy your trust in your husband, but we both know that something is not right about this whole situation."

Charlene stood quietly thinking for several moments. To her knowledge, Zack had never lied to her during their marriage. He was a truthful man. Even if he thought the truth would hurt her, he'd always been honest. But his reaction to Mabel Joe at the hospital was unnerving. That feeling intensified when she'd found the picture. Pondering Vanessa's request, she realized that Zack had never asked her not to go into the basement. It was just a mutual understanding between them that it was his private domain. He'd told her that he did not like to be disturbed while working out, and she'd always respected his wishes. Based on that logic, Charlene reasoned that if she went down there now, she would not be going against his wishes. She turned to Vanessa. "Okay, let's go do it now before I lose my nerve."

The two of them trotted down the stairs into the kitchen and over to the basement door. Charlene opened the utility drawer next to the sink and retrieved her keys. First, she unlocked the padlock. She tried to do it alone, but it took the strength of both of them to raise the iron bar. Next, she unlocked all of the deadbolts and turned the tumblers. Finally, she put her key into the lock on the basement door. Pausing to take a deep breath, she looked over at Vanessa. "This just feels wrong. We shouldn't do it."

"Girl, I just broke a sweat lifting that bar," Vanessa said indignantly. "We are going in. Now go ahead and open the door."

Charlene inhaled deeply and turned the key in the lock, then pulled the basement door open. As soon as she did, Zack walked into the kitchen.

Startled, both Vanessa and Charlene quickly scampered away from the open basement door. "Honey, what you doing home?" Charlene asked.

Zack looked back and forth at the two women and then the basement door before answering. "I forgot my iPad. Why is the basement door open? I've told you it could be dangerous if the boys went down there."

"Um . . . the boys are at school, and um . . . Vanessa wanted to see what kind of equipment you have down there. She's thinking of building a gym in her home." Charlene barely squeaked the lie out, and it seemed to burn her lips as it left her mouth.

Zack looked them both over again once more. "Sure, go ahead and show her the whole layout, but don't forget to lock the door when you're done. I'm going upstairs to get my iPad. I have a meeting downtown." He started to leave the kitchen, but then he stopped and turned around. "Oh, I'll probably be a little late for dinner."

As soon as he was gone, Charlene rushed over and closed the basement door, and locked all of the locks.

"What are you doing? He said it's fine if we go in," Vanessa whispered.

"That's exactly why I'm not going down there. It proves that he has nothing to hide, and I should not be snooping around. Help me get the bar back down."

Reluctantly, Vanessa took the edge of the bar, and they both heaved it into place. She crossed her arms across her chest in frustration as she watched Charlene place the padlock on the door and return the keys to the drawer.

Outside the kitchen door, Zack stood watching and listening. Once he was sure they'd locked up the basement, he grabbed his briefcase and left the house feeling grateful that his wife has so much trust in him. As he got into his car, he made a mental note to change all of the locks on the basement door.

Chapter Fifteen

"Honey, we're going to be late if you don't hurry up," Brandon yelled. Tia was in her private bathroom getting ready for the *Revelations* cast finale party.

"I'm dressing for two. I'll be out soon," she yelled through the door.

"Fine, I'll be waiting for you downstairs," he said before leaving the bedroom.

Inside the bathroom, Tia stood posing in front of her full-length mirror admiring her naked body. Whenever she had the luxury of removing the padding, she could not help gazing into the mirror at her lean and trim physique.

Over the past few months, she had found that padding her figure to appear increasingly pregnant was the worst part of the whole plan. After years of Pilates and a strict diet, she hated that she now had to hide the figure she'd worked so hard to maintain. It was especially difficult for her during the summer when she wanted to wear short shorts and midriff tops. Attending the cast party at Evangelist Hyatt's home that summer had been humiliating for her. Instead of being able to show off her washboard abs in a tiny string bikini, Tia had to wear a one-piece bathing suit dress with padding underneath. Brandon told her that she looked beautiful, but Tia felt fat and ugly. But she took consolation in the fact that unlike real pregnant women, her weight was artificial, and each night before taking a shower, she had the luxury of shedding it all to strut her stuff in front of the mirror.

During the past few months, Tia also learned that being pregnant had perks that she had not expected. Quincy had encouraged her to fake morning sickness. "Look, girl, you are supposed to be sick every morning. Tell Brandon that you are nauseated, then go in the bathroom and make throwing up sounds," he had said.

"That's disgusting." Tia's nose sneered up at the thought of it.

"Maybe so, but if you expect your husband to believe that you are pregnant, you are going to have to simulate the symptoms."

The following Sunday morning, Tia did as he asked. After Brandon left for church alone she was elated to realize that being sick allowed her to skip service. From that day forward she used her pregnancy as an excuse to get out of all sorts of church business. Brandon felt she should not be on her feet too much, so he took over her duties at the soup kitchen, and replaced her as a Sunday School teacher. When the Ladies League announced their clothing drive, Brandon sent over two church ladies to help Tia sort through clothes to donate. With her feet propped up, Tia worked the two women like Hebrew slaves. They not only cleaned out all four of her closets, but they also agreed to rub her feet and legs after she pretended that they were swelling.

Although his constant prodding and reminders were annoying, Tia was actually grateful that Quincy was helping her through the entire process. He kept in contact with the surrogate and went with her to every doctor's appointment. He also helped Tia run interference with Brandon to be sure that he conveniently missed all of her pretend appointments. Even Tia had become excited when Quincy delivered to her an ultrasound that confirmed the baby was a boy.

One morning she'd gone into her bathroom and realized that she was out of feminine hygiene products. She'd already pushed the intercom and was prepared to wail Sophia's head off for not replenishing them, when she suddenly realized that her maid thought she was pregnant and did not need them. Tia began to panic as she wondered how she could get more. There was no way that she'd walk into a store and buy them. Even when the TV cameras were not following her, everywhere she went, someone in Atlanta recognized her from the show. The gossip blogs had written a story on the last pair of shoes and matching purse that she'd bought, so she knew they'd report it if she bought anything else. Feeling desperate she called Quincy.

Half an hour later, he arrived at her home wearing tight jeans, a hot-pink tube top, a lime-green feather boa, and 3-inch stiletto heels. In his hand he was carrying a large shopping bag. He swished his hips up the stairs and into her bedroom without waiting for Sophia to announce him. "Here you go, girlfriend," he said with a big, boisterous smile.

Tia gave him a big hug of gratitude. "You are a lifesaver."

"Gas to get to the store . . . ten dollars, two boxes of feminine hygiene products . . . twelve dollars, the look on the old biddy's face at Target as I pranced up to the register and bought them . . . priceless," he said. The two of them doubled over on the bed in laughter.

At last, through with admiring her body in the mirror, Tia grabbed her six-month pregnancy padding and put it on. She began to step into her royal-blue strapless sequined gown, but remembered that she couldn't get it over her belly. Instead, she had to pull it over her head. As she struggled into the dress, she wished she could call for help. *How do fat women get dressed every day?* she wondered just as she was finally able to get the dress to slide past her hips.

She emerged from the bathroom and pressed the intercom to summon Sophia to escort the makeup artist upstairs that she'd hired and to put on her shoes. That was her favorite pregnancy perk. Instead of trying to reach around her stomach, she simply sat down in a chair while Sophia placed the shoes on her feet for her. Tia loved every moment of it. There was just something about having people kneeling at her feet that made her feel all warm and tingly inside.

Growing weary of waiting, Brandon returned upstairs to check on Tia's progress. "Honey, I've been dressed and waiting for over an hour. Can we go now?" he asked.

"No. Ming is here, and she has to do my makeup and hair."

Brandon shook his head. In all the years that they'd been married, Tia had always been high maintenance. He smiled politely at Ming and went back downstairs. He knew that it would be at least another half hour before they'd be ready to depart.

To pass the time, he decided to call his parents. His mother picked up the phone on the second ring. "Brandon, honey, I thought you were attending a finale party tonight in Atlanta," she said.

"I am. I'm just waiting for Tia to get ready. You know my wife likes to make an entrance."

"Oh, how is Miss Thing enjoying her pregnancy?"

Brandon chuckled. His mother had referred to Tia by that nickname since the day they'd first met. "She's fine, Mom, and so is the baby. Did I tell you it's a boy?"

"Are you sure? You've been saying it's a boy all along."

"Yes. Tia had an ultrasound last month, and it was confirmed." Brandon had wanted to be there to hold her hand through the whole thing, but he'd been out of town. When he returned, Tia presented him with the ultrasound picture. He had it framed and hung on his office wall.

"It's a boy!" his mother yelled out. "Brandon and Miss Thing are having a boy."

Brandon heard applause, screams, and cheers in the background. "What's going on?"

"Your father and I are throwing our own finale party right here at the house. Your brothers and sisters are all here, and the grandkids. I'm so glad that you gave us that big-screen TV for our anniversary."

Brandon felt a twinge of sadness mixed with jealousy. As much as he liked his cast mates, he'd much rather be sitting in the middle of his mother's den floor watching the last show with all of his loved ones. In his mind, he could imagine the food that his mother had cooked. He was sure she had her kitchen counter weighed down with fried chicken wings, honey-glazed meat balls, pigs in a blanket, and sweet & spicy shrimp. His siblings would be in charge of the side dishes. He could almost taste his big brother's famous red cabbage coleslaw and the fried corn he just knew his sister had brought. "It sounds like you guys are having a ball," he said.

"When are you coming to visit, son?" Brandon's father picked up the phone extension and joined in the conversation.

"Dad, I would love to come home for Christmas, but I don't think Tia will be up to traveling. She'll be almost eight months by then. But I promise we'll be home in the New Year. As soon as the baby is old enough, we'll bring him to see you."

"How'd you jump all the way to Christmas? Thanksgiving is next week. The show is done filming, so can't you come then?" Brandon's mother asked.

Brandon sighed. "I wish I could, but the church is serving the homeless on Thanksgiving Day. It's one of our biggest projects of the year. As the pastor I have to be there, and I really want to be there."

"That's my boy. You have always put other's needs above your own. We are proud of what you are doing with your ministry, Brandon. Just be sure to give us a call that day," his dad said.

Brandon smiled. "Yes, sir. I promise. So what's going on back there?"

As he listened intently, his mother did a rundown of all the family business. One of his sisters had received a promotion on her job. Another was laid off, but she was making ends meet by selling handmade jewelry online. He had a niece who'd made varsity cheerleader and another had been crowned homecoming queen. His namesake nephew was the latest star on the high school basketball team. Brandon's oldest brother along with his wife had just returned from a Caribbean cruise, and his parents had enrolled in a computer class at the local senior citizen center. While he waited for Tia, his mother also told him all of the happenings in his old neighborhood. She was excited that a new Church's chicken had been built less than a block from their house and their local church had just purchased new pew Bibles.

After more than an hour on the phone with his mother, he heard Tia's heels clicking as she came down the stairs. "It sounds like my wife is finally ready to go. I love you guys."

"We love you too," his parents said in unison.

Brandon hung up the phone just as Tia arrived downstairs taking his breath away. "You look absolutely gorgeous," he said. He took her hand and linked it into his arm to escort her outside.

"Brandon, you rented a limo?" Tia asked as they stepped onto the porch. The long stretch pearl-colored limousine sat parked in their driveway. A man dressed in a black chauffeur's uniform stepped out and held the door open for them.

"It wasn't me. It's a gift from Julian. He wanted the entire cast to arrive in white limousines for the party."

Tia grinned and stepped inside. Brandon got in beside her, and the driver closed the door behind them. Brandon cuddled up close to Tia, then placed his hand on her tummy. Tia pushed him away and slid to the other side of the long seat. "Brandon, you are going to mess up my dress and makeup," she said protesting.

"I just wanted to see if the baby would kick for me."

"He's been kicking all day. Just let him sleep so I can enjoy the party," she snapped.

He laughed. "My mother warned me about pregnancy mood swings. Okay, sweetie, I'll leave you two alone."

Tia breathed a sigh of relief. It irritated her that Brandon was constantly touching her belly and wanting to feel the baby move. The first time he had asked, she had covered her mouth to fake nausea and run from the room. After he left the house, she called Quincy and begged for his help. "Brandon wants to feel the baby kick. I told you this plan would not work. How am I supposed to make a sponge belly kick?"

"Wow . . . I didn't think of that. Just give me a few days. Try to stay away from him and I'll come up with something."

A few days later, he called to tell her he had found the answer. He asked Tia to come over to his studio immediately. Tia was lying across her bed in the midst of an afternoon nap. She stretched and yawned like a Siamese cat. "This had better be good. I was asleep. You know us pregnant women like to sleep a lot."

"Then you've been pregnant your whole life, because you've loved to lie around and sleep away most of the day since we met."

Tia giggled. "Yea, but now nobody questions me about it. I love it."

"Stop being so lazy and get over here," he said and hung up the phone.

When she arrived, he was busy showing a customer the fabric he'd chosen for her living room, so Tia went into his back office and waited. Sitting on his desk she noticed a lavender bag with the name Dirty Diana's on the front. She grabbed the bag and was just about to peek inside when Quincy walked in. "You are *so* nosy," he said, snatching it away.

Tia laughed. "Okay, you said you had the answer to the baby kicking. What have you got?"

Quincy reached into the bag and pulled out a long, slender massager. "Here it is," he said proudly.

"Thanks so much, but I have my own toys at home," Tia laughed loudly.

"It's not a toy, silly. Put this inside the belly padding and turn it on. The rippling effect of the massager will go through the pad and feel just like a baby moving around in your stomach. After Brandon is through feeling the baby, just excuse yourself, go to the bathroom, and turn it off."

Tia stared at him in disbelief; then she grinned. "Quincy, you are an evil genius."

That trick had worked successfully several times. Tia had even turned it on before getting into bed several times. The distraction of the baby kicking made Brandon forget about asking her for sex. After he dozed off, she'd sneak into the bathroom and turn it off. But Tia had not included it in her padding before dressing for the party. Wearing a full-length gown, she knew it would be too difficult to reach inside and turn on and off, even in the privacy of the bathroom. She decided that Brandon was just going to have to get through one night without having his son kick for him.

They arrived at the party, and the driver pulled behind an identical white limousine and parked. Brandon and Tia stepped out just as another white limousine pulled in directly behind them and also parked. The entire cast was in attendance, along with Anderson, and they each walked the red carpet along the driveway up to the front door of Danita's estate as the paparazzi's flashbulbs lit up the sky like lightning on a hot summer night.

Chapter Sixteen

Yolanda stepped out of the limousine provided for them and waited for Jimmy. She knew he was hesitating because he was adamantly against coming at all. It wasn't until their attorney advised him that he was contractually obligated to do publicity for the show that he finally relented and agreed to attend the party.

The past two weeks had been the most strained and difficult that Yolanda could remember in her marriage. After she'd told him about Julian and he'd run out, she helped the camera crew gather up all of their equipment while making excuses for Jimmy's behavior. She waved good-bye to the crew; then she fixed dinner and waited for Jimmy to return. The roast chicken she prepared for dinner sat warming in the oven until it shriveled up and dried. Sadly, she realized that Jimmy was not going to be home for dinner. She tossed the chicken out with the trash and told JJ to order a pizza for him and Priscilla. "Your father is working late. I'm sure he'll be home soon," she said, trying her best to reassure them.

"Did he call? It's not like him to stay at the church and not call," JJ said. He grabbed a large slice of pizza from the box and watched the cheese stretch, then took a big bite.

"Um . . . I talked to him earlier . . . don't worry."

It didn't take much to convince JJ, and after eating four slices of pizza, he grabbed a bag of potato chips, two sodas from the fridge, and a handful of cookies to take to his room for a snack. "I've got an algebra test tomorrow. Prissy, can you come help me study?"

"I will when you learn to pronounce my name right," Priscilla said.

When they were small children, JJ found pronouncing the name Priscilla difficult. So as a two-year-old, he'd shortened it to Prissy. Although he was older and could easily pronounce her name now, he sometimes forgot how much she hated it. He rolled his eyes behind her back before correcting himself. "I mean, Priscilla, will you come help me study?" he said.

"Yeah, I'll be up in a minute. I wanna talk to Momlanda first."

JJ stuffed two Oreos into his mouth and grabbed several more; then he left the kitchen.

Yolanda stared out of the kitchen window, hoping that any moment she'd see Jimmy's car coming up the driveway.

"Momlanda, what's really going on?" Priscilla asked.

Still staring out of the window, Yolanda gave her a halfhearted answer. "Nothing, honey, everything's fine."

Priscilla turned to walk out of the kitchen. Halfway out, she changed her mind and turned around. "I heard you and Dad arguing earlier. Just tell me the truth."

Surprised, Yolanda turned away from the window and stared at her. "What did you hear?"

"I heard you crying, and I heard Dad yelling. I know that something is going on, just tell me what it is."

"It really doesn't concern you. This is grown folks' business, and it's between me and your dad."

Priscilla crossed her arms across her chest and rested her weight on one hip, displaying a classic teen-ager-filled-with-attitude pose. "Oh, really? Don't you mean it's between you, my dad, and Mr. Washington? Is that why you were so upset that he gave me a ride home today?"

"I swear to you, it's not what you think. Just stay away from Mr. Washington. He is not who you think he is. You really don't know him at all."

"No, Momlanda. I think it's *you* who I really don't know."

As Priscilla turned and left the kitchen, Yolanda wanted to chase after her and explain, but she was too concerned about Jimmy to think about anything else. She'd never seen him as angry as he was when he left the house. Sitting down at her kitchen table, she bowed her head and prayed.

"Lord, I am so ashamed of the woman that I've been. For the past several months, I have made excuses for my behavior while emotionally cheating on my husband. My mind was filled with dreams of being a movie star, and I completely lost sight of the woman that I should be. I am so sorry. Please forgive me, Father. Please help Jimmy to find it in his heart to forgive me too, and please, Lord, stop him from doing something today that he will regret."

Yolanda sat up in her bed that night waiting for Jimmy and continuing to pray. Shortly after midnight, she heard his keys in the door. Her first instinct was to rush downstairs and try to talk to him, but she decided to wait for him to come to their bedroom. Quietly, she waited as she heard him climb the stairs and walk down the hallway. His footsteps stopped at their bedroom door for a few seconds; then they continued. The next sound she heard was the door of their guest room opening and closing as Jimmy went inside.

She got out of bed and grabbed her bathrobe. As she was putting it on, her cell phone began beeping to alert her of a text message. She picked up the phone, and saw that the message was from Julian.

"I saw your husband today. Now that your marriage is over, we can finally be together. I love you."

Yolanda ran into her bathroom, dropped the phone into the toilet, and pressed the handle to flush it. Through tears streaming down her face, she watched it swirl around in the bowl until it disappeared.

When she returned to her bedroom, she wished that getting rid of Julian could be that easy. Taking off her robe, she decided against going to the guest room, and instead, climbed into her bed. She buried her face in a pillow and cried herself to sleep.

The next morning, she made breakfast for the children and sent them off to school as normal. Jimmy came downstairs shortly after they had left.

"Good morning," she said, sounding a bit too cheerful.

"Good morning." Jimmy's response was cut and dry. He picked up a piece of toast from the platter on the table and smeared strawberry jelly all over it. "Can you please call a plumber to come over today? There is something wrong with the bathroom in our bedroom. It seems to be clogged."

"Yes, I'll call right after breakfast."

Jimmy balanced his toast in one hand and awkwardly leaned in to kiss Yolanda on the cheek. "Have a good day," he mumbled.

"Jimmy, we have to talk. Please don't leave."

"There's nothing to talk about. I think you said everything that needed to be said yesterday."

For the next week, they coexisted in their home, barely speaking to each other. He returned to their bedroom, but the cold shoulder he gave her made it seem as if she was still alone. Then the invitation arrived for the finale cast party.

"We're not going," Jimmy told her as soon as she pulled it out of the envelope.

Yolanda was disappointed, but she didn't protest. The next morning, she called Anderson to decline.

"I appreciate the call, but you don't have the option of not coming," Anderson said.

"You don't understand. My husband refuses to go to the party, and I would be uncomfortable coming alone."

"Look, Yolanda, I know that there was some friction between your husband and Julian. I don't know all the details, but I know that you asked to be released from your contract."

"That's right, and my husband doesn't want to have anything else to do with *Revelations*."

"I'm sorry to hear that, but the contract is iron clad. You both agreed to attend publicity events at the producer's discretion. So I expect to see you both at the party."

When Yolanda told Jimmy about the conversation, he immediately called his attorney and set up a meeting. After speaking with him, he came home and filled Yolanda in on the details.

"Julian has threatened to sue us if we don't attend this finale party. It seems that they have enough footage to complete the show without bringing the cameras back into our home. So if we go to this party, that will complete our obligations."

"Um . . . I spoke to Charlene Morton this morning, and she said that the network has already agreed to do a second season."

Jimmy glared at her. "I am *not* doing another season. We never should have done this one. If it's that important to you, then you can do it without me."

"No, I don't want to do it. It's not important to me at all." Yolanda nervously chewed on her bottom lip. "The only thing I care about is you and our kids."

"Do you really mean that?"

"Yes, I really do. Everything that's happened has shown me just how important you and the kids are to me. I made some stupid mistakes, and I'm so sorry. Can you please find it in your heart to forgive me?" she pleaded.

He reached out and pulled her into a hug. "I forgive you," he whispered.

Yolanda felt better, but as they prepared for the party, she could feel the level of tension in their marriage steadily rising again. Jimmy had told her about his last encounter with Julian, and they both were worried about what would happen when the two men stood face-to-face again.

After he finally stepped out of the limousine, Yolanda entwined her hands with Jimmy's as they walked into Danita's mansion. Wearing a Carolina Herrera Floral Ball Gown, Danita stood at her front door and greeted each guest as they entered. "Yolanda, you look lovely," she said. They exchanged air kisses on both cheeks.

"Thank you." Instead of purchasing a new gown and running the risk of irritating her husband further, Yolanda had borrowed a cocktail dress from one of her church members. It was a simple black-and-white ruffled dress with a modest hemline. Standing next to Danita she felt inadequate as she smiled for publicity photos.

"Bishop Snow, you look wonderful in your tuxedo," Danita said. "Is this Hugo Boss?"

"Um . . . I'm not really into designer labels. I just picked out one that fit."

Danita threw back her head and laughed loudly. "Well, you picked out a great one," she said before turning to greet her next guest.

Instead of mingling with the other guests, Jimmy led Yolanda directly to their seats on the front row of the viewing room. They were just about to sit down when Anderson approached them. "I'm glad to see you," he said.

Jimmy lightly shook Anderson's hand, then took his seat. "You didn't really give us a choice in the matter, now, did you?"

"You're right. I didn't. I'm a producer, so my first concern is for the success of my show. But I've got good news for you."

"What's that?"

"Julian was called out of town suddenly on business, so he won't be attending the party. You can relax and enjoy yourselves."

After he walked away, Jimmy breathed a sigh of relief. Yolanda sat down beside him, and he grabbed her hand and held it in his lap. "I'm so glad he is out of town. I have to admit I wasn't convinced that I'd be able to control my temper tonight. That's why I sat in the limo for so long. I was praying for strength."

"Don't relax just yet. I've known Julian for a long time. He doesn't give up easily."

"You're probably right, but he's not here now. So let's just enjoy the final show, and then we can move on with our lives."

The lights dimmed, and the rest of the cast took their seats. Yolanda tried to relax but something in her spirit would not allow it. She had not heard a word from Julian since the text message he had sent before she drowned her phone. Not hearing from him terrified her almost as much as hearing from him, because she knew it meant he was up to something. Yolanda believed that Julian was like a cheetah stalking his prey. He'd lay low and quiet, seemingly out of sight until the precise moment arose. Then he would pounce on his victim and rip them to shreds. As she stared at the screen, Yolanda suddenly realized that that moment had come. Unbeknownst to her, Julian had videotaped all of their lunch dates. With her cast mates and husband watching, Yolanda saw herself on the screen laughing and having the time of her life with Julian.

As soon as the scene switched to Brandon Kitts helping the youth of his church with a car wash, Yolanda felt Jimmy slip his hand out of hers. Without looking over at him, she knew that he was furious. She tried her best to remain calm as she felt all eyes in the room were no longer on the screen but positioned directly on her.

The show continued on as each minister was featured in their segments, and then it returned to Yolanda and Julian. Unable to move, Yolanda watched as her worst nightmare played out before her on the screen. She watched the two of them in the limo as Julian leaned over and kissed her. The kiss seemed to go on forever, until finally the credits began to roll and the screen froze with her lips stuck to Julian's.

Chapter Seventeen

As soon as the lights came on, Jimmy stood up from his chair and rushed out of the room, leaving Yolanda sitting alone in her seat. He ran out of the front door, and as soon as he stepped on the porch, the waiting paparazzi spotted him and surged forward. He dropped his head and pulled his coat up to cover his face. As their flashbulbs went off, he pressed his way through the crowd until he was behind the velvet rope and continued walking until he was at the end of the driveway. Driven by shame and humiliation, Jimmy looked both ways, trying to decide what to do. Then he began walking down the street.

Julian stood lurking in the shadows watching the partygoers. As soon as he saw Jimmy leave, Julian slid out of his hiding place and walked up the driveway of Danita's estate, wearing a long black trench coat, black pants, and a black chauffeur's cap. Walking up to the third limousine in the line, he lightly tapped on the window. The young driver who had been dozing sat up and rolled down the glass.

Without a word, Julian drew back his fist and punched him directly in the face. The driver slumped over unconscious. Julian looked around to be sure no one was watching; then he opened the door and pushed the driver to the other side of the seat and climbed in beside him. He reached into his trench coat pocket and pulled out a gag and some wire. It only took him a few moments before he had the driver bound and gagged and slumped over in the front seat.

Julian covered the driver with his coat. He rolled down the partition and leaned into the backseat, where he placed a bottle of champagne and a note on the seat. After he put everything into place, he closed the partition and waited behind the steering wheel for his beloved Ophelia to return alone to the limousine.

He kept the window separating them rolled up and did not look back at her as she got into the limousine and sat down. Fearful of her recognizing him, he pulled his hat down lower and slowly drove to the end of Danita's driveway. Just as he was about to pull out into the street, the driver groaned and began to wake up. Julian reached over him and opened the passenger door and with one swift kick of his foot, he shoved the bound man out of the car onto the driveway. He watched him tumble into the ditch. Then he slammed the door and sped off down the street.

As he continued walking, Jimmy noticed one of the white limousines from the party go past him. A few yards away it stopped and began backing up until it was directly beside him. The window came down, and Zack Morton stuck his head out. "Get in the car, Bishop," he said.

Jimmy was too angry to respond, so he kept walking as the limousine followed him moving at a slow crawl before it stopped again. Zack stepped out and held open the door. "Get in, Bishop. It's cold out here."

Another white limousine went racing past them as Jimmy reluctantly got in. He was surprised to see Brandon sitting inside. He slid over and made room for Jimmy.

"Were you really gonna walk all the way home?" Zack asked.

"I don't know what I was going to do. I just needed to get out of there," Jimmy replied.

"That's obvious, because your house is in the opposite direction. It's a good thing we came this way first," Brandon laughed, trying to lighten the mood.

"I looked at that screen, and I all could see was red." Jimmy took several deep breaths, trying to calm down.

Brandon nodded. "We understand. That's why we came looking for you. Just so you know, Yolanda gave us the Cliffs Notes version of what's going on with you guys and Julian."

"She told me that he kissed her, and she immediately pushed him away, but that kiss seemed to go on forever," Jimmy said. "I believed her, and I forgave her. Now I feel like a complete fool."

"You shouldn't. What you saw tonight was the work of clever editing. We all know that it didn't really happen that way," Zack said.

"Maybe so, but something happened. My wife was so intent on being a TV star that she compromised our marriage and our family. Everyone in my congregation watched this show tonight, not to mention my children."

"Do you honestly believe that your wife cheated on you?" Brandon asked.

Jimmy hesitated before answering. He knew that what he'd seen on the screen was probably manipulated by Julian to get back at them. He sighed. "No. I'm positive that nothing happened between them."

"Then that's all that matters. There will be a lot of gossip and rumors, but as long as you know the truth, you guys can get through it," Brandon assured him.

"I guess you're probably right. It just made me so angry when I saw it that I couldn't think straight. I knew I had to get out of there before I did something crazy." Jimmy sighed again. "Would you guys mind heading back to the party so that I can talk to Yolanda?"

"She's probably gone by now. Charlene and Tia were going to make sure she got home safely while we came looking for you. They should be there by the time we get to your house," Zack said.

Jimmy felt deeply grateful that his cast mates had come to his rescue in his time of trouble. He was also somewhat surprised. Although they had worked together for months, and there were no problems between them, he didn't realize the bond that they'd formed. Silently, he thanked God for the friendship. Then he expressed it openly. "I really want to thank both of you for coming after me. I overreacted, and it's good to know that someone has my back." He held his arm straight out and did a fist bump with Brandon, and then with Zack.

They pulled in front of Jimmy's house and parked directly behind the other limousine. The three men got out and went inside. Charlene and Yolanda were seated in the family room sharing a glass of tea. As soon as she saw him, Yolanda ran to Jimmy, and he hugged her tightly. "I'm sorry," they both said.

"Don't apologize to me," Yolanda said. "This whole mess is all my fault. I should have known Julian was up to something when he didn't show up for the party."

"I'm sorry for walking out like that. I promise you we are going to get through this together." They kissed and held each other tightly.

Zack held out his hand to Charlene. "Come on, honey, I think the crisis is over, and we should leave these two alone."

"I agree," Brandon said. "We should get going too. Where's Tia?"

"I don't know. She didn't ride with us," Charlene answered.

As soon as Brandon and Zack had left to search for Bishop Snow, Tia realized that she did not want to hang around and babysit Yolanda. She wasn't surprised at all that something was going on between Yolanda and Julian. Tia felt that it certainly would explain why Yolanda had suddenly shot to the forefront of the show. Not only that, but Tia could care less about the whole thing, as none of it held any benefits for her. The padding was shifting inside her evening gown, and she was beginning to itch and sweat. All she wanted to do was go home, take it all off, and hop into a hot shower. So while the other ladies were hovering over Yolanda, she snuck outside and jumped into the first limousine that she saw. She was about to give the driver instructions when she noticed a bottle of champagne and a note sitting on the seat.

"For my star," it read.

It figures, Tia thought. *Julian didn't leave champagne in our car for us. This must be for his mistress, Yolanda. Well, it's mine now.*

Tia had not had a drink since she began pretending to be pregnant and champagne was her absolute favorite. Since she was alone, she decided to pop the bottle open and take a few sips before giving the driver her address. She did not notice that the cork was already loose, and it had been previously opened. After gulping down a few sips, she felt woozy, so she put the bottle down. Before she realized what was happening, Tia slumped over in the seat and blacked out.

As Julian sped down the highway on his way out of Georgia, Tia lay unconscious in the back of the limousine, unaware that she'd been drugged and kidnapped.

Chapter Eighteen

Danita sat in her living room feeling excited as she waited for her daughters to come down the stairs. The four of them had a full day of fun planned together. Danita had tickets to the Coca-Cola Museum and the Georgia Aquarium. Afterward, she planned to take them to dinner and, if time permitted, a movie. The girls were out of school for the Thanksgiving holiday, and Danita wanted to be sure to spend as much time with them as possible.

Although Danita continued to pray and believe that she would not lose custody of her girls, she also wanted to prepare herself and the girls for the possibility. The previous week she'd had a visit from the caseworker appointed by family court. Danita felt angry and humiliated as they poked around her home and asked her all sorts of personal questions. It all seemed ridiculous to her. It was obvious that her girls were well taken care of and deeply loved. The caseworker questioned Danita about her need for a chauffeur, housekeeper, and nanny.

"Well, the chauffeur drives me and the girls around town. I have always been afraid to drive in Atlanta traffic. Before I could afford a driver, I took cabs. I'm also the minister of a large congregation, and I don't have time to cook dinner or clean this big house, so I employ a housekeeper to help me with those things. Vivian has been with me since Summer was born. She loves the girls."

"With such a large ministry, how do you find the time to spend quality time with the girls?" the caseworker asked.

"I'll admit it's hard. But I make sure that I'm home in time to put the girls in bed each evening. If I have to travel, then I take them and Vivian along with me. The girls are also involved in ministry at the church as well, so that they can spend time with me at the church. All three of the girls sing in the church Sunbeam choir."

The caseworker didn't show any emotion that Danita could detect. She simply asked questions and wrote notes in the notebook she carried. "Why did you make the decision to allow TV cameras into your home and to film your children?"

"I did *Revelations* to further my ministry. After my husband's death, my congregation suffered, and I thought being on the show would help me to reach more people. But I have to point out that the girls have minimal screen time. They are not exploited in any way."

The questions went on for over an hour, making Danita feel as if she were on trial once again. After speaking with her, the caseworker also spent time speaking with each of the girls, and with Vivian. Danita was not allowed to listen in on their interviews, and it took all of her restraint not to ask what they'd talked about. But instead of prying, she decided to pray and trust that God would work it out for her.

Danita had always been a good mother to her daughters. But now that she faced the possibility of losing them, she was making an extra effort to be a great mother. After she had completed plans for the finale party, she'd made arrangements with the caterers to come back and serve a traditional Thanksgiving dinner for them that included a turkey and all the trimmings.

Autumn's favorite food was macaroni and cheese, while Winter and Summer both loved sour cream mashed potatoes. Danita insisted that the caterers include both dishes in their dinner. Prior to the court decision, Danita had made plans for the girls to spend the entire week with Ben's family, but she rescinded that offer after they petitioned for full custody. Instead, she and the girls planned to eat dinner together, before going to Brandon Kitts's church to help with feeding the homeless. Due to her pregnancy, Tia was unable to assist Brandon, so Danita had volunteered to be there along with the girls. She felt it would be beneficial to them to help those less fortunate.

Even though the season had ended, Danita was grateful for the friends she'd made while filming *Revelations*. She was also happy that, unlike many other reality shows, they had never sunk to cheap antics and over-the-top sleazy drama. At least they had not done any of that until the final show. None of the cast could understand why Julian had decided to turn their family show into tabloid television. Yolanda Snow had tried her best to explain the nature of their previous relationship, but Danita still found it mind-boggling that Julian had allowed his personal feelings to affect the show.

The front doorbell rang, and Danita wondered where her housekeeper was. It rang again, and she reluctantly went to answer it.

"Can I help you?" she asked the police officer who was standing at her door.

"I'm investigating the carjacking that occurred here last evening. May I come in?"

"Yes, of course, please come in." Danita led the officer into her home through the foyer to the living room. Politely, she offered him a seat while trying to hide how nervous she was. Since her trial, just being in the presence of police officers made Danita edgy.

"Mrs. Hyatt, we got a call this morning regarding an unidentified man found bound and gagged in a ditch at the end of your driveway."

"That's right. He was found by my security guard this morning when he reported for duty. He untied him and called you guys. Do you know who he is, or how he got there?"

"He is a driver for Huntington Limousine Service. He says that he was carjacked last night outside your party. He was waiting for his riders to return, when someone knocked him out and stole the limousine."

Danita covered her mouth in surprise. "Is he okay?"

"He's been taken to a local hospital to be checked out. What type of party did you have here last night, Mrs. Hyatt?"

"It was a finale party for the cast of *Revelations*. The only people invited were the cast members and our producer. But the driveway was packed with reporters and fans. Maybe somebody saw something."

"What about you, Mrs. Hyatt? Did you see anything?"

Danita shook her head. "No, I was inside the whole evening. Julian Washington owns the TV station, and he hired the limousines as a gift to the cast because he was unable to attend. There was a . . . um . . . incident at the party, so Bishop Snow and his wife did not return to their limousine. Instead, they rode with other cast members. Everyone just assumed that the driver left with an empty car. We had no idea it was stolen."

"I need the names of all of the other cast members who were here last night."

"Sure. They are Apostle Zack Morton and his wife Charlene, Bishop Jimmy Snow and his wife Yolanda, and Reverend Brandon Kitts and his wife Tia, and of course, as I stated, our producer, Anderson Carter."

"Thank you for your time, Mrs. Hyatt. We'll be speaking with the other cast members later today." The officer stood up, and Danita escorted him to the front door. "Thanks for your help," he said before leaving.

Just as she closed the front door, Danita's three daughters came bounding down the stairs followed by their nanny, Vivian.

"Mommy, we're ready to go," Winter squealed. She was so excited that her little brown face was glowing.

"Let's go," Danita said.

By the time they returned home late that evening, the girls were exhausted and Danita, Vivian, and Philippe had to carry them up the stairs to their beds. Except for the few moments that they'd encountered the paparazzi's cameras, the entire day was perfect in Danita's opinion. She could not remember the last time that she and girls had enjoyed themselves so much. "Please God, let us have many more days like today," she prayed as she watched them sleeping peacefully.

Chapter Nineteen

"Do you guys have any clues about where she might be?" Charlene asked the police officer.

"That's why I'm here, to try to get some answers."

As he opened his basement door and turned to lock it, Zack Morton was stunned to find a police officer standing in his kitchen. He didn't hear the whole conversation, but he sensed that something was terribly wrong.

"What's going on?" he asked.

"Bo, this officer is here because—"

The officer held up his hand and interrupted Charlene. "Ma'am, I'll explain it to him."

Zack's eyes darted back and forth between Charlene and the police officer. "I didn't have anything to do with her disappearance. I barely knew Mabel Joe Stevens," he blurted out.

"I'm not here about Mabel Joe Stevens," the officer said.

"Um . . . okay . . . can you please tell me what's going on?" Zack asked. He turned his back to Charlene and faced the officer.

"Mrs. Tia Kitts is missing. No one has seen her since the cast party that you all attended the other evening. Her husband filed a missing person's report after she didn't come home that night."

"Really? We had no idea." Zack was fidgeting and shifting his weight back and forth from one foot to the other.

"Did you see Mrs. Kitts leave the party?"

"No, I didn't. I think I left before she did, but I really don't know." Zack folded, then unfolded his arms.

The officer looked him up and down. "Why are you so nervous?"

"I'm . . . not . . . nervous," he stuttered.

The officer looked around the kitchen until his eyes fell on the door to the basement. Zack had only locked the door and had not yet clicked all of the locks or put the bar into place. "What's down there?"

"My personal gym."

The police officer stepped closer to the door. "You don't mind if I take a look around down there, do you?"

"Do you have a warrant?"

The officer looked Zack up and down again. "Do I need one?"

"You are here about Mrs. Kitts. We haven't seen or talked to her since the party. There's no reason for you to go into my basement. Is there anything else my wife and I can help you with?"

The officer reached into his pocket and pulled out his business card. "Just give us a call if you hear from Mrs. Kitts." He held the card out to Zack, but when he didn't take it, the officer laid it on the counter and left.

Zack turned to the basement doors and locked all the locks, then put the bar in place. He sat down at the table and suddenly noticed that Charlene had left the room. Zack sat alone in the kitchen for twenty minutes before Martin and Luther came running in. They grabbed their coats and hats from the rack by the door.

"Where are you guys going?" he asked.

"Chucky Cheese!" they both yelled.

Zack was confused. Charlene had not mentioned to him that she had plans to take the kids anywhere that morning. She also had not served him breakfast for the first time since they'd married. "Where's your mom?" he asked Luther.

"She's getting Coretta dressed. Can you zip up my jacket, Dad?"

Zack helped both boys put on their hats and coats. He was contemplating whether to go upstairs and talk to Charlene when he heard a knock at his back door.

"Vanessa, what are you doing here?" he asked as soon as he opened it.

"Charlene called and asked if I'd take the kids out for a while. Is she upstairs?" Without waiting for an answer, Vanessa walked past him and up the stairs. A few moments later, she returned carrying Coretta. "See you later, Zack," she said as she took the children and went out the back door.

Zack rushed out of the kitchen and up the stairs to the master bedroom. Charlene was sitting on the side of the bed holding a picture in her hands. He knew what it was, but decided to play dumb. "Honey, are you okay?"

"I asked Vanessa to take the kids so that we could talk alone. What happened to Mabel Joe?" she asked calmly.

"I don't know. Like I said, I barely knew her. I heard you and that cop say someone was missing, and I just assumed that's who you meant. It's no big deal."

She turned to look at him, and he could see tears forming at the base of her eyes. "You promised that you'd never lie to me. Just tell me the truth, Zack. Where is she?"

Slowly he walked over to the bed and cautiously sat down. "I swear to you, I have no idea where Mabel Joe is."

Charlene held the picture up. "What are you doing with this picture?"

"Um . . . Mabel Joe gave it to me."

"When?" she demanded.

Zack sighed. "I had lunch with her after I saw her that day at the hospital. I . . . I had lunch with her . . . and she gave me that picture. I haven't seen her since."

"You said you barely knew her, but you had lunch with her. Now she's missing, and you have her picture. That sounds fishy to me, Zack."

"I didn't recognize her at the hospital, but later I remembered her. So I called and invited her to lunch. You're not jealous, are you? That woman is old enough to be my mother."

"Of course not. I just don't understand why a woman you barely knew would give you a family photo, then suddenly disappear."

"I . . . I don't know what you're getting at."

"Why, Zack? Why did Mabel Joe give you this picture?"

"What difference does it make, Charlene? It's just a picture."

Charlene stood up. "Fine. If you won't tell me, then I'll just have to turn this over to the police. Maybe they can use it to help find Mabel Joe."

He grabbed her by the arm. "Are you kidding me?"

She snatched her arm away. "No, I'm not. You might have been the last person to see her alive." Charlene picked up her phone from the dresser.

"Charlene, don't call the police!" he yelled.

The urgency in his voice frightened her. "Oh my God! Did you do something to her?" Holding tightly to the phone, Charlene rushed to the other side of the room.

"No . . . of course not!" Zack stood up to go to her, and she backed farther away. "Listen to me . . . I did not do anything to Mabel Joe." He watched her standing in the corner of the room trembling and crying. "Charlene, are you . . . are you afraid of me?"

"I'm afraid of what you've done." She opened the phone to dial, and he suddenly lunged at her, snatching it from her hands.

"Zack, what is wrong with you?" Charlene screamed. She turned to run from the room, and he blocked her exit. Quickly, she backed up into the furthest corner of the room as tears rushed from her eyes. "Please, don't hurt me," she whimpered.

Zack held his hands up as if to surrender. "Charlene, I've never put my hands on you, and I never would." He saw fear in her eyes and face, but she did not speak. He sat down on the bed and stared at his hands, realizing that the last thing he wanted was for Charlene to fear him. He heard his grandmother's voice. *You are who you are Zack Morton. Just be who you are.*

Without looking at Charlene, he spoke. "I have this picture because . . . Mabel Joe thought that I'd like to have it." He paused and waited for her to respond. When she didn't, he continued. "She said that she thought it would mean a lot to me."

"Why?" Charlene asked.

"The little boy in the blue necktie is Mabel Joe's son. She told me that he died in Iraq." Zack paused again and took a deep breath. "The other little boy is . . . he's me."

Charlene took another look at the picture. "These are two little black boys in this picture." She took a closer look. "Well, one of them is definitely black, the other one could be Hispanic maybe, but he's not white. So there's no way he could be you."

Zack took another deep breath and blew it out slowly. "My mother was African American, and that racially ambiguous little boy in the picture is me." He leaned forward and placed his middle finger on his eyeball. Slowly, he removed his contact lenses and laid them on the nightstand. He blinked several times, and then looked into Charlene's eyes. "Does he look like me now?" he asked.

Charlene's jaw dropped. "You wear blue contact lenses? For the past twelve years, you've been wearing blue contact lenses?"

Zack nodded his head. "I've worn them since I was about sixteen. I also dye my hair. The natural color is dark brown."

Charlene carefully sat down on the bed beside Zack, still staring at the picture, and noticing for the first time that the boy had a striking resemblance to her own sons. "I don't understand. Who are those people in Asheville that you claim as family? I know that Roscoe is not your real dad. But your mom, brother, and sister are as white as you are."

"Nancy is not my mother. She's my stepmother. My mother died when I was six months old. My dad married Nancy before my first birthday. When I was three, Kyle was born, and when I was five, Meagan was born."

Charlene shook her head. "None of this is making sense. Are you telling me that all these years you've been passing for white, but you're not white?"

Zack stared at the floor, as he finally told Charlene his life story. "Yes . . . you see, my father died when I was nine years old. Up until that point, I had been raised as a white kid and I believed that Nancy was my mother. After my dad died, she had trouble making ends meet and felt that she couldn't afford to raise three kids. Of course, she chose to keep her own, but she sent me to Atlanta to live with my maternal grandmother. All Nancy told me was that my real mother was dead, and that I was going to live with her mother. I can't even describe what it was like. I stepped off that Greyhound bus expecting someone who looked like me to be waiting, and instead, I saw a woman as big around as a potbellied stove, and just as black."

"Zack, is that you?" she asked.

"Yes, I am. Who are you? Are you my granny's maid?" I must have hurt her feelings, because she suddenly got a disturbed look on her face.

"No, boy. I'm your granny. Now get your bag and let's go," she said.

Charlene used tissues to dab at her tears as Zack kept talking.

"Living in Atlanta was a major culture shock for me. My grandmother's house had belonged to her family for many years. Downstairs she had a beauty salon where she worked to make money, and we lived upstairs. Mabel Joe lived next door, and her son was my only friend. The kids used to called me Vanilla Chocolate, and I got beat up almost every single day, until he showed me how to defend myself. It was also the best time in my life. Nancy had never hugged me, or told me she loved me, or that she was proud of me. Basically, she just tolerated me. But I thought that was how all mothers acted. It wasn't until my grandmother showed me what it was like to be truly loved that I realized what I'd been missing."

Zack looked over at Charlene and noticed that she'd stopped crying. He stopped staring at the floor and looked over at her as he continued. "Shortly after I turned fifteen, my grandmother suffered a debilitating stroke and had to enter a nursing home. Because she couldn't take care of me anymore, I ended up back in Asheville with Nancy, Kyle, Meagan, and Nancy's new husband, Roscoe." Zack shuddered at the thought of his stepfather. "He used to torture me."

"What do you mean?"

"He gave me spoiled food, on purpose, just to see me throw up. Then he'd hide things in his hand and beg me to shake it. I never wanted to because I knew he was up to something, but he made me."

"You mean like a joy buzzer?"

"No. I mean like baby snakes, snails, or fire ants. He got a kick out of watching me scream and try to get the things off me. If I refused to touch his hand, he'd hide them in my underwear drawer or my bed. At night, I would hear Roscoe and Kyle talking about me and plotting the next horrible thing they were going to do to me. The whole experience made me distrustful of people, food, and just life in general. I know it's irrational now, but it's who I am."

"He did all of that just because you were a stepchild?"

"No. He hated me because he knew I was black. When I returned to Asheville, I was a different person. My grandmother had introduced me to new foods, new music, and the love of God. So I listened to Luther Vandross, Whitney Houston, and Donnie McClurkin, while my siblings were playing The Judds and Reba McEntire. I wanted to eat fried chicken, corn bread, and collard greens with sweet tea. But Nancy cooked things like tuna casserole and veal parmesan. I also started to feel the call to ministry, so I began attending a black church like the one I attended in Atlanta, where they sang upbeat gospel music and I could feel the presence of the Holy Spirit. Nancy thought I was being a rebellious teenager, and maybe in some ways, I was. But all I really wanted to do was be who I was."

"Being black is not about the kind of music you listen to or what you eat or even how you worship God. You should know that, Zack."

"I know that now. But at fifteen, all I wanted to do was embrace being black in the only ways that I knew how. For five years in Atlanta, I had been the black kid who looked white, and then I moved back to Asheville and became the white kid who acted black. Nancy and Roscoe didn't like my behavior at all, and they refused to allow it. They said that I embarrassed them and that people were beginning to talk. So they gave me an ultimatum. I either had to stop acting black or move out."

Zack stopped talking to look over at Charlene. He was unable to read the look on her face. He desperately hoped that she understood, so he kept talking. "So I conformed to who they wanted me to be. Nancy suggested that I dye my hair, since she, Kyle, and Meagan are all blonds, so I agreed. The contacts were her idea too. I became the white son that she and Roscoe wanted. The Zack Morton they created finished high school and attended college. The funny thing is, they still hated me. If I didn't have my faith, I never would have made it through. That's the one thing they couldn't take from me, my love for God. They were not happy when I decided to enter the seminary. But I went through the motions for them, and whenever I could, I would travel to Atlanta to visit my grandmother at the nursing home."

"So they made you pass as a child, but that doesn't explain why you continued to live a lie for all these years." Charlene shook her head with disapproval.

"Honestly, I don't even remember when I made the conscious decision to pass. Maybe I never did. I just grew weary of always having to explain who I was. Roscoe and Nancy made me look white, but when I wasn't around them, I didn't act like it. They never knew that I was dating black girls or that all of my friends were black. The last time that I visited my grandmother, she told me to just be the person that I was inside, because the outside didn't matter. Honestly, I was so

confused at that point that I really didn't understand
what she meant. She died a few weeks after that, and I
inherited the house that she had run her beauty salon
out of. I moved back here and started my first church
in that building. By that time, all of the old neighborhood people like Mabel Joe who knew me as a kid had
moved away. Everyone assumed I was a blue-eyed soul
brother, and I never bothered to correct them."

"What about Mabel Joe? What happened to her?"

"I honestly don't know. We had lunch, and she gave
me the picture . . . And I told her that you didn't know
about my grandmother or my past, and I begged her
not to tell you."

"Is that all?" Charlene could sense that Zack was still
holding back information.

"I gave her $10,000 to keep my secret. She probably
took the money and left town, but I swear I don't know
where she is."

"Oh my God, Zack, you didn't?"

"I'm sorry, Charlene. I was just so afraid of what
would happen if you found out. But I'm telling you everything now. No more secrets."

Charlene turned to look at him. "What are you hiding in the basement?"

"Nothing . . . everything . . . Sometimes I just go
down there to look at my photo album with the pictures of my mother and grandmother. I never knew my
mom, but I miss my grandmother so much. I do have
a gym and a shower in the basement. Um, but after
sleeping in contacts all night, I go down there to rinse
them out and put clean ones in. I also keep my hair dye
down there too, so I can touch it up and make sure the
roots don't show. I didn't want to let you or the boys see
me doing that. But I was just being vain. I don't have to
do any of that."

"I wear weave, braids, and sometimes wigs, Zack, and you've seen me au natural many times. You did that to keep us from knowing that you were passing for white. Don't try to sugarcoat it now." Charlene stood up and went to the closet. She pulled out a suitcase. "I want you to leave. I don't know who you are anymore."

"Honey, no. I'm the man you fell in love with. I'm the man you married!"

"I married a blond, blue-eyed white man who told me that race didn't matter. But obviously it mattered so much that you chose to deny your own." She went to the chest of drawers and dug out Zack's underwear and threw them in the suitcase. Next she went to the closet and began packing his pants and shirts.

"Please, don't do this! You always told me that you married a man and not a color. I'm still that man, Charlene. It shouldn't matter what color I am."

"You're right. It shouldn't matter, but it did to you. It mattered so much that you've spent twelve years hiding it from me. It mattered so much that you spent $10,000 to keep me from finding out. I fell in love with a man of God who believed in honesty. You have been lying to me since the day we met!" She continued putting his clothes into the suitcase.

He begged and pleaded with her, but Charlene was through listening. Finally, he realized his words were no good. "Stop! I'll do it myself," he said. Zack took the clothes from her and finished packing. Solemnly, he carried his suitcase down the stairs and left the house.

Chapter Twenty

Brandon knelt in front of his living-room sofa and prayed. He was going out of his mind with fear and worry for Tia and their unborn son. That night of the cast party when he arrived home, he searched the entire house for her, but she was nowhere to be found. He tried calling her cell phone, only to find it ringing upstairs in their bedroom. Unable to sleep, he sat up the entire night hoping and praying that she'd walk in any moment. His mind was filled with all sorts of thoughts. A part of him wondered if she'd left him. His love for Tia was unconditional, but in his heart, he knew she didn't feel the same way.

Throughout their marriage, he'd tried everything he could think of to make her happy, and he felt that at times she experienced pockets of enjoyment. But he knew it wasn't enough. He'd hoped that things would change after she became pregnant and that having a child would bring them closer together.

He checked their bedroom and nothing had been disturbed in their closets. As unhappy as he suspected she'd been, he was convinced that she'd never leave him without taking her Louis Vuitton purses or her Prada pant suits. Early the next morning he finally decided to call the police but was angered by their refusal to do anything. An officer with no concern in his voice told Brandon that adults had to be missing for at least forty-eight hours before a report would be filed. Exasperated, he'd called Quincy in hopes that he'd heard from her.

"The Periwinkle Palace, where your dreams become reality and your reality feels like a dream. How may I help you?" he said, as he answered the phone.

"Quincy, this is Brandon Kitts."

The surprise almost caused Quincy to drop the phone. In all of the years that he'd been friends with Tia, he and Brandon had never held a conversation without her present. "Hey, Brandon, what's going on?" he asked cautiously.

"Tia is missing. She never came home from the cast party last night. Please tell me that she's with you."

Quincy immediately grabbed a chair and sat down. "What happened? Did you two argue or something? Why wouldn't she come home?"

"No, everything was fine last night. I left the party with one of the other ministers, but no one knows what happened to Tia. Man, I'm worried sick."

"Oh my stars! That's not like Tia at all. Have you called the police? I don't mean to alarm you, but I know my girlfriend. She wouldn't leave without talking to me."

"The police won't do anything for at least forty-eight hours. If you hear from her at all, Quincy, please call me on my private cell phone. I'm going to be sitting right here all day."

"I will, I promise. Don't worry. I'm sure she's fine," Quincy said before hanging up the phone.

Next, Brandon called Danita Hyatt in hopes that she knew what time Tia left the party.

"I'm sorry, Brandon, I was so busy consoling Yolanda that I didn't see her leave at all," she said.

"Thanks, Danita. Could you ask your security guard if he saw her leave in a car or something?"

The mention of her security guard caused a lightbulb to turn on in Danita's head. "There was a carjacking the night of the party. My security guard found one of the limo drivers beat up and lying in a ditch. Oh my God, I hope Tia wasn't caught up in that."

"You're kidding me?" Brandon's heart began racing "I've got to call the police back and tell them this new information. Thanks, Danita."

A police officer showed up at Brandon's home two hours later and asked him a multitude of questions, but nothing they said offered him any assurance. Over the next couple of days, they questioned the limo driver and the entire cast that attended the party, but no one knew anything.

After praying, Brandon stood up and took a deep breath. He was due at his church in a few hours to help his church ministry to feed the homeless and low-income families for Thanksgiving. His wife had been missing all week, but he knew that he couldn't let his church family or those in need down. Just as he was putting on his coat, his front doorbell rang and he rushed to answer it, anxious for news about Tia.

"Hey, Brandon, I stopped by to see if you wanted me to take over for you at the church today?" Zack said.

"No, thank you. I'm not doing Tia any good by sitting around this house worrying about her. I was just about to leave for the church."

"Well, in that case, can you use an extra pair of hands? I'd be happy to help."

Brandon was surprised. "I thought that you and Charlene were planning a big family dinner at your house today."

Zack sighed loudly. "We were but . . . the truth is Charlene asked me to leave yesterday. I spent the night at a hotel, and I called her this morning, but she doesn't want to talk to me. So I thought that rather than sit around feeling sorry for myself I should help someone else."

Brandon invited Zack inside and sat quietly while he told him the whole story. "I'm blown away by all this. I've never met anyone who was passing," he said after Zack was done.

"I'm not anymore. The contacts are gone, and I'm letting the color grow out of my hair. I remember how much I hated it when my stepparents made me do it. You'd think that when I moved to Atlanta I would have stopped immediately, but continuing it was easier."

"I can understand that. Most black people have wondered what it would be like to be white and have life be easier, even if only for a few moments."

Zack shook his head. "No, that's not what I mean. Of course, life has been easier as a white man in many ways, I suppose. But I was tired of being different. I got sick of being asked all the time, what are you? I never hated being black. I hated not looking black, but I loved everything else about it." Zack suddenly looked at Brandon. "I'm sorry. Here I am laying my problems in your lap when you have your own. Has there been any word on Tia?"

"No, the police believe that she may have been kidnapped by the person who stole the limo, but so far there have been no ransom demands or anything. I would give any amount of money to have her back and know that she and the baby are safe. But I am not going to sit here moping, and neither are you. Let's get to the church."

They arrived at the church, and both men temporarily forgot the turmoil going on in their lives while they busied themselves setting up tables and putting out chairs with the help of the other church volunteers.

Around noon, Danita and her daughters arrived to offer their assistance. Brandon assigned the girls the task of putting out paper plates, cups, napkins, and plastic forks, while Danita put on an apron and helped set up the food serving line.

Everything was prepped and in placed by early afternoon. Brandon went to open the main doors and let the diners in, and he was surprised to see Bishop Snow and his family standing in the doorway at the front of line. "Hey, you guys, this food is for the homeless," he said, teasing them.

"We came to offer some help, and also, Yolanda and I need to speak with you privately. We might have a clue about Tia's whereabouts," Jimmy said.

"Come in. Um . . . Priscilla, would you and JJ help out in the serving line? Danita can show you where to find aprons and plastic gloves."

He pointed the teenagers in the direction of the kitchen; then Brandon hurriedly opened the double doors wide so that the people waiting outside could enter. His plan had been to greet each person individually as he or she entered, but he was so anxious to talk to Jimmy and Yolanda that he abandoned that idea. Instead, he told Zack to take over and make sure that everyone was greeted and stayed in line in an orderly fashion. Then he asked Yolanda and Jimmy to follow him as he left the gymnasium and went down the hallway to his private office. It was located only a short distance from the gym, but it felt as if he'd walked a mile by the time he arrived. He offered them both a seat and anxiously waited behind his desk to hear the news.

Yolanda spoke first. "I told you guys at the cast party that I had a prior relationship with Julian before Jimmy and I met and got married, and that's why he put that footage into the show. What I didn't tell you was that Julian has been stalking me for several years. I thought I'd gotten away from him, but he found me again through the show. Most people do not realize it, but he's a very dangerous man."

"I don't understand. What does that have to do with Tia?" Brandon asked.

Jimmy pulled a piece of paper from his pocket and handed it to Brandon. "I got this letter in the mail yesterday."

Dear Jimmy,

By now I'm sure that you've seen the last episode of Revelations *and you understand my love for Julian. I'm sorry that you had to find out this way, but it was the only way that I knew to show you how I truly feel. Our marriage is over, and I am leaving you to be with Julian. He is the only man that I've ever loved or will ever love. Please don't bother to look for me, because I don't want to be found. All I want is to be with Julian forever, as we were meant to be. I want you to know that there are no hard feelings, and I hope that one day you'll be able to forget me.*

Yolanda

Brandon stared at them with a perplexed look on his face. "Yolanda, why would you write a letter like this, and again, what does it have to do with Tia?"

"I didn't write that letter. We believe Julian typed it and mailed it. It was his intent to make Jimmy think that I'd willingly left him."

Brandon was still confused, and he was quickly becoming agitated. "This is all very interesting, but I am worried about my wife. Please tell me what all this has to do with her."

"We think Julian kidnapped Tia," Jimmy said.

"What? That's the craziest thing I've ever heard. Even if he was stalking your wife, there would be no reason for him to kidnap mine."

"It all fits together. The limousine that was taken was the same one that Yolanda and I arrived in. The carjacking happened shortly after I left the party on foot. We believe that Julian paid someone to take the limousine because he thought that Yolanda was inside alone. The person probably didn't realize they had taken Tia instead," Jimmy answered.

"Have you talked to Julian? What does he have to say about these accusations?" Brandon asked.

"No. Instead of calling him, we gave a copy of the letter to the police. They tried to reach him, but were unable to find him. Anderson says he's in London on business," Jimmy answered.

"But we don't believe him," Yolanda added.

"So let me get this straight. Julian was stalking Yolanda, and you believe he sent this letter. You also believe he is behind Tia's kidnapping, but he meant to take Yolanda instead?"

Jimmy and Yolanda both nodded their heads.

"What you are saying may be true, but there's one thing that doesn't make sense," Brandon said.

"What's that?" Jimmy asked.

"Tia's been missing for several days. Surely whoever took her has realized who they have by now. If she isn't the one they wanted, why haven't they let her go?"

"We can't answer that because we simply don't know," Yolanda said. "But I'm positive that Julian is behind this. This letter was mailed after the party, and I didn't write it. What sense would it make for me to send a Dear John letter to my husband when I'm still with him? Don't you see that Julian mailed this because he planned to have me with him when it arrived?"

"I do. I'm just trying to understand why he or whoever he's working with hasn't let Tia go. She's pregnant for goodness' sake. I'm so worried about her and the baby. What benefit could she possibly be to Julian now?"

Yolanda reached out and took Brandon's hand. "I'm so sorry. I feel like this whole thing is my fault. But as horrible as Julian is, I don't think he would hurt Tia. It's me he wanted. He has no beef with her."

"You said he's dangerous. How dangerous is he?"

"I . . . I don't really know," Yolanda answered.

"Tell him about the text messages, Yolanda. He has a right to know," Jimmy said.

Brandon looked frantically at them both. "What messages?"

"Over the past few months after I had refused to see him, Julian sent me very disturbing text messages." Yolanda paused as she tried to gather the courage to finish. "Several times he threatened to kill me."

"How could you continue filming the show after he threatened your life? Did you tell the police this when it happened?"

"No. I didn't tell anybody. I'm sorry. I just kept hoping that he was bluffing, and maybe he was. Besides, like I said, it was me he wanted. That still doesn't mean he will harm Tia."

Brandon sat back in his chair and tried to process the information. "What about Anderson? Do you think he's covering for Julian? Is he involved in this?" he asked.

"I don't think so. I think he's telling us exactly what Julian told him to say. He hasn't spoken to him since before the party," Jimmy answered.

"Thank you . . . thank you so much for telling me this, and also for telling the police," Brandon said. He turned to Yolanda. "Don't blame yourself. There's no way you could have known what Julian was planning or that Tia would be a part of it. Besides, we don't know for sure that Julian had anything to do with it at all."

"I'm convinced that he's behind it, but maybe you're right. We are jumping to conclusions when the most important thing is finding Tia and getting her home safely," Jimmy said.

Brandon returned to the gymnasium following his conversation with the Snows and took his place in the serving line. He was scooping out a large spoonful of mashed potatoes to place on the next plate when he suddenly noticed a commotion near the front door. He immediately left the line and went over to investigate.

"Reverend Kitts, is there any word on your wife, Tia?" he heard a reporter yell.

"Do the police have any leads?" another reporter shouted out.

Flashbulbs went off as several reporters tried to barge into the building and get photographs. Brandon had promised the individuals and families who dined at the church that day that they would receive explicit privacy. Because many of them were homeless or underprivileged, he did not want to exploit their stories on the evening news. Holding up his hands, he commanded the attention of the reporters. "Please, I'll answer your questions, but I have to ask you to take all of the cameras outside. These people have a right to their privacy," he said.

Brandon summoned Zack and Jimmy's assistance and the three of them forced all of the reporters outside of the church to the parking lot. Once outside, he climbed up into the bed of his red Ford pickup and stood to face the reporters in an informal press conference. There were too many reporters present for him to entertain questions, so he decided to make a brief statement. "I am thankful for all of the concern and prayers for my wife, Tia Kitts," he said. "At this time, the police have very few leads, and we have not heard anything from her. As you know, my wife is expecting our first child, so I am especially anxious that she is found safe. If you think that you may have information that could help, I urge you to contact the police. Thank you." Brandon knelt down to climb out of the truck, then suddenly stopped and stood up. "I'd also like to state that I will be establishing a reward fund. I am offering $250,000 to anyone who can provide information that will lead to the safe return of my wife."

The reporters continued to yell questions as Brandon climbed down and returned inside the gymnasium. For the rest of the day, he helped to serve the meals, mingled with the diners, and tried his best to be as thankful as the holiday required. On the outside, he was full of strength and faith, as he did his best to be a blessing to those less fortunate. On the inside, he was full of doubts and fear as he tried desperately not to break down in tears at any moment.

The last diner left the gym around 9:00 P.M., and Brandon stayed around to help the janitorial staff lock up the church and turn off all the lights. As he walked out to his truck, he dreaded going home to an empty house. Out of the blue, he remembered his promise to call his family and wish them a Happy Thanksgiving.

It seemed to Brandon that his mother answered before the phone rang one time.

"I've been sitting by this phone all day waiting for you to call," she said.

"I'm sorry, Mom. I got busy at the church and completely forgot."

"Why didn't you let someone else take over the dinner today? You have so much going on with your wife missing and all. You didn't have to do that."

"But I wanted to do it. It was much better than sitting in the house alone all day."

"Of course, I understand that. After dinner, we all joined hands and prayed for her and the baby. God is in control, son. Just remember that."

Brandon felt his emotions bubbling to the surface once again. Although he was speaking to his mother, his pride blocked the tears and wouldn't let them fall. "I know, Mom. Listen, I'm just leaving the church after a long day, so I'd better get home. Give Dad my love."

The next morning, Brandon awoke in his empty bed, and for a few seconds, he forgot that Tia was gone. Then he reached for her, and his hand landed on the cold, empty sheets. Leaning down he sniffed her pillow. He could still smell the faint scent of her perfume. He was lying on the bed inhaling her scent when he heard Kirk Franklin singing "Hero" and suddenly realized that his cell phone was ringing. He snatched if off the nightstand and answered anxiously. "Hello?"

"Reverend Kitts, we've located your wife," the police officer said.

Chapter Twenty-one

"Momlanda, can I drive today?" Priscilla asked, as she walked into the family room where Yolanda was waiting for her.

"That's fine with me. Are you ready to go?"

Priscilla nodded her head and put her arms into the sleeves of her coat. "I told Jennie we'd pick her and Lavette up on the way."

"Pick them up for what? Priscilla, this is usually *our* day to spend together, just you and me."

For the past several years, Priscilla and Yolanda had started a family tradition of going shopping on Black Friday. In previous years, the two of them would wake up very early and venture out to the malls in time to catch the early bird specials and sales. They would spend the entire day together buying things they really didn't need, eating fattening foods, and enjoying what Yolanda felt was quality time together. It was the perfect girls-only outing, and they'd return home to Jimmy and JJ eating leftover turkey sandwiches and trying to find yet another football game on TV.

It was especially important to Yolanda this year because she felt that she and Priscilla needed some time to talk. Although Jimmy had forgiven her and they were working on getting things back on track with their marriage, Priscilla was extremely upset at her actions and relationship with Julian. When the finale aired, Priscilla had been at a friend's house bragging about her celebrity parents. That night, she returned home under a cloud of shame and embarrassment. While JJ's peers were more concerned with the upcoming football playoffs and what girl they were going to ask to the Winter Ball, Priscilla's were focused directly on the affair they believed was going on between Yolanda and Julian. Their constant teasing of Priscilla had caused a rift between mother and daughter that Yolanda desperately wanted to repair.

"I just thought it would be fun to have them come along. What's the big deal?" Priscilla answered.

"It's not a big deal. I just didn't know that you'd ask them, that's all. Let's start out with them, and then later, we can drop them off and the two of us can have dinner together. I'm sure your dad and brother can survive on leftovers."

After picking up her friends, they arrived at the mall an hour later. As they went from store to store in Lenox Square Mall, Yolanda felt completely isolated and alone. The three girls giggled, looked at cute boys, and tried on outfits. Not once did they ask Yolanda her opinion on the outfits or invite her into the conversation they were having. The only time Priscilla spoke to her was to ask for the credit card when it was time to make a purchase or to hand Yolanda her bags to carry. Several times Yolanda tried to interject into the conversation by suggesting they stop at a particular store or that Priscilla try on an outfit that Yolanda liked. Her ideas were met with rolling eyes, blank stares, and sucking teeth.

Yolanda leaned on the second-level railing of the mall and looked down at the shoppers below, feeling rejected and left out. To her right, she noticed a huge display of presents with a jolly Santa Claus seated in a huge chair. She smiled as she remembered the first

time she and Jimmy had taken their kids to the mall
to have their photo taken with Santa. JJ had cried and
screamed because he wanted no part of Santa's lap.
Priscilla, on the other hand, was the perfect child. She
smiled for the camera and hammed it up like an old
pro. After that, she'd had a tradition of taking a yearly
photo with Santa Claus until after she turned twelve
years old. By then, she thought she was too old. As she
stood watching Santa and reminiscing, Yolanda suddenly heard the girls behind her.

"Hey, let's take a picture with Santa Claus," Lavette
suggested.

Yolanda stifled a laugh as she waited for the other
two girls to veto that idea. To her surprise, they both
happily approved. "Yeah, that would so cool. We can
put it on our Facebook pages," Jennie agreed.

The three girls stood in line with their compacts in
hand to check their makeup and hair. A blond teenager dressed in a green elf costume with red and white
striped tights took their money and led them over to
Santa. Yolanda stood back and watched as they took
their places on his lap and around him.

"Come on, Momlanda," Priscilla said, inviting her
into the picture.

Yolanda found a safe spot to lay their packages, then
happily joined the girls standing beside Santa Claus.
They moved around and did several different poses
before finally leaving to allow the next child in line
his turn. It had taken almost all day, but Yolanda was
finally able to shake the feeling of being the oddball.
She suggested that their next stop should be a place
where they could find nice frames for their photos, and
the girls actually agreed. Yolanda was ecstatic. As they
stood by the printer waiting for their photos to print
out, Yolanda suddenly heard a scream coming from
behind her.

"That's her! That's Yolanda Snow from *Revelations!*"

She turned around and another scream went pulsing through the mall. "Oh my goodness, it's really her!"

Before she could stop it from happening, Yolanda was swamped by a sea of people screaming her name while asking for autographs and photos with her. The feeling of euphoria that swept over her was something Yolanda had never known was possible. As long as she could remember, she'd dreamed of being famous. As a child, she'd stand in her bedroom and practice saying her Oscar acceptance speech while holding up a bottle of lotion. In high school, she dreamed of the day when she'd have paparazzi following her every step and fans clamoring for her attention. With all of the commotion surrounding Julian and the strain it had placed on her marriage and family, Yolanda had completely forgotten the reason she'd so desperately wanted to do the show in the first place. A young black boy around the age of ten held up a piece of paper to her and it all came rushing back. "Can I have your autograph, please? You're my favorite person on the show," he said with a shy smile.

"Of course, I'll sign it." She looked out into the crowd. "I'll sign them all!" she said, beaming.

For almost an hour, Yolanda smiled and posed for camera phone pictures, signed autographs, and even kissed a few babies as if she were running for president until mall security arrived and began to disperse the crowd.

"Mrs. Snow, we need you to follow us and go out the back entrance so that we can clear this area. It's beginning to get congested and dangerous," one of the guards said.

"Okay, I just have to get my daughter and her friends." Yolanda began to look around for the girls, and then suddenly realized that she had not seen them at all since the crowd gathered. "Priscilla?" she yelled over the crowd.

"We'll find her, but first we have to get you out of here," the guard said.

Yolanda turned and smiled and waved once more to the crowd. Flanked by two security guards, she made her way through the mall, down to the food court, and out to the back parking lot.

"I've radioed the valet. He's going to bring your car around for you," the guard said.

"Thank you, but I need to find my daughter and her friends first. The last time I saw them, we were all standing next to Santa's workshop."

Before he could respond, the guard received a call on his radio from the valet station. After answering he turned to Yolanda. "They said your car is gone. Apparently your daughter and her friends have already picked up the car and left. Do you want me to call a cab for you?"

Feeling flabbergasted, Yolanda could not respond. She could only nod her head.

Yolanda arrived at her home an hour later. She paid the cab driver and stormed angrily into her house. "Priscilla Monique Snow, get down here right now!" she screamed.

"She's not here," Jimmy said.

Yolanda stomped into the family room where Jimmy was sitting in his leather recliner. "Don't tell me she's not back from the mall yet? That girl is going to be grounded until she's wrinkled and grey. How dare she leave me like that?"

Jimmy laid down the magazine he was reading. "Calm down. Priscilla came home over an hour ago. She told me what happened at the mall, and I gave her permission to go over to Lavette's for the rest of the day."

"What do you mean she told you what happened and you gave her permission to leave? Did she tell you that she took my car and left me stranded at the mall?"

Jimmy nodded. "She also told me why she left you. Aren't you interested in knowing?"

"There is no excuse for what she did. I'm sure she gave you some lame explanation. Then she batted those long eyelashes and gave you the puppy-dog eyes, but I am not falling for it. When she gets home, she's going to be grounded for the next month."

"No, she's not."

Yolanda stared at him, stunned. "*What?*"

"I said you are not going to ground her for a month. You really need to calm down and just listen for a few minutes."

"Listen to what? I just came in and told you that Priscilla left me at the mall, and you are sitting here defending her without even listening to my side of the story. You've never gone against me when I chose to punish one of the children. What is going on with you?"

"I was just about to ask you the same question."

"You don't have to ask me that. I just told you that Priscilla and her friends got into my car and drove away from the mall without me. They didn't ask if it was okay. They didn't say they were leaving. They didn't say anything to me at all."

"That would have been kind of hard to do with all your adoring fans in their way, don't you think?"

"So I signed some autographs. What does that have to do with anything?"

Jimmy gestured toward a chair, inviting her to sit down. "This shopping day has been a family tradition between you and Priscilla for years. Now I understand that you had no control over being recognized in the mall, but you could have handled it better."

"I know that it's a family tradition, and I was really looking forward to our day together, but she wanted those girls to come along, and I agreed. Then she and her friends ignored me all day. They barely said a word to me, and when I spoke, they acted as if I'd committed a cardinal sin."

"They were being teenagers. Did you *really* think she wanted to try on a frilly lace dress in front of her friends? She's seventeen, not seven. You've been shopping with Priscilla and her friends before. Was it really that different?"

"Well, no, but I just felt so left out. I wanted to spend the day with Priscilla. It's our tradition."

"And she wanted to spend it with you too, especially after all the tension that's been going on around here lately."

"If that's true, then why did she leave me? Tell me why."

Jimmy laughed. "Oh, so *now* you wanna know?"

"Stop teasing and just tell me." She tossed a throw pillow at him.

"She was upset because you guys had planned to get frames for your photos, then drop the girls off and the two of you were going to dinner. But you forgot about all of that to pose for pictures and sign autographs. She stood there for half an hour waiting. Don't you think that's a bit much?"

"What was I supposed to do? Just turn all those people away? They were fans of the show. The last thing I wanted to do was be rude to them. Being rude to your fans can kill your career."

"What career, Yolanda? We are done with that reality show, and you don't have a career. You don't have to be rude to people, but you are getting caught up in this whole celebrity lifestyle and making bad decisions because of it."

"You don't understand, Jimmy," Yolanda pouted.

"You're right. I don't understand. I have no idea why you would care more about photo ops and autographs than you do about your relationship with our daughter. Even with all of the turmoil being on television has brought into our lives, you are still basking in the glow of your own starlight. Our daughter was embarrassed and ridiculed because of your actions on this show, and you left her standing alone to watch you being cheered by your fans? I don't understand that at all." He stood up to leave the room. "By the way, I already grounded her for one week because regardless of how hurt she was, she was still wrong to leave you the way that she did."

"If you grounded her already, then what was the reason for this whole conversation we just had?"

He looked at her with sadness in his eyes. "Pride goeth before destruction and a haughty spirit before a fall."

"And what does that mean, Pastor?" she asked sarcastically.

"That's something you are going to have to figure out on your own, Yolanda," he said before leaving her alone.

Yolanda slumped back into the couch and tried her best to figure out the scripture Jimmy had just recited. As much as she loved him, it annoyed her when he recited scripture, then left her to figure it out. She'd much rather he say it plainly, but Jimmy rarely did. She was still thinking it over when Jimmy came running down the stairs half an hour later.

"I just got a call from Brandon. The police found Tia. Get your coat and let's go."

Chapter Twenty-two

Charlene stuck her fork into her third piece of sweet potato pie. She slid it into her mouth and swallowed without even tasting it before digging in and taking another bite. Since she'd been a teenager, Charlene had been an emotional eater. By her sixteenth birthday, her clothing size matched her age due to her inability to find another way to deal with her issues.

After medical school and during her residency, she managed to conquer her weight problem with diet and exercise, but the emotional eating was still a part of her life. Whenever she failed a test, she ate. If her superiors were displeased with her work, she ate. The morning after she experienced the death of a patient for the first time, she ate. All of the turbulent moments of her life had been punctuated with eating binges. But those moments had been few and far between. Thankfully, after meeting and marrying Zack, things had been so perfect she'd never had a reason to eat a whole box of Mallowmars in one sitting. But now that he was gone, she found herself absorbed in food once again.

Her children were spending the remainder of the holiday week with her parents, while she carried on a clandestine affair with leftover turkey and mashed potatoes. After that, she'd consumed a can of cranberry sauce, two bowls of green beans, four dinner rolls, and a half pan full of broccoli casserole. Now she was lying in her bed, polishing off the last of the sweet potato pie and hoping that her sister had forgotten to take the last few slices of her homemade coconut cake.

During their family's Thanksgiving dinner the day before, Charlene had been stunned at her family's reaction to her asking Zack to leave. As they sat around the dinner table, she could hardly believe the words coming out of their mouths.

"You put your husband out because you found out he's *black?*" her mother asked.

"No, Mama, it's not because he's black. It's because he lied to me about being white. All this time that I've known him, he's been pretending to be someone else."

Her brother, Peter, laughed. "I've always said Zack was the blackest white man I'd ever met. He loves soul food, gospel music, basketball, and thick women. I bet next, we are going to find out that Bill Clinton is passing too."

"It's not funny. How can you sit here and make jokes about it? Zack has been passing for most of his life. I can't believe I'm the only one bothered by this," Charlene complained.

"I understand that you are upset that he's been hiding this from you. But unless you've walked a mile in his shoes, you have no right to judge him. I'm confused sitting here listening to this story. I can only imagine the life of confusion he's lived," her mother said.

"So he was confused, I get that. But why couldn't he confide in me?"

"He did, and you threw him out of his home," her father chimed in.

"But, Daddy, that was after living with him for twelve years believing he was white. He's been hiding in the basement dying his hair and putting in contacts all this time. He paid someone ten grand to keep his secret. How could he keep this from me for so long?"

"He couldn't tell you on your first date because he had no idea where this relationship was going. After you became serious and decided to marry, it was too late. If he'd told you at that time, you would have reacted exactly the same way as you are now," her father chided her.

"Daddy's right," Peter added. "You expected him to share something with you that nobody even shared with him until he was ten years old. It's a secret that his family still doesn't talk about. You are always ranting about how much you love Zack, but you have no compassion for what his life must have been like."

"His life has been made easier by passing. I understand that."

"Has it really? Let me ask you this. Has his family even seen Coretta yet? Or a better question might be, do they even *want* to?" Peter asked.

"Zack is not close to his family, and they've always had a problem with the fact that he married a black woman. They are the ones who made him pass in the first place. So no, they haven't seen Coretta, and they probably don't want to."

"Charlene, think about it." Peter poked her in the forehead to emphasize his point. "If they don't want to see your children, can you imagine what kind of life Zack had having to *live* with those people? They hated his blackness and made him hide it."

"You're right, but why did he continue to do it after he moved to Atlanta?"

"They are still his family. Until he married you, they were all that he had. You make it seem as if the choice was obvious and easy. I'm sure that it wasn't," Peter said.

"We never liked the fact that you married a white man, but that didn't make you turn your back on us.

Family ties are sometimes complicated, but you hang in there with love and understanding. I'm certainly not going to sit here and defend his dishonesty. It was clearly wrong. The man painted himself into a corner, and I understand that you feel betrayed, but is *that* enough reason to end your marriage?" her father asked.

Charlene didn't answer him. Instead, she grabbed the last turkey drumstick from the table and stuffed it into her mouth. Rather than deal with her feelings about Zack, she had continued to eat almost nonstop.

Now she was lying on the bed swirling her fork around the empty pie tin, wondering what else she could find in her kitchen to eat when she heard a knock at her back door. She tied the sash on her tattered blue terry cloth robe and slipped her feet into a pair of bunny slippers. One of the bunny's ears was missing, but they were warm and comfortable, so she put them on anyway and trudged downstairs.

I'm going to fire Marty, she thought as she saw Vanessa standing on the other side of the door. She'd given him specific instructions to not let anyone past the gate because she wasn't in the mood for company. "What do you want?" she asked grumpily.

"Stop playing, girl, and open this door," Vanessa ordered.

Charlene unlocked the door and walked away so that Vanessa could let herself in while she went to the refrigerator in search of her new best friend. There were no more leftovers from Thanksgiving dinner, so she grabbed a pack of sliced ham and the jar of mayonnaise from the fridge. Then she grabbed a loaf of bread from the bread box, sat down at the table, and began making sandwiches. "Want one?" she asked.

"Why don't you stop eating all this food and call Zack?"

"I don't want to talk to him."

"Girl, please. I've known you your whole life, and I know that when you eat like this, it's because you are upset."

Charlene piled three slices of ham on her sandwich and took a big bite. "I'm upset because my husband lied to me."

Vanessa sat down at the table and pushed the food out of Charlene's reach. "Look, I'm the last person that you'd think would defend Zack, but I really think you are being too hard on him."

"You too, Vanessa?"

"What do you mean, me too?"

"Yesterday at dinner, Momma, Daddy, and Peter were all defending him. For all of these years none of you have given two flips about my husband, and now, you all are taking his side over mine. It's crazy."

"We *are* on your side, Charlene. The fact that we've all put aside how we personally felt about Zack all these years should tell you something. We've had our issues, but we all know that Zack is not a bad person. He's weird, with his sneered-up nose and refusal to shake hands, but weird is not bad. It's just who he is. Frankly, I don't understand why you asked him to leave."

"Okay, let me say this *really* slowly so you can get it. My husband has been pretending to be white for years, when he's really black."

Vanessa shrugged her shoulders, "So?"

Exasperated, Charlene went back to the fridge and grabbed a six-pack of her son's chocolate fudge pudding and a spoon from the drawer by the sink. She sat down again in front of Vanessa. "What do you mean, so?" she asked between bites.

"What is it that you always say to me?" Vanessa paused, then continued while doing her best impersonation of Charlene. "Zack is a good man, and he loves me. What difference does it make what color he is?"

Charlene scraped the bottom of the pudding cup, and then opened another one. "It really doesn't matter to me what color he is. How come nobody understands that it's the dishonesty that I have an issue with?"

"To be perfectly honest, I don't believe you for one minute."

"I beg your pardon?" Charlene rolled her neck. "What do you mean you don't believe me?"

"I don't believe you. I know you, girl. I think that you've enjoyed being in an interracial relationship and all the attention that goes along with it. Now that you know the truth, you realize that you aren't special anymore. You are married to just another brother like the rest of the sistas."

Charlene shoved in two more spoonfuls of pudding before answering. "I'm so ashamed, but you're right. When Zack told me he isn't white, I felt . . . I felt disappointed. Isn't that awful? I mean I was mad that he'd been dishonest, but I was suddenly disappointed that I didn't have the white man that I married."

"Are you saying you only married Zack because you thought he was white?"

"Of course not, I love him with all my heart. It's just that . . . being the wife of the blue-eyed soul brother has been nice. Zack is well respected in this community, and let's be honest, a large part of that is because he's white. Even the producer of *Revelations* chose him primarily because he was a white man with a predominantly black congregation. I just feel that our life has had some things that we might not have enjoyed if people knew he was black."

"If you feel that way, just imagine how Zack must have felt every day of his life."

"But it's wrong, isn't it? I mean, it's self-hatred."

"I don't know. I think that sometimes we have to live with the cards that life deals us. Zack's cards were all jumbled, and he took the easiest route. I'm sure there are those who would say he's a sellout or whatever, but they don't know Zack. You do."

Feeling sick from all the food she'd inhaled, Yolanda sat back in her chair. "So I guess I'm supposed to just go on with my marriage as if nothing has happened? I don't know if I can do that. What if he's hiding something else?"

"Do you really believe that?"

"No. I'm just confused. And I feel sick. Why did I eat so much?"

Vanessa giggled. "I have no idea, but what you need to do is get out of this funky robe, take a hot shower, drink an Alka-Seltzer, and call your husband."

After Vanessa left, Charlene took her advice regarding the shower and Alka-Seltzer, but she wasn't sure about calling Zack. Before she could talk to him, she needed to deal with her own feelings. Instead of the telephone, she picked up her Bible and called on God to give her some comfort. As she flipped through the pages, she felt compelled to stop at Galatians 3:26.

For ye are all the children of God by faith in Christ Jesus. For as many of you as have been baptized into Christ have put on Christ. There is neither Jew nor Greek, there is neither bond nor free, there is neither male nor female: for ye are all one in Christ Jesus.

After reading the passage and praying for clarity, Charlene carefully picked up the phone and called Zack. He arrived an hour later, and Charlene was surprised that he didn't bring his suitcase. He walked into the house and took a seat on their living-room sofa as if he was a guest.

"So what did you want to talk about?" he asked.

"Um . . . We need to talk about everything. You need to know that I've told Martin and Luther about . . . well, I told them that Nancy isn't their natural grandmother."

"Really? What was their reaction?"

"Surprisingly, it didn't really matter to them. They wanted to know when you were coming home and if we are getting a divorce."

Zack folded his arms across his chest. "I've been wondering the same thing myself."

"You have to realize how surprising this whole thing has been for me. For the past few days, I've felt like I was shell-shocked. It really hurt me to find out that you haven't been honest with me throughout our marriage."

"I do realize that, and I'm very sorry."

"Please, just let me finish. One of the reasons that I was hurt was because I felt disillusioned with our marriage."

Zack nodded his head. "I know. I let you down."

"No. You didn't let me down. I felt that way when I realized that I really enjoyed being married to a white man. It's horrible to say, but I wasn't sure if I could deal with being the wife of a black man."

"I don't understand. You told me that I was the first white man that you'd ever dated. You even turned me down at first because you said that you were not with the swirl."

"I know it sounds crazy, but somewhere inside me, I felt that you were the perfect man, not in spite of being white, but because you were white. Somehow, during our marriage, I'd created this profile of the perfect man, and part of that perfection was that he was white."

"Wow, I had no idea you felt that way."

"Neither did I until the feelings surfaced."

Zack stood up. "Okay, I guess I understand. I wish I could continue to be that white man that you want, but I've lived a lie too long. Now that I've told the truth, I can't go back." He sighed as he walked toward the door. "Let me know when I can come back for the rest of my things."

"Wait, Zack, please don't leave. I didn't mean that the way it sounded. I was only trying to explain my feelings."

"I understand your feelings. I've heard them my whole life from Nancy and Roscoe. White is better. I get that, but it's not who I am anymore. It's funny. All this time I really thought you loved me, and not my blond hair and blue eyes."

"I do love you, Zack. That's why I called you. This situation has been confusing for me, but the one thing that I know for sure is that I do love you."

He turned away from the door and faced her. "Do you love who I am now, or who you thought I was?"

"I love Zack Morton. The man who wouldn't take no for an answer when I refused to go out with him ten times. The man who opened doors, pulled out chairs, and treated me better than any other man I'd ever dated. I love the man who proposed to me by walking into my office wearing a tuxedo and carrying a dozen red roses. I love the father of my three beautiful children, who loves and protects us no matter what. I even love the fact that your nose works overtime and you won't shake hands with people. It's a part of who you are, and I love it. I don't care about the hair, or the eyes, or even what color box you check on the census form. I love you, and I just want us to start over."

Zack walked over and pulled Charlene into a hug. "I promise that I will never ever keep anything from you again."

"You can go by the hotel tomorrow and get your things." She grinned. "The children are gone, and they won't be back until Sunday afternoon. We have the whole house to ourselves."

Zack grinned too and took Charlene's hand into his. She was following him up the stairs when his cell phone began ringing. "I'll ignore it," he said.

"No, it might be important. Go ahead and answer."

He answered the phone and had to hold onto the stair railing to keep from falling over as he listened. "I'll be right there." He hung up the phone and turned to Charlene. "That was Brandon. They've found Tia, but it's not good news."

Chapter Twenty-three

"No, I don't want anything else," Julian replied to the convenience store clerk. He picked up the bag of potato chips and soda that he'd just purchased and walked outside. As he stood on the side of the building eating the chips and watching the patrons go in and out, he knew that he needed to get out of Atlanta as fast as he could. He scratched the razor bumps that were forming on his chin since he'd shaved off his beard. A woman near the gas pumps glanced in his direction, and he pulled his wool stocking cap down so that it covered his eyebrows, and hiked up the collar on his black peacoat. His teeth chattered in the cold, crisp November air as he tried desperately to figure out his next move.

His body trembled from his head to his toes with a mixture of anger and regret as he thought back over the past week. By this time, he'd planned to be lying on a fake fur rug in front of a roaring fireplace next to Ophelia. But none of that was possible anymore. Julian thought he'd come up with the perfect plan as he had happily driven away from the cast party and deep into the mountains of Virginia.

Prior to the party, he'd set everything into motion. Unbeknownst to Anderson, he'd taken over the editing of the show and included the footage of him kissing Yolanda that he had secretly videotaped. He was positive that once Bishop Snow saw his wife in such a compromising position, her marriage would be over.

Rather than attend the party, he had waited outside until he saw Jimmy leave. As he watched him angrily walk away from the party, he couldn't help but think of how stupid the man was being by not calling a cab. But Julian really didn't care. All he cared about was that Yolanda would return to the limousine alone. He still did not understand why Tia Kitts had gotten into the back of the limousine instead and thrown his entire world off-kilter.

Julian had driven up the long, winding dirt road that led to what he referred to as his and Ophelia's enchanted cabin, humming "Endless Love." On the way, he'd made one stop to mail the "Dear John" letter to Jimmy, ensuring that Yolanda would be with him forever. After they arrived, he decided to take their luggage inside and allow her to continue to sleep in the backseat. Julian had packed enough of his clothing to last for several months and purchased the same amount for Yolanda.

Inside the cabin, he placed their bags in the master bedroom, and then he returned to the limousine to unload the food. The cabin was located in a secluded area where the nearest store was over ten miles away, and the closest neighbor was at least twenty miles away. It was the perfect spot for them to be alone, while he made her fall in love with him all over again.

He had opened the limousine door and leaned in to gently wake her, when he suddenly realized that things were not as they should be. She was lying on the seat facedown. Instead of waking her, he reached in and placed his arms under her legs, then lifted her out of the limousine. "Tia!" he screamed, and immediately dropped her onto the ground. She landed on her bottom with a loud thud, but still did not wake up.

Julian cursed under his breath and picked her up again and carried her inside. She was still knocked out as he placed her into a chair in the living room. A light snow began to fall, so he went out back to chop wood for the fire. By the time he returned inside an hour later, Tia was just beginning to regain consciousness. Rubbing her eyes, she looked around. "What's going on?" she asked.

"You are ruining my life and my plans, that's what," he angrily answered.

Tia looked around the unfamiliar cabin. "The last thing I remember was drinking champagne in the back of a limousine. How did I get here? Julian, tell me what's going on," she demanded.

"Shut up!" he screamed at her. "Everything would have been perfect if you had not gotten your stupid behind into that limousine. So just shut up!"

"Who do you think you're talking to? Where's the phone? I'm calling Brandon to come get me right now!" Tia stood up and began walking around looking for a telephone, but she sat down again because she felt woozy. She put her hand to her head. "You drugged me," she accused.

"Don't blame me because you were too dense to get into the right limousine. Now, I told you to shut up. Do it or I'll be forced to shut you up!"

Tia suddenly heard the threat in Julian's voice and saw the rage blazing in his eyes. "Just let me call Brandon so I can go home," she begged.

"You're not going anywhere. Sit down and shut up."

Tia ran to the door and tried to open it. Realizing it was locked, she turned to look at Julian. "Why are you doing this? What do you want with me?"

"I *don't* want you. You got in the way, and now I just have to figure out what to do with you. I need time to think."

Tia returned to the chair and slowly sat down. "Please just let me go. I'm pregnant."

Julian laughed loudly. "I've worked in television since I was nineteen years old. Do you really think I don't know a padded belly when I see one? Just because you managed to fool that idiot you married doesn't mean you have everyone fooled."

"You . . . you're crazy." Tia tried her best to look indignant.

"I'm not the one carrying around a six-pound bag of foam. Go in the bedroom and you'll find some clothes you can change into. Do it quietly, and don't try anything stupid."

Rolling her eyes, Tia obeyed. Inside the bedroom, she heaved and strained, trying to push open the window. She failed to get it open, so she began looking around the room for something to break it with. In the dresser drawer, she found a box of chocolates and a note. She took a bite of the candy while she read the note.

Dear Yolanda,

I know this transition is difficult and you miss your family. But I love you, and I promise to make you happy,

Julian.

"So he planned to snatch Yolanda and got me by mistake," she mumbled to herself. Also in the drawer she found a hairbrush that she took to the window. She looked outside and noticed that the ground and trees were covered in snow, and it was still falling. *Even if I get out, where am I going to go?* Instead of running, she decided that she'd try to reason with Julian. She took off her dress and the baby bump pad and replaced them with a pair of jeans and a T-shirt that she'd found in the suitcase. She smiled at Julian as she walked into the living room.

"Did you leave your baby in the bedroom?" he asked mockingly.

"Okay, you got me. I'm busted. So you know my secret, and I know yours. If you don't tell mine, then I won't tell yours."

"My secret?" Julian looked at her strangely. "What secret is that?"

"I found the note in the bedroom. I know that you intended to bring Yolanda Snow here instead of me. Just take me home and I'll keep my mouth shut about this, as long as you don't tell Brandon about the . . . the baby."

"You must think I fell off the turnip truck. My relationship with Yolanda is no secret. It was broadcast to the entire world on *Revelations*."

"But I'm the only one who knows that she wasn't going to come up here willingly. That's your business, and I don't care. Just let me go."

Julian thought for a moment. He was just about to agree to Tia's arrangement when he suddenly remembered the letter he'd mailed. Even if he let Tia go, the letter had tipped Yolanda and Jimmy off to his plan. *They probably have the police searching for me and Tia at this very moment,* he thought. "Yolanda was planning to come here with me willingly," he lied. "She's probably angry with me now because she thinks I stood her up. So shut up, Tia. You don't know what you're talking about."

"I'll explain everything to her. I'll tell her it was all a big mistake. Come on, Julian. Just let me go."

"No. Now quit talking and leave me alone."

Tia returned to the bedroom and retrieved the hairbrush. Before entering the living room, she practiced swinging it several times. *These guns are gonna knock that fool out,* she mused. She walked into the living room, and Julian was bent over near the fireplace, placing logs on the fire. Quietly, she crept up behind him.

Without any warning, he spun around. "I told you, don't try anything stupid. Give me the hairbrush!"

Tia's eyes widened, and he pointed toward the television. Peering at it, she realized it was closed circuit and the camera was in the bedroom. Grudgingly, she handed the brush over. "You are a sick, twisted, crazy freak and—"

"Watch your mouth, Tia," he warned, interrupting her. "You are no prize yourself. Just go sit down somewhere and be quiet."

"No. I want to go home, and I want to go now! You can't keep me here. I know my husband has called the police, and any minute now, he's going to be here with the cavalry to save me! You are psychotic, Julian."

Tia continued ranting on and on and whining about going home. Her words disintegrated, and all Julian heard was the annoying sound of her voice grating on his nerves until he could no longer stand the sound of it, and he snapped. "I said shut up!" he screamed. Julian grabbed Tia by both arms and slammed her into the wall. Her neck flipped back like a bobblehead doll, and her head struck the wall. "Do not say another word, do you understand me?" he seethed. Tia did not answer, so he shook her and screamed again. "Do you hear me, Tia?" Julian watched as Tia's eyes slowly rolled back in her head. Quickly, he released her and watched her body fall to the floor. "Tia, stop playing," he warned her. He knelt down on the floor next to her. *Oh my God, what have I done?*

Julian sat in the cabin for the next several days until the stench from Tia's corpse was more than he could stand. At first he had thought of running. He knew that he had more than enough money to book a flight and leave the country. But then he realized that if Tia's body was found in his cabin, he'd be the first, last, and only suspect. The next plan he thought of was to dump her body outside in the snow. If he did, he knew it would be spring before anyone located her. But again, he didn't want her to be found on his property and implicate him in her death.

Julian believed that killing Tia had been an awful accident. It wasn't intentional; therefore, he didn't intend to take the blame. Finally, he decided that running was his best option, but first he had to get her body as far away from his cabin and property as possible. On Thanksgiving morning, he got up early and took a long, hot shower. Still dripping wet, he slathered lather on his face and shaved his mustache and beard. Once his face was smooth as a baby's bottom, he put lather on top of his head and shaved himself completely bald.

Julian then wrapped Tia's body in a bedsheet and loaded it into the trunk of the limousine. Next to her, he tossed in the pregnancy padding and her ball gown she'd worn to the party. Then Julian drove back to Atlanta. He removed everything from the limousine that could remotely connect it to him and parked it in an empty parking lot and walked away.

Now as he stood outside the convenience store, he searched for a suitable car to take in order to make his exit. A twenty-something black woman got out of her late model Honda and went into the store. Julian approached her car and noticed she'd left the keys dangling in the ignition. Then he also noticed she had two rug rats asleep in the backseat.

Moving along, he decided against another carjacking and walked to the Marta Train Station. He took a seat in the back away from all of the other passengers, while still trying to decide on his destination. It was too late to leave the country; he knew he was probably a wanted man. Instead, he decided to continue running, indefinitely.

Chapter Twenty-four

Danita pulled a black glove on her left hand and then repeated it for the right hand as she prepared to attend Tia Kitt's funeral. While she and Tia had not grown close, Danita's heart ached for Brandon. She knew firsthand what it felt like to lose a spouse under mysterious circumstances. Over the past several days, she did her best to offer him support and comfort and was pleasantly surprised that the whole cast of *Revelations* had rallied around him.

The police had found Tia's rotting body in the trunk of the limousine that had been stolen from the cast party five days prior to the funeral. The police were not sure, but several of the clues found in the limousine pointed to Julian Washington being responsible. After dusting the car for fingerprints, they found one thumb print that had been confirmed as Julian's. Their next step was to question the driver who had been carjacked. After looking over the pictures that the police provided, he felt that Julian looked familiar, but he was unable to swear that he was the same person who'd knocked him out. Without any other evidence, the police were reluctant to issue a warrant for Julian's arrest. Instead, they put out a search for him as a person of interest, in the hopes that he'd come forward to clear his name. So far, that had not happened.

Danita could not get over the fact that he seemed to have vanished off the face of the earth. After several hours of questions by the police, Anderson decided that he did not want to be implicated in any crime; therefore, he finally stopped telling the cover story and admitted that he had no idea where Julian was. He had not heard from him since before the finale party and he assured the police that he would contact them if he did.

Philippe pulled up to the mortuary and let Danita out in front. She was wearing a simple A-line black dress, with two-inch heeled black pumps, black gloves, and a black hat with a small veil. It was the same outfit she'd worn to her husband Ben's funeral. As she entered the doors, she was surprised to see Ben's alleged mistress standing among the crowd of spectators outside the mortuary. Danita assumed she was either nosy or a fan of the show, but neither mattered to her at that moment. The size of the crowd inside surprised Danita, as she'd been told that this would be a private service. Then she remembered how many siblings, nieces, and nephews that Brandon had and realized that they were the mass of people that she saw.

She walked over to Yolanda Snow, feeling grateful to see a familiar face. "Hello, Yolanda, how are you?" she asked.

"Um . . . Hello, Danita," she answered.

Danita noticed that Yolanda's eyes were red from crying. "I'm sorry, I didn't realize that you and Tia were so close," she said.

"It's not that. I mean, I liked Tia. It's just that I can't shake the feeling that it was supposed to be me lying in that box. Julian intended to kill me, and Tia somehow got in the way," she cried.

"Have the police named him as a suspect?"

"Not yet, but I'm positive that he's responsible. I just hope they find him soon."

Danita put her hand on Yolanda's shoulder. "Stop worrying. If Julian is responsible, I'm sure he's miles away from here."

"I guess you're right. I feel so bad for her, though. What kind of animal kills a pregnant woman?"

Danita leaned in and lowered her voice. "You mean you haven't heard?"

"Heard what?"

"Brandon told me that Tia wasn't really pregnant. The police found some type of padding in the car, and then the autopsy confirmed it. There was no baby."

Yolanda eyes bugged out in surprise. "No, I had not heard that. I'm really ashamed, but I haven't been around Brandon much at all. Jimmy has spoken with him, but I feel so guilty about Tia's death that I've just been avoiding him."

"Isn't Jimmy coming to the funeral?"

"Yes, he had to finish up some business at the church first. He's meeting me here."

"Let's go find a seat before Brandon's family takes up the whole place. We'll save a spot for him," Danita suggested.

They entered the chapel and found three seats on the same row as Zack and Charlene Morton. They waved politely, then took their seats. In silence, they watched as Brandon entered with his mother on his left and his father on his right. Each of them held on to his arms as if they believed he would topple over if they let go. Although they were positive his heart was shattered into tiny pieces, he showed no emotion. There were no tears or loud outbursts. He simply looked straight ahead as they led him to the front and helped him into a pew. They were followed by the rest of Brandon's family. Danita thought it was odd and sad that none of the mourners was related to Tia. After the family was seated, Jimmy entered and found them just as the choir finished singing "We'll Understand It Better By and By." Quietly, he slipped into his seat.

Brandon's associate minister began the service by reading a scripture that was familiar to them all from John 11:25–26.

Jesus said unto her, I am the resurrection, and the life: he that believeth in me, though he were dead, yet shall he live. And whosoever liveth and believeth in me shall never die.

During the service, he spoke of God's ultimate plan for eternal life. He advised those who had accepted Christ to grieve with the hope that one day they'd see Tia again, while admonishing those who were lost to get right before it was too late.

Following the services, they were all invited to attend the repast that was being held in the gymnasium of Brandon's church. Danita was chatting with Charlene Morton as they waited for the caterers to bring their food to the table. She looked in the direction of the door and once again she saw her late husband's alleged mistress. This time the woman managed to get past security and was barreling across the gymnasium, headed straight for Danita. "I need to talk to you. It's important," she said.

Danita was so stunned she didn't know how to respond. "What . . . What could you possibly need to speak to me about?"

"They lied, and they double-crossed me. When I went to court, I thought they was gonna take you for every dollar that you got. I ain't know they was gonna try to take yo' kids. We needs to talk," she said.

Danita cringed as the woman who had spoken so eloquently in court was now standing in front of her butchering the English language. She was also creating a scene as she stood in the middle of the room in a bright yellow sundress and sandals. It was as if she believed it was the middle of the summer instead of the end of November. "Fine, let's see if we can find a room where we can speak in private," she finally said.

Danita followed the woman into the ladies' lounge, where they found a woman standing at the sink washing her hands. They stood staring at each other without speaking until the woman exited the bathroom.

"First of all, let me say that I ain't the kind of woman you think I am. I wasn't having no affair with your husband. As a matter of fact, I barely knew the man. I'm a single mother, and I got kids to feed. I just want you to understand that," the mistress said.

"I knew it. I knew Ben would never cheat on me. Why did you lie in court? I don't understand."

"Miss Joy made me do it. She was my supervisor at the cleaning company where I worked. One night she caught me taking a nap on the job. I just knew I was done, but she said she'd make a deal with me. She told me that she needed me to come in court and pretend to be your husband's mistress. I ain't wanna do it, cuz like I said, I'm not that kind of woman. But she threatened to have me fired if I didn't go along with it. And she told me that once the case was settled, she would give me some extra money, you know, for my trouble."

"You said they double-crossed you. What did you mean by that?"

"That no good heffa, Joy, fired me anyway. Two days after we was in court, she called me in the office and let me go. She said it was because of cutbacks, but I know better. So I asked her when was they gonna get the settlement money because they won the case. I figured I could really use it because I was out of a job. That's when I found out that they didn't ask for no money from you."

Danita nodded. "That's right. Is that why you're here? Did you plan on asking me for money?"

"No. Just hear me out. Like I said, I'm a single mother, and I got kids to feed. I heard they was trying to have you declared unfit so they could get yo' kids. That's just trifling. You done lost yo' husband; you need to be with yo' kids."

"Right, as long as I pay you for the information?" Danita eyed her suspiciously.

"No. To be honest, it's not like that. I think it's wrong that they trying to do this to you, and I wanna help. That's my word from one single mother to another. I'll go back to the court and tell the judge the truth, and if you see fit to pay me for that, then I'd appreciate it cuz it's hard not having a job. But I'm not trying to sell you information. I just wanna help."

Danita smiled. "Well, let's start by you telling me your name. I'm sorry I wasn't really listening when you gave it in court."

"It's Gretchen Jenkins. I know it's strange to see a black woman named Gretchen, but I was born in Germany while my daddy was in the Air Force."

Charlene Morton entered the bathroom and interrupted them. "Is everything okay in here?" she asked cautiously.

"It's great," Danita answered. She turned to Gretchen. "Are you hungry? I know they've got tons of food out there. Won't you join us for dinner, and then we'll finish our talk."

Gretchen nodded her head.

She followed Charlene out of the bathroom. Danita stood back for a few moments. "Thank you, God," she said before following them out.

Chapter Twenty-five

When she returned home that evening, Yolanda went upstairs and knocked on Priscilla's bedroom door. "Come in," she heard her say.

"Can we talk?" Yolanda asked through the half-opened door.

Priscilla sat up on her bed and grabbed the remote for her TV and clicked it off. "Sure. Come on in."

Yolanda took a seat on the bed beside Priscilla. "I think I owe you an apology," she said.

"I'm listening."

"I was hoping you'd make this easy on me, but I guess I deserve the attitude. I'm sorry about what happened last week in the mall. I got caught up in the frenzy, and I'm really sorry that I forgot all about you. Will you forgive me?"

"I will if you tell me the truth about something."

"I've always told you guys the truth. What do you want to know?"

Priscilla looked directly into her eyes. "Did you really have an affair with Mr. Washington? I mean, the clip of you kissing him is all over YouTube. You and Dad said it was edited, but it looked real to me."

"The truth is the kiss was real, but *he* kissed *me*. I pushed him away immediately. What you saw on television was edited. He made it look as if we were kissing for a long period of time, and that's not true. He wanted your father to believe that we were having an affair, and then he intended to kidnap me."

"But he got Mrs. Kitts instead, right?"

"That's what your father and I believe, but the police are still working on the case."

Priscilla nodded her head. "Momlanda, how do you know if you're being stalked? I mean, do they just follow you around?"

"Has someone been following you?"

"It's not about me." Priscilla hesitated. "It's Lavette. She broke up with Nehemiah last year, but he won't let go."

"What has he done?"

"He calls her all the time. Sometimes if we're at the movies or out to eat, he'll show up out of nowhere. One time he told her he'd kill her if she didn't take him back, but then he said he was just playing around."

"Honey, listen to me. Lavette needs to have her mother call the police. I want you to call her today and tell her that," Yolanda said. Her voice was filled with urgency.

Priscilla shook her head. "He's just annoying, not dangerous."

"I know it may seem like that now, but she has to do something before things get out of hand. I used to believe that Julian was not dangerous. Even when he was sending me text messages saying that he would kill me, I didn't believe it. I'm sorry now that I didn't take him seriously."

"Okay. I'll talk to her later. Oh yeah, and I'm sorry too. I shouldn't have left you at the mall like that. I was just so mad."

"Well, you don't have to worry about anything like that again. The show is over, and after a while, people will stop recognizing me when we go out. But even if they do, I promise that I won't act crazy like that again."

"Oh, I forgot to tell you, Mr. Carter called while you were out. He said that he needed to talk to you guys about the show. He said something about a 'special.'"

Yolanda was livid. As if it wasn't bad enough that Anderson had not attended Tia's funeral, she could not believe he had been making phone calls about the show. She left Priscilla's room and went down to the family room to tell Jimmy. He was on the phone when she walked in, so she took a seat and waited.

"That was Anderson on the phone," he said after hanging up. "He wants the cast to get together to film a special Christmas show."

"You've *got* to be kidding me. I *know* that you told him that there's no way that we'd be involved."

"Actually, I didn't say that. I mean, that was my first reaction, until he explained to me what he wants to do."

"Jimmy, I'm shocked. *You* are the one who's been against being on television from the beginning."

"I know, but this is different. He wants it to be a tribute show honoring Tia's life. He plans to invite each member of the cast to gather and offer our memories of her. He's also having the production team put together a montage of clips of her from the show."

"Honey, I don't mean to sound uncaring, but who in the cast even has any memories of Tia? She was always so standoffish. Besides, if they edit her footage the way that they did mine, it won't be a tribute, it will be another massacre."

Jimmy sighed. "That's not gonna happen. He also told me that the police have officially named Julian as a suspect in Tia's murder. They've issued a warrant for his arrest. I think Anderson is trying to distance himself from Julian and this crime as much as possible."

"Thank God. Do they have any idea where he is?"

"No, but they have some leads. Julian owned a cabin in Virginia, and they believe that's where the murder took place. They've also questioned his family in Greenburg, but they say that they haven't seen him or heard from him. He's apparently on the run."

"I remember that cabin. It was so far back up in the woods, the squirrels needed scooters to get there. I always hated that place. Julian called it romantic, but to me, it was just creepy," Yolanda said, shuddering.

"Well, I told Anderson that we'd consider doing the show, but only if Brandon agrees. I won't do anything that's going to put him through any more grief or pain."

"Honey, Danita told me today that Tia had been lying about being pregnant. She said the autopsy confirmed that there was never a baby."

"Yeah, Brandon told me about that. It was difficult for him to lose Tia, but finding out she'd been lying to him for months about the baby just devastated him. I mean, how can he grieve for her when he's so angry about what she did?"

"I think we should do the show," Yolanda said.

"Now, why doesn't that surprise me," Jimmy smirked.

"No, you don't understand. This time, it's not about me getting in front of the camera and trying to be the star of the show. I can't help but to feel somewhat responsible for what happened to Tia."

"I've told you before, you can't blame yourself. Julian is a crazy man, and he's the only one responsible for this crime."

"Jimmy, last night I had a horrible dream."

He looked at her with concern. "You tossed and turned all night. I'm surprised that you slept at all."

"After the dream I was so shaken up that I couldn't . . . I was too afraid to go back to sleep. It was so real."

"Do you want to talk about it?"

"I dreamed that Julian came back for me. He told me that he was sorry for what happened to Tia, but that I was next. He said, 'I love you to death.' Then he shot me. It was so real that I felt a burning in my chest, like a bullet was searing through my flesh. I fell, and I just kept falling and falling and falling until I woke up."

Jimmy pulled her into his arms. "It's okay, honey. It was just a dream."

"I know, but he's still out there somewhere. I'm so sorry that I let my desire to be famous bring so much pain into our lives. Tia didn't deserve to die because of my ambition."

"That's not why she died," he assured her.

"I was just upstairs talking to Priscilla, and she has a friend who's being stalked by an ex-boyfriend, but she's not taking it seriously. I didn't take it seriously either, and I can only imagine the many women out there who don't. Even when I did call the police on Julian, they were really nonchalant about it."

"What are you trying to say?"

"We need to do this show and bring some attention to the crime of stalking. We need to let those young women out there who are getting the late-night phone calls and text messages know that they need to take these threats seriously. Even if Brandon doesn't want to do the show, we need to talk him into it."

"Honey, aren't you forgetting that Julian was verbally and physically abusive to you as well? That was probably a sign of what was to come."

"No, that's my point. We need to point out the signs of an abuser and possible stalker. Jimmy, you are always talking about how you want your church to minister to those with real-life issues. This is as real as it gets. We've got to do this show for every scared woman out there, but most of all, so that Tia's death is not in vain."

Jimmy nodded. "Okay, I'll talk to Brandon about it."

Two days later, Brandon reiterated his answer. "No, I don't want to be a part of this show," he said emphatically. "I want to move on, and I want to forget it. Can't I just do that in peace?"

Zack Morton sat at his office desk looking over at him. Their meeting had only begun a few minutes earlier, and Brandon had already said no to the show five times. He'd also said no to Jimmy and Yolanda Snow, as well as Danita, when they had asked. Zack was their last hope of getting a yes out of him. "I understand that you want to move on, but as a minister, you know that part of the grief process is channeling your grief into something positive."

"I'll be honest with you, Zack. In the past when I've sat in my office and counseled people who were grieving, I've said the same thing. Now that I'm on the other side of the desk, I realize just how ineffective this is."

"Okay, since you're being honest, tell me the real reason that you don't want to do this show. I know that you loved Tia, so why are you so against honoring her?"

Brandon shifted his weight in his chair and continued brooding. "You wouldn't understand. Yes, I loved Tia, but Tia didn't love me."

"What are you talking about?"

"The sad thing is that I've always known how she felt, but I wouldn't accept it. I just kept praying to God that one day she'd stop faking that she loved me and actually start loving me for real. It never happened. Right up until the day she died, she was playing me for a fool," he said. He tried to fight it, but tears began rolling down his cheeks.

Zack reached across his desk and quietly handed Brandon a tissue. Patiently, he waited as Brandon dabbed at his tears and blew his nose before speaking again. "I didn't know Tia that well, but I do believe that she loved you."

"If she loved me, then why did she play such a cruel joke on me? She knew how much I wanted to be a father. Pretending to be pregnant like that has to be the vilest, cruelest thing she could think of. If she loved me, she would have been honest with me."

"Look at me, Brandon. Look into my eyes."

Brandon glanced at Zack, then turned his eyes back to his lap. "My dad used to ask me to look into his eyes when he wanted to emphasize a point. I'm not a teenager, so you don't have to do that."

"No, that's not what I mean. I want you to look at the difference in my eyes, and in my hair."

"I know they are brown now instead of blue. And I can see your roots growing into your hair. What does how you look have to do with me?"

"I was dishonest with my wife for my entire marriage. I set out to make her and everyone else believe that I was something that I was not. I know I was wrong, but I swear to you, it had nothing to do with how much I loved her."

"So tell me why you did it? I was raised to tell the truth. My parents never tolerated me or my siblings telling even a small lie. So you'll have to excuse me if I don't understand the logic behind lying to someone that you love."

"There is no logic behind it. I can't speak for Tia, but for me, I did what I did in order to please the people who claimed to love me. My stepparents wanted a white son, so I gave them a white son. Even though he wasn't real, I justified my actions by telling myself that it was what they wanted."

"No offense, but that's pretty lame. I suppose you are trying to say that Tia lied to me and wore padding because I wanted a baby so much."

"Like I said, I can't speak for Tia. But don't you think that your desire to be a father might have affected her actions just a smidgen? I know you've taught Sunday School. One of the first lessons we teach is that once you tell a lie, you have to keep telling more lies in order to cover for the first one until you have a huge ball of incomprehensible lies. I know from experience that you don't want to keep doing it, but you also have no idea how to stop it."

"I wanted to be a father because I love kids and I believe in family. That does not justify what she did."

"It doesn't. I totally agree. I'm not trying to justify it at all. I'm just trying to help you understand it, so that you can deal with it." Zack paused and picked up his Bible. He turned to Ephesians 4:32. "I know that I shouldn't have to read this to you, but I feel that you need to hear it.

And be ye kind one to another, tenderhearted, for-giving one another, even as God for Christ's sake hath forgiven you.

Zack closed his Bible and looked over at Brandon. "I'm sorry for what I did, and I'm thankful to God that my wife has forgiven me. You've got to forgive Tia. You said that you want to move on. The first step to that is forgiving your wife for what she's done."

Brandon covered his face with his hands as he broke down and cried. "I loved her so much, and now she's gone. Being mad at her keeps me from missing her," he sobbed.

Zack stood up from his desk and walked over to Brandon. He knelt on the floor beside him and lay his hand on his arms, and he began to pray. He allowed Brandon to continue sobbing as he petitioned God on his behalf. When he was done, he returned to his seat and quietly waited for Brandon to pull himself together.

"I'll do the show," Brandon said. He blew his nose.

"Are you sure? I know that's initially why I asked you to come here, but the last thing I want to do is put more pressure on you. I'm your friend first. Don't worry about the rest of the cast, I'll handle them."

"No, I'm sure. I want to honor my wife, and I know that the viewers of the show want to honor her as well. I've received a ton of cards and letters from people since this happened. They all loved Tia."

"Um, you announced on the show that she was pregnant. How do you want to handle that with the tribute show?"

"It's not a problem. The police have told me to keep it under wraps because the fewer people who know, the better. I've only shared it with the cast and, of course, my family. We are all positive of Julian's guilt, but they think we need to keep a lid on the details of the crime, just in case. Anyone with too much information could be a suspect."

"I thought Julian was the only suspect."

"He is, but they think he may have had some help."

Zack nodded. "I'll call Anderson and the others and let them know we have a green light on the show."

Chapter Twenty-six

Brandon sat in his living room staring at the lights that were twinkling on his Christmas tree. It had only been up a week, but according to his family's tradition, he planned to take it down the next morning. His mother would have a fit if he allowed a Christmas tree to be up in his house when the New Year rolled in.

His traditional celebrations would continue into the New Year, and he'd invited Zack and Charlene, along with their family, to have New Year's Day dinner with him. His housekeeper was planning to cook a traditional dinner that included black-eyed peas, collard greens, and corn bread. They laughed at him when he told them that Zack would have to walk into the house first, but according to Brandon's mom and her down-home superstitions, it was bad luck to have a woman enter your house first in the New Year. He'd also invited Danita, but she and her girls were spending the holidays at a cottage she'd rented on Martha's Vineyard. Jimmy and Yolanda Snow had also declined his invitation because they'd accepted an invitation to dine with the parents of JJ's girlfriend, Teresa.

Celebrating the holidays without Tia had been extremely difficult for Brandon, but his family and friends had helped make it memorable and special for him. The *Revelations* Christmas Special aired a week before Christmas. Anderson had arranged for the cast to meet at a rented mansion, where they gave the illusion of enjoying a holiday dinner together. The set was decorated with garland, red bows, and a huge Christmas tree surrounded by gifts. Danita's girls, along with Charlene and Zack's children, opened gifts provided by the show. During the interview segments, they each spoke from their heart about Tia. Brandon was humbled by the fact that several of the memories shared were things that he did not know had transpired. He knew that his wife had her faults, and he was pleased to hear so many wonderful things about her.

At the end of the show, Yolanda Snow did a brief public service announcement regarding the dangers of not reporting an abusive partner or stalker. She was joined by Brandon as he announced that the four churches featured on *Revelations* would be joining together to form a program for battered women. Its purpose would begin with counseling and eventually lead to a shelter for those needing a way out. The police also added in a Crime Stoppers number for viewers to call if anyone had any information on Julian's whereabouts.

Brandon spent Christmas with his family in his hometown of Tulsa, Oklahoma. He arrived on Christmas Eve, and his mother and sisters were busy in the kitchen preparing cakes, pies, ham, turkey, and a myriad of delicious foods for Christmas dinner. Later, he and his brothers were up until five A.M. assembling bicycles and dollhouses for all of the kids. Seeing the looks on their faces filled him with joy and sadness. While watching them, he prayed that one day God would bless him with a family as big and loving as the one his parents had.

The day after Christmas, he returned home in order to spend the rest of the holidays with friends in Atlanta. Brandon turned off the tree lights and went upstairs to his bedroom. After saying his nightly prayers, he climbed into bed and dozed off almost as soon as his head hit the pillow. In the wee hours of the morning, his phone rang, waking him up. "Hello," he mumbled.

"Brandon, this is Quincy. If you want to see the birth of your son, you need to meet me at Piedmont Hospital right now."

Brandon, still groggy and half-asleep, replied, "Quincy, what are you talking about?"

"I will explain everything when you get here, but you have to hurry or you're gonna miss it."

"I'm going to miss what? You're not making any sense."

"Ugh! Listen to me. I know that you know that Tia wasn't really pregnant when she died. But she did plan on giving you the son you wanted. We hired a surrogate, and she's gone into labor early. Just get down here!"

Still feeling confused and numb with this information, Brandon stumbled out of bed and got dressed while trying to make sense of what he'd just been told. The last time he'd seen Quincy was the day that he found out Tia was dead. Since they were best friends, he decided that it would be easier if he went to Quincy's shop and told him the news in person. As soon as Brandon walked into The Periwinkle Palace that day, Quincy began crying and flailing his arms wildly. "Oh my God, what happened? You've *never* been here before, so I *know* something bad must have happened to my girlfriend," he cried.

Brandon tried his best to calm him down and get him into the back room so that they could speak privately, but it was no use. While several confused customers looked on, Brandon broke the devastating news to him, and then spent the next half hour trying to calm him down as Quincy ran, cried, ranted, and screamed, totally hysterical. Since he was unable to calm him down, Brandon had no other choice but to lock up the store and drive Quincy home to his partner, Nicky.

A few days later, Quincy called and told Brandon that he would not be attending Tia's funeral. Instead, he asked if he could just stop by the mortuary and spend some time alone with her. Brandon had agreed and had not spoken to Quincy again.

When he arrived at the hospital, Quincy was waiting to escort him up to labor and delivery. "I'm so glad that you're here. I just spoke to her doctor, and it's going to be awhile, but she's definitely going to deliver." He grabbed Brandon's arm. "Let's go."

"No. You need to explain everything to me first," Brandon said, pulling his arm away. "Who's going to deliver, and what is this all about?"

Quincy motioned for him to follow him into the waiting room where they both sat down. "I may as well start at the beginning. Tia wanted to give you a child, but the truth is, she couldn't get pregnant."

"We could have kept trying. She didn't have to resort to tricks."

"No, you don't understand. Tia had her tubes tied before she met you. You could have tried forever, but she never would have gotten pregnant."

"That's impossible. She was pregnant two years ago, but she miscarried."

Quincy shook his head. "No, she wasn't. She just pretended to be because you wanted it so much. Then she faked the miscarriage and hoped that would stop you from wanting to try again for a while."

"Just when I'd found peace and had begun to forgive her, I found out she's been lying to me for years." Brandon sighed. "So, are you telling me that she never wanted kids with me? It was all a game?"

"No, she wanted to give you a baby, she just couldn't. So she came to me for help."

"No offense, but why you? I know you were best friends, but you don't seem to be the best option for this kind of problem."

"I'm not a biological woman, but I know what it's like to want to give your man a child and not be able to."

Brandon suddenly regretted his choice of words. Spiritually, he believed that Quincy's lifestyle was wrong, but he also felt that it wasn't his place to judge him. In all the years that he'd known him as Tia's best friend, he'd tried to understand him, rather than condemn him. "I'm sorry. I didn't mean to be rude. So Tia came to you, and then what happened?"

"I've had friends who used surrogates to build their families, and Tia knew this. So we decided to find one to carry the baby for her. That's who is upstairs about to deliver. She knows that Tia is dead, and she still wants to give you the baby."

"Why didn't Tia just tell me the truth? We could have hired the surrogate together, then at least the baby would really be ours. I mean, we talked about it, and I even made a few deposits at the sperm bank, just in case."

"Because she'd been lying to you for so long she was afraid of how you'd react to the truth. So she came up with this plan. The baby isn't really Tia's, but it's really yours."

Brandon's eyebrows crinkled with confusion. "I don't understand what you mean."

"Tia told me that your family has very strong genes and that you'd be suspicious of a child that did not look like you. So the woman upstairs was impregnated with your sperm that you donated for you and Tia to use later on, in case you had conception problems. She's giving birth to your son."

Unable to contain his excitement a moment longer, Brandon demanded that Quincy immediately take him to labor and delivery to meet the surrogate. Still feeling slightly confused, Brandon stood in the doorway and just stared at the surrogate woman for several moments before finally entering the room.

"This is Myrna," Quincy said, finally breaking the awkward silence that stood between them.

Myrna winced in pain before weakly smiling at them both.

Brandon continued to stare at the beautiful black woman lying in the bed. Her hair was dark brown and curly surrounding her light brown face. Brandon thought she looked a lot like his favorite singer, Jennifer Hudson. He slowly approached the bed like a nervous teenager on his first date. "I'm Brandon Kitts," he said politely. He extended his hand to her.

"Hi, Brandon," she said. "This is weird. We've just met, and now we're having a baby together."

The three of them laughed.

"Tia gave me the check to pay Myrna a few weeks before she . . . well . . . anyway, we both felt that it was only right that you be here. Your son is going to be born real soon," Quincy said.

A few hours later, Brandon held Myrna's hand as she gave birth to Brandon Tianté Kitts. Being seven weeks early, he was tiny and frail, but the doctor declared that he was healthy. Brandon cut the umbilical cord with trembling hands and fidgeted impatiently while the nurses cleaned and checked the baby. Just when Brandon thought he'd burst with anticipation, they finally laid the infant into his waiting arms. For weeks, he'd fought back tears of grief, but as he stared in his son's tiny face, he allowed the tears to flow freely. His heart swelled with so much pride, joy, and unconditional love that Brandon was sure he'd burst. "Hello, son," he said as he grinned from ear to ear.

Epilogue

One Year Later

Zack Morton trotted up his basement steps and closed the door before entering his kitchen. Charlene stood at the stove scrambling eggs, while Martin and Luther sat waiting at the table. Coretta swung her pudgy legs back and forth as she sat comfortably in her high chair.

"Daddy, what time does the party start?" Luther asked.

"Not until later this afternoon. After breakfast, we're going to go shopping and pick out a present for him."

"Cool. I say we get him a super soaker water gun," Martin said.

"He's only a year old; he can't play with a super soaker water gun. Maybe we can get him an educational toy," Charlene suggested as she placed eggs on everyone's plate.

"Mom, don't do that to him. He's too little to be educated. How about a toy drum? He loves to pound on things," Luther suggested.

"I think that's a great idea," Zack agreed. He dug into his eggs and smiled at his family. The past year had been one of their most difficult, but he was thankful that they'd come out of it feeling closer than ever to each other.

The previous Christmas he received a beautiful card decorated with palm trees from Mabel Joe Stevens that read:

Greetings from Hawaii
Dear Zack,
I have to thank you so much for giving me the money to keep your secret. As you always said, God does everything for a reason. I took the money and immediately flew to Hawaii to see my grandchildren. As it turns out, my daughter-in-law was sick, and she really needed my help, so I decided to stay. I have never been happier. This island is like paradise. Thank you so much for my blessing.
Love,
Mabel Joe Stevens

After reading the postcard, Bo contacted information to find a phone number for the address listed on the postcard and asked to speak with Mabel Joe. After thanking her for the card, he let her know that she was listed on Atlanta's missing persons list. Mabel Joe laughed.

"You mean to tell me folks been looking for me?" she asked.

"Yes, ma'am. It's been on the news, and there are flyers up all over town. Why didn't you tell someone where you were going?"

"It never occurred to me that I needed to tell anyone. I hated that job at the hospital, and I don't have no family back there. But it does my heart good to know that folks care, even when I didn't think that they did. I'll make a phone call and let the authorities know that I'm okay," she said before hanging up the phone.

During February of that year, Nancy had passed away, and Zack took his entire family to Asheville to pay their last respects. His brother and sister had no idea that he'd stopped passing, and both stood with their mouths gaping open when he drove up to their single-wide trailer and stepped out of his car with dark brown hair and brown eyes. Zack thought that he still looked more white than black, but they did not agree.

His brother screamed for his stepfather. "Roscoe, get out here! Zack's home!"

Roscoe stepped out onto the porch and stared at Zack. He looked him up and down before taking a seat on the porch steps. Zack felt completely unwelcome, so he turned around and told Charlene and the kids to stay in the car.

"What have you done to yourself?" Kyle asked. "You are dark as an Injun. Are you trying to be a Cherokee?"

"I think you mean Native American. And no, I'm not passing as anything anymore. This is what I look like."

"You can't go to the funeral like that," Meagan insisted. "Momma would not be able to rest in peace if she knew you looked like this."

"This is who I am, Meagan. My mother was African American, and so am I."

Roscoe stood up, then walked down the steps and stood face-to-face with Zack. "You know I ain't racist, but some of the people who are gonna be at this funeral are. It's bad enough that you married a black gal and had a bunch of mongrel chirren. You will not walk into my wife's funeral looking like a niggrah." He spat tobacco on the ground and stared defiantly at Zack.

Zack hated the way Roscoe combined the words *Negro* and *nigger* to make up his own version of the horrible word. Regardless of how he pronounced it, Zack felt insulted. "I'm sorry you feel that way, Roscoe. My family and I will just go to the mortuary and say goodbye before we head back to Atlanta."

"You do what you gotta do," Roscoe said coldly.

Zack got back into his car and drove away. Instead of going immediately back to Atlanta, he decided to spend some time in Asheville and show his family where he'd grown up. They took a tour of the downtown area and drove by the historic Biltmore estate. Then they checked into a nice hotel for the night. The next morning, Zack went alone to the funeral home and said his final good-byes to Nancy. As he did so, he realized that he was also saying good-bye to the person she'd made him become. He felt sorrow for her death, but he couldn't help feeling elated that he was finally free from all of the hurt and pain she'd caused in his life.

Over the next several months as his appearance changed, Zack heard the rumblings of gossip within his congregation. It took a bucket of courage and a boatload of prayer, but by late May of that year, Zack decided that it was time that he told his congregation the truth. Except for the occasional snide remarks, the majority of them had accepted the news with little fanfare.

His marriage to Charlene was stronger than it had been in years. Although he continued his morning workouts, he'd asked Charlene to join him in the gym. They worked out together and grew closer as a couple. He still kept the door locked to keep the children out, but he reduced it to only the small lock on the door. He also finally took the photos of his mother and grandmother from the basement and put them in their rightful places on the mantle along with their other family photos. The boys enjoyed hearing about their family, and Zack was both proud and ecstatic to be able to share it with them.

As soon as they finished eating their breakfast, Zack, Charlene, and the children piled into the car to go shopping for a birthday present for Brandon's son.

***

In her mansion, Danita stood in the front entryway yelling up the stairs for her daughters. "If you girls don't hurry up, you are going to be late for the birthday party," she yelled.

"Summer is hogging the bathroom mirror," Autumn yelled back.

Vivian stepped to the top of the staircase and looked down at Danita. "I'll have them down in just a few minutes," she said.

Danita went into the family room and lounged on the couch while she waited. It had only been a few weeks since the court rendered a decision, but she was completely thankful that she'd won full custody of her girls.

Gretchen spoke with the court-appointed liaison assigned to Danita's case and told them everything she knew about Ben's family. Although they'd told the judge they were not after Danita's money, that was not the complete truth. Joy was in financial trouble due to gambling debts, and she desperately needed a way out. Danita did not understand why they had not simply asked for money in the wrongful death suit, but Joy had a much more complicated plan in mind. Joy knew that even if the family won the suit, her parents would receive the bulk of the settlement and she would not be able to ask them for money without revealing the truth about her gambling problem. So she talked them into seeking custody of the children instead.

According to Gretchen's testimony, her next plan would have been to request child support payments from Danita. Because of her parents' age, she knew that she'd most likely be named as their legal guardian and Danita would have to pay the money directly to her. She also knew that she could easily ask for several hundred thousand dollars in support per month by stating that the girls had a right to maintain their present lifestyle. Unfortunately, she had not counted on Gretchen speaking with Danita and recanting her statements.

With Victor's help, Danita was able to appeal the wrongful death decision, and she had won. Shortly thereafter, she'd received the news that the custody battle was over and no one would be able to take her kids.

Following the verdict, Danita picked up her phone and contacted Ben's parents. "Hello, Mother Hyatt, it's me, Danita," she said.

"Um . . . Hello. Wow, I never expected to hear from you."

"I know, and I must admit that I never expected to be making this phone call. First of all, let me say that your actions in court were deplorable. Ben would never have approved of the tactics that you all used against me."

"I'm really sorry about that, Danita. My husband and I are truly sorry. I can't apologize for Joy, but I know that she's ashamed as well."

"I understand that, and I appreciate your apology." Danita paused as she gathered her nerve. "The reason I'm calling is to find out if you'd like to see the girls over the Christmas holiday. They will be out of school for two weeks."

Ben's mother was stunned. "After everything that's happened, you *still* want us to see them?"

"I want what's best for my children. You're their grandparents, and they love you. I won't keep them away from you, ever. I promise."

Her mother-in-law thanked her profusely before setting up a date and a time to pick up the children. Danita knew that she'd made the right decision. God had forgiven her for her anger, and she knew that she had to forgive them as well.

"Mommy, what did you do with little Brandon's present?" Autumn asked. She and her sisters were finally dressed and standing in the doorway.

"Philippe put it in the trunk of the car. It's too big to carry," Danita answered.

The three of them had chosen a handmade rocking horse with a lifelike mane. It was white trimmed in blue.

"Well, let's hurry up and go. I can't wait to see him ride it," Autumn answered as they all walked out the front door.

Jimmy, Yolanda, Priscilla, and JJ were the first to arrive at Brandon's home.

"I'm so glad you guys are here. The clown cancelled, Costco lost my cake order, and the helium tank is not blowing up the balloons," Brandon said. "I knew I should have let my mother plan this party."

"Where is she? Don't tell me your mother is missing the party?" Yolanda asked.

"Unfortunately, my mother is. Dad had surgery on his hip and can't travel. But we are going to Tulsa next week, and she's having another party there with the whole family."

"Don't worry. Priscilla and I will go to Publix and get a cake. JJ has a clown outfit that he wore for the school carnival, so we'll pick that up too," Yolanda offered.

"Let me take a look at that tank, Mr. Kitts. I bet I can make it work," JJ chimed in.

As they all rushed off to their appointed tasks, Jimmy followed Brandon into the house. "I really wanted to do an outdoor party, but it's too chilly this time of year," Brandon said as they entered his great room.

"It looks nice in here. You're doing a good job," Jimmy said.

"He hasn't done *anything* but give orders," Quincy complained. He walked into the room carrying a roll of blue crepe paper. "I'm barely six feet tall even in three-inch heels, but I hung all of these streamers."

Jimmy was still amazed at the friendship that had formed between Quincy and Brandon since the birth of his son. The first time he'd seen Quincy at little Brandon's christening, he felt compelled to ask why they'd grown so close.

"He's a good person with a good heart," Brandon had said. "Besides, if it wasn't for him, I would not have my son. He didn't have to call me that night. Myrna had been paid by Tia before she died. She could have put the baby up for adoption, and I never would have been the wiser. I owe him a lot."

"But you're a minister. Aren't you worried about how this looks?" Jimmy asked.

"My granddaddy used to say that you gotta catch the fish before you can clean it. My prayer is that I can positively influence Quincy's life."

Jimmy had discovered over the past year that Brandon was right. Quincy attended church services regularly at Brandon's church, and when he did, he dressed conservatively in a suit and a tie. He was still over-the-top at other times, but they both could see a change in him. For the party, he'd chosen skintight leather pants with a multicolored sweater and stiletto pumps. Jimmy walked over and offered his assistance to him with hanging streamers.

Brandon was directing them to hang the streamers more to the left when his cell phone began ringing in his pocket. "Hello,"

"Hi, Brandon, it's me, Myrna."

"Sweetheart, we are almost done setting up for the party. Where are you?" he asked.

"My plane is delayed, but I should be home before the party is over. Give our son a kiss for me. I'll be there as soon as I can," she replied.

After meeting her at the hospital the night his son was born, Brandon had tried unsuccessfully to fight the strong attraction he felt to his son's mother. At first, he'd told himself that it was just gratitude for her carrying his son, but soon, he had to admit that it was much more. By the time, little Brandon was six months old, he'd finally gotten up the courage to ask Myrna on a date. The two had been almost inseparable since. Brandon had not expected to fall in love again so soon after Tia's death, but he was certain that Myrna was the woman he'd prayed for all of his life. On Christmas Eve of that year the two of them had exchanged vows in front of Zack Morton, with Quincy standing by as best man. The day before their son's birthday, she'd flown to California for the funeral of a family friend.

"Do you want us to wait for you before we start?" he asked.

"No, don't disappoint the children. Just be sure to save some cake for me."

Two hours later, all of the guests had arrived and gathered around the table with the birthday boy sitting at the head. He was dressed in a baby blue sweater with blue jeans and white sneakers and had pulled the party hat off of his head, busily tearing it apart as his guests looked on. Suddenly, Myrna burst through the door carrying a large birthday present just as Brandon came in carrying the cake that Yolanda and Priscilla had purchased. A single candle shaped like the number one sat glowing on top.

"Okay, everybody, who's going to lead the birthday song?" Brandon asked as he placed the cake on the table.

Little Brandon immediately reached for it and put a huge dent in the icing with his tiny fingers.

"Y'all better hurry up. This kid is ready for the cake," JJ said laughing.

"I'll start," Priscilla said. "I'm in the choir at church."

Singing off-key, she led them all in a rousing yet pitiful rendition of "Happy Birthday." They all clapped and cheered as Martin and Luther helped little Brandon blow out the candle.

"I want a *big* piece," Luther said.

Charlene and Danita began cutting pieces of cake to serve just as the front doorbell rang. Brandon rushed to answer it and was surprised to see Anderson. "What are you doing here?"

Anderson held out a brightly wrapped package. "I brought a present for your son."

"Thanks." Brandon took the package and began to close the door.

"Can a brother get a piece of birthday cake?"

"Sure. But first, let's cut to the chase. What's the *real* reason you're here, Anderson?"

Anderson shoved his hands into his coat pocket. "Look, I knew that everyone from the show would be here, and I'd like to talk to you all."

Sighing, Brandon let him inside his home. "Okay, but make it quick. It's my son's birthday." Brandon led Anderson into his home office. "Have a seat. I'll go get the others."

Brandon asked Myrna, Priscilla, and JJ to be in charge of the other children, then invited the entire former cast of *Revelations* to join him in the office with Anderson.

"Well, look who decided to finally crawl out from under that rock he was hiding under," Zack said.

No one from the cast had spoken to, or seen, Anderson Carter since the taping of the Christmas Special Show in tribute to Tia that had been done over a year earlier. Due to Julian's disappearance, his family had taken over the corporate offices of The Washington Broadcast Network and cancelled plans for a second season of *Revelations*. Unlike Julian, they seemed to be content with allowing the station to be a collage of old reruns and game shows.

"I wasn't hiding. I was trying to make a living after Julian's sister fired me," Anderson answered.

It had been over a year since she'd heard from or seen him, but the sound of Julian's name made Yolanda's intestines tremble. "Has his family heard from him at all? I know the police haven't found him," she asked.

Anderson shrugged. "If they have, they didn't tell me. You guys know I had nothing to do with all of that madness Julian was involved in. I was just trying to do my job."

"I'd like to get back to my son's party, so for the last time, Anderson, why are you here?" Brandon asked.

"Julian's sister contacted me. Although it's been over a year since the last episode, the station has been overrun with requests to bring the show back. I'm here to ask . . . no, to beg, you guys to agree to it." He looked expectantly around the room.

"I'd love to do it again," Danita said. "I can honestly say that it helped my ministry at the church. Not only that, but it also added some positivity to reality television."

Zack looked over at Charlene, and she nodded her head. "We're in. I'm starting a new outreach ministry that I'd love to see featured on the show," he said.

"What about you, Brandon?" Anderson asked.

"Sure, why not? I got a lot of positive feedback about Tia's tribute show. I think the fans would be glad to see our son."

Everyone's eyes turned to Yolanda and Jimmy.

"Bishop Snow, I know this has to be a difficult decision for you and your wife after the last show," Anderson said, "but I assure you that Julian was solely responsible for that and it will never happen again."

Jimmy cleared his throat. "Well . . . I—"

Yolanda interrupted him. "I'm not really interested in doing a television show anymore. If my husband agrees to this, I want it to focus on his church and the new ministries they are implementing this year."

Jimmy smiled and took her hand into his. "We both would be glad to do the show. One of our newest ministries is the Tia Kitts Memorial House for battered and abused women. It should be open in time for the first show."

Anderson was elated. Before calling Julian's sister to tell her the good news, he followed the rest of them into the dining room for little Brandon's party. JJ had changed into his clown costume and was leading the kids in a game of pin the tail on the donkey, while Priscilla tried to clean the cake icing out of her hair that little Brandon had thrown at her.

Three months later as the cast gathered at the W Hotel to celebrate their premiere, Julian sat alone in the corner of a secluded bar hundreds of miles away, staring at the television screen as the new season of *Revelations* premiered.

Reader's Group Guide Questions

1. Are you a fan of reality television?

2. *Faking Reality* has four core characters that are pretending in their lives. What were your feelings regarding the secrets they held?

3. Have you ever felt angry at God the same as Danita? If so, how did you handle that anger?

4. Yolanda Snow's actions were fueled by ambition. Do you believe that sometimes God gets lost in the lives of those looking for fame?

5. What were your thoughts on the friendship between Tia and Quincy?

6. Did you have a favorite character in *Faking Reality?* If so, who was that character?

7. Did you have a least favorite character in *Faking Reality?* If so, who was that character?

8. When Zack's secret was revealed, whom did you agree with, Charlene or her family?

9. Have you or someone you loved ever been stalked by a former lover/husband/wife?

10. Do you feel stalking and abuse are subjects that the church is not adequately dealing with?

11. Does your congregation offer counseling/shelter to stalked/abused women?

Bio

Zaria Garrison is a Black Expressions Bestselling Christian fiction author. Her debut novel, *Prodigal*, was nominated for Christian Fiction Book of the year 2010 by SORMAG (Shades of Romance). Zaria was also nominated for Christian Fiction Author of the year. She is co-owner and staff writer of *EKG Literary Magazine*, an online magazine geared toward all members of the literary community. Zaria can be reached online at zaria@zariagarrison.com.

Notes